Other Books by George Seaton

Listening to the Dead

Big Diehl: The Road Home

Big Diehl: Comes a Peace

Finding Deaglan

Whispers of Old Winds

Shane Thorpe Knew Jesus and Rode Bulls

Finding Skylar Hand

The White Buck
and other stories

George Seaton

For those who may appear in these pages, (you know who you might be), and, of course, for David and Kuma.

To my editor, Jerry Wheeler, who consistently manages to make decent books better.

The White Buck and Other Stories

Copyright © 2020 George Seaton. All rights reserved.

No part of this work may be reproduced or utilized in any form or by any means, electronic or mechanical, including photocopying, microfilm, and recording, or by any information storage and retrieval system, without permission in writing from the publisher.

Published in 2019 by George Seaton

Pine, Colorado

https://www.gmseatonauthor.com/

ISBN: 978-1-6546570-4-8

This collection is a work of fiction. Names, characters, places, and incidents are products of the author's imagination or are used fictitiously.

Notes:

"The Cinnamon Boy" first appeared in *Out In Colorado II*. Broomfield, CO: Rocky Ridge Books, 2015

"The Flies of August" first appeared in *An American Memory*. USA: Wilde City Press, 2014.

"The White Buck" first appeared in *Found*, an anthology of Rocky Mountain Fiction Writers. Ed: Mario Acevedo. Montrose, CO: RMFW Press, 2016.

"The Story of Myrtle Roady" first appeared in abridged form in *Year's End*. Ed: J. Alan Hartman. USA: Untread Reads Publishing, 2012.

"Simple Gifts" first appeared in *An American Memory*. USA: Wilde City Press, 2014.

The White Buck
and other stories

Contents

The Cinnamon Boy

The Cow

An Intended Life

The Flies of August

The White Buck

Clowns Never Cry

Simple Gifts

Fixing Fence

The Story of Myrtle Roady

"Nothing if given to mankind, and what little men can conquer must be paid for with unjust deaths. But man's grandeur lies elsewhere, in his decision to rise above his condition. And if his condition is unjust, he has only one way to overcome it, which is to be just himself."

"Camus at Combat: Writing 1944-1947" – Albert Camus

The Cinnamon Boy

*O*h, Danny boy. *I would have you standing naked before me, a string of gardenias hanging from your neck, a sprig of hyacinth in your hair. I would tell you to turn this way and that way, and then I would ask you to tell me your secrets through the afternoon as we sat on floor pillows, a meager fire barely crackling and hissing before us. We would open whiskey and believe the aroma from the bottle is like that which wafts from Kentucky boys working the mash. As we sipped, we would tell stories about those crackers in their threadbare overalls. We would see them entwined, their voices softly atwang, barefooted and bedazzled by their lusts, their overalls shucked, the immediacy of their steamy aroma effused from each to the other. Then, as night caressed us, we would lie upon pillows and sip, oh, a deeply red wine from swarthy Italian grapes, and I would touch your skin, your hair, my lips to yours.*

Whaddaya think, Danny boy? You up for that?

I have tried to write you into a story, you know. I cannot do that. My characters, you see, come mostly from my imagination. I build them from whole cloth, though I daub them here and there with quirks, imperfections, fears, strengths—the essential stuff of boys I have known or wish I had known throughout my life. Can one ever truly know another? My characters are amalgams, mixtures of this and that, conjured into believable presences who creep through my stories as black words on white paper or from beaming screens; phantoms that are either captured as real in readers' minds, or discarded as trite and too overly affected to be believed. But you, well... The Delivery Boy Cometh. *Hah! How's that for a title? Thing is, Danny boy, I can't even begin to shape you into words. You're too...um, real, I guess would be the operative word. And I don't write biographies.*

I suspect you've already loaded my order into your truck and are headed this way. I'll tidy up a bit before you get here. I'll air the place out, sweep the doormat of pine needles, gather sweet spring water for your pleasure, columbines for your hair.

///

Black Irish from his daddy, an obscure Italian pedigree from his mother, here is Daniel Flynn, twenty years old, working a summer job at Flynn's Market and Hardware in the mountain town of Vail, Colorado, from where he drives this morning. His destination is fourteen miles north into the Eagle's Nest wilderness area where the writer resides alone and is presumably waiting for his supplies. The writer's order of foodstuffs—wine, bourbon, cigarettes, writing paper, printer ink cartridges, and miscellaneous hardware items—are secured in the truck's bed by a tarp and bungee cords. Daniel maneuvers the F250 over the ruts and rocks that spot the less than well-kept single lane dirt road leading part way to the writer's cabin. He also pulls an ATV atop a small trailer. The ATV will get Daniel and his load the rest of the way to the writer's door, where the delivery charge will nearly equal the cost of the supplies.

Trying to avoid scraping the truck against errant branches of thickset pine and spruce trees along the side of the road, Daniel brakes a bit, carefully eases to the left or right, and grimaces when contact is unavoidable. The faint scratches will be obvious to his father who will inspect the truck when he returns to Vail, and who will ask the inevitable question: "Why weren't you more careful?"

After fourteen miles, the road ends at the Pinecone Lodge's

pebble-packed parking lot. The lodge is open from mid-June through late-September to paying customers eager to get back to nature for a few days—hop on a horse, paddle a canoe, live in a tent, and shiver through frigid mountain nights.

Daniel steps out of the truck, tugs at his beige cargo shorts that have ridden up almost painfully during the trip, stomps his hiking boots to enhance the loosening, stretches, and scans the area. Horse wranglers are out, one tending to the hoof of a roan-colored mare tied to one of three hitching posts. After he delivers the supplies to the writer, he'll hang around the corrals for a while. Maybe talk to Gary, the wrangler he met last summer who once offered to help him get the supplies up and over the hill to where the writer lives from June to October. Before politely refusing Gary's offer, Daniel had considered the possibilities of spending some time with the boy, who appeared to be only eighteen or nineteen, whose blue eyes perhaps spoke of craved intimacies, whose ash-colored jeans exposed in precious subtleties what lay beneath the fabric. Whose smile enchanted.

Daniel backs the ATV out of the trailer, then unhitches the trailer and pulls it out of the way, next to the truck. He moves the supplies from the truck to the ATV's cargo basket where he re-covers them with the tarp and straps the bungee cords around the load.

"Shoulda put my order in, too," Gary says as he approaches Daniel.

Daniel turns, sees who it is, smiles, and picks at his blue T-shirt where his sweat has stuck the fabric to his skin. "Hi, Gary. I was going to see if you were around after I delivered this stuff."

"Saw you pull in." Gary's soft leather chaps nicely frame his crotch, which he deftly adjusts with a cupped hand. "If I'd had your number, I woulda called to see if you could bring me some stuff up here. Save me a trip to Vail."

"Should have given it to you last summer." Daniel says. "You have your phone with you?"

Gary fishes his cell from his shirt pocket. "What's your number?"

Daniel gives him his personal number, and Gary punches it in.

"Good deal," Gary says. "You come up about every two weeks for Mister White?"

"Just about. If you need something, I could come whenever. If I bring it up with Mister White's order, you won't have to pay for delivery."

They both turn their heads toward the corral when a shouted voice calls, "Gary."

"I gotta go." Gary puts his phone back in his pocket, begins to walk back, stops and turns to Daniel. "Come by before you leave?"

"Yeah. I'll do that."

"If I'm not babysittin' a bunch a folks on a pony ride, I should be here. Tell you what, you got *your* phone handy?"

Daniel reaches into his pocket and pulls out his phone.

"Here's my number. Just give me a call when you're done and headin' back down."

Daniel saves Gary's number. "Okay. Shouldn't be very long."

"See yah," Gary says as he turns and continues to walk back to the corral.

Daniel watches that ass, the treasure tightly framed like the front, and feels the swell from within his cargo shorts, deftly making his own adjustment.

///

The cabin, quite spacious for being so isolated, is three miles into the Eagle's Nest wildness area, accessed only by a trail once used by the Ute, deer, elk, and bears. Or, that is the lore of the place. Deeply rutted, the trail is thrice intersected by streams less than a foot deep. It narrows in places where lodgepole pine, fir, and aspen trees crowd in, and is further constricted in places by magnificent boulders to one side and thickets of trees on the other. The leavings of the pine beetle's voraciousness spots the sides of the trails with brown trees, some fallen, some still standing, some ancient—dead gray and still as death itself.

Mister White sits on one of the two rough-hewn pine Adirondack porch chairs. His gray hair is pulled tight on the sides, the end of a ponytail drapes his shoulder. His fingers caress the glass stem of a tall glass, a cigarette between two fingers. As Daniel stops the ATV, Mister White stands up, a scarf around his neck, the ends hanging to his sides, a white t-shirt asking the question, "Either/Or?," his beige Dockers secured at his waist with a woven multi-colored rope.

"Hello, Mister White," Daniel says, slipping off the seat and stepping to the ATV's bed.

"Danny," Mister White says as he steps off the porch and crosses his arms. "How was the journey? And I've told you before to call me Dick."

Daniel unwraps the supplies. "Good. The trail could use some work, but it's still passable."

"Should get some Boy Scouts to clean it up. Or, maybe some robust, large-thighed Campfire Girls, huh?"

"Yeah, that, or I could do it," Daniel says, lifting a box.

"Oh, I like that idea." Mister White steps back onto the porch and opens the screen door. "Just put it on the kitchen counter."

Daniel walks into the parlor, where two colorful Indian blankets cover a sofa. A pine coffee table is centered on an oval green and brown area rug. A red vase sits atop the coffee table, within which mountain columbines spread their petals, all purple and white. Large pillows form a semi-circle in front of the rock-faced fireplace.

"Would you like some lunch?" Mister White says as Daniel passes him and walks back through the parlor. Mister White steps onto the porch, and again holds the screen door open.

"Thank you, but I have to get back. More deliveries to make, and I've got to close up the store later." Daniel hefts another box and carries it into the house.

Mister White lets the screen door close. "Your parents won't be there? No one else to close the store?"

Daniel sets the box next to the other on the kitchen counter and nods. "They're going to Denver for their anniversary. Getting a hotel room and going out to dinner. And, yeah, we've got other employees, but my dad…" Daniel raises his hands, shakes his head. "My dad wants me to do it."

"Family business and all that, I guess?"

"Yeah. What are you working on, Mister White…Dick? I read your last book and really liked it."

"Ah, yes. The demon-cum-priest thing. Or was it the other way around? I don't know. I send them off to Miss Ham in New York and forget about them. They become errant and tiresome children once I've finished with them. How'd you like it, Danny?"

"It was good. Took a while to get through it. But it was good," Daniel says as he again walks back through the parlor.

"You gave it a glorious review on Amazon, of course?"

"Ah," Daniel says as he steps onto the porch. "I haven't done that yet. But I will. I promise."

"I'll be watching for it." Mister White leans against the screen door to keep it open.

Daniel grabs the last box from the ATV and carries it into the kitchen. "Okay," he says, "that's it."

Mister White stands in the parlor, sticks his hand in his pocket, and pulls out a wad of bills. "You're sure you can't hang out for a minute? Have a drink?" He extends the money to Daniel.

"That's not necessary. Mom will bill you." Daniel shakes his head as he walks past him. "But, thank you. And no, but I've got to get going." He steps onto the porch.

"Danny, don't leave me this way." Mister White stands under the doorframe, his hand still extended. "I'd feel…dirty in a way if you don't take it. It's only"—he studies the bills in his hand—"forty-two dollars."

"Really, I can't—"

"Here." Mister White grabs Daniel's hand, stuffs a twenty into it, and then puts the rest of the money back in his pocket. "I'll see you in a couple weeks?"

"Sure," Daniel says. "Thank you. Oh, and let me know if you want me to clean up the trail." He steps off the porch to the ATV.

"Most assuredly. You be careful now on your journey home."

Daniel starts the motor and waves as he turns the ATV around and heads back down the trail wondering, not for the first time, if all writers are as weirdly kind as Mister White.

///

Did you see me feign nonchalance, Danny boy? Once, I would have pled, a lachrymose mien that probably disgusted more than it cajoled the desired response from boys I once desired to grace my bed. Now, well, all I can do is stand aside as you enter my space, make your delivery, and smile at me as though I am just a customer. Yet I suppose that's all I am. Wouldn't do to have me pawing at you, or better yet, beguiling you with the charms I do possess but find silly to haul out for the mere delivery boy. Did I say mere*? Sorry. That's not the correct word. I do have a prissily caustic side I hope you never see.*

*I once fucked a mere boy who had not eaten for three days. I wasn't much older than he and I had never missed a meal. I found him early one morning on the beach at Fire Island Pines. He had slept on the sand, and as the sun rose, I saw him from my little balcony, curled into himself as if begging a return to the womb. I approached him quietly, studied him—so terribly handsome, quite smudged on the face and arms from I know not what. Perhaps he'd fallen in the scrub during the night. Perhaps he'd been…*used *the night before. When he opened his eyes, I shaded them with my hand against the sun's glare, and he raised his hand as if beseeching alms, a beggar pleading kindness from a stranger.*

Anyway, I took that boy to my little house—paid for from the fruits of my first brilliant tome—and put him in the shower, fed him, and fucked him. Oh, we shared a little nose candy before, a little wine, and then I fucked him. Just like that. Sent the boy away before tea dance time. It was so easy then, Danny. Seems they fell from the sky, right into my arms. Later on, well, much later on, it wasn't that easy. Oh, I was revered for my talents. Boys wanted to be near me. But, you see, Danny, after a while it was only the studious boys, the ones who'd read my books who wanted my, um, essence. I'd aged. I'd snorted too much. Drunk too much. Ate too much. Yes, and I became as I've said, lachrymose, shamelessly pleading with the prettiest boys to spend the night. I never paid for it, however. Never once did I pay. A point of personal pride, I don't mind saying.

But you, Danny boy... Oh, would you sit on my face? Would you let me lick the crevice where your prize resides, darkly hidden and surely disused to this point of your life for the delightful purpose I'd make of it? No. I suspect not. You are, after all, just the delivery boy, huh?

The thought of you cleaning up the trail intrigues me. Better yet, you and my little cowboy, Gary, could do it together. Have I told you about Gary? No? Well, suffice it to say, Danny, he could tell you a thing or two about...life.

///

Daniel watches Gary assist a group of older women climb down from their horses. One by one, Gary grabs the horses' bridles and guides them to the dismount block. He takes the reins from the women, explains the proper method for dismount, stands with his arms ready to catch them if they falter, smiles large, and tells each one, "You're doin' fine. Just swing that leg over."

The women, all giddy from their slog up and down the hill while atop too gentle, too tired, too bored horses aged almost to retirement, gather in a circle once they plant themselves upon the ground. They recount their adventure to one another, their voices squawking delight as they adjust their too tight jeans and flap the bottoms of their shirts or blouses to cool their tummies.

Gary waves at Daniel.

Daniel, leaning against a hitching post, waves back, and watches as two other wranglers assist Gary in unsaddling the horses, leading them to the pasture where their hay and water awaits.

"So, how'd it go?" Gary says as he walks toward Daniel, taking off his gloves and sticking them in his rear pocket.

"Good," Daniel says. "I got up the hill okay."

"Mister White sober?"

"Seemed to be. Why?"

"Oh," Gary takes his weathered cowboy hat off and wipes his forehead with his arm, "I've seen him not so sober."

"You know him?"

"Sure. He comes down here sometimes and hangs around. S'pose he gets cabin fever ever once in a while. Hey, you wanna get a hot dog or somethin' at the lodge?"

"Yeah, that'd be great."

They sit across from one another on the lodge's homey picnic table, hot dogs, sodas, and chips before them, Gary's hat next to him on the bench.

"Grew up in Wyomin'," Gary says, wiping mustard from his mouth. "My daddy has a ranch outside of Laramie—cows, horses, the whole deal. Graduated high school two years ago, and since my parents had come up here to the lodge a couple times when I was a kid, I thought I'd see if I could get a job with the wranglers. Go back home when the season ends."

"You want to go to college?" Daniel asks.

"Nah, never had a desire. I think horses is where my future is. Maybe I'll just stay on the ranch for a while during the winter, though my daddy is pissed I'm gone when he needs me the most. Hell, he can hire some men to take my place while I'm gone. You goin' to college?"

"Yeah. I work at my parents' store during the summer."

"Gathered that." Gary puts the last of his hot dog in his mouth.

"Sorry. I guess that's obvious."

"So… Mister White treat you all right? Give you a glass a wine or somethin'?"

"He offered," Daniel said. "Really didn't have time to… I don't know. Sometimes he seems a little too friendly, if you know what I mean."

"Yeah, he's the friendly sort."

"So, you've been up to his place?" Daniel asks.

Gary shakes his head. "No. Never been."

Daniel looks at Gary, sees that he's turned his eyes away and is looking off toward the lake that stretches out from just below the deck of the lodge's dining room. "You ever get into Vail?"

"Sometimes." Gary turns back to Daniel. "So many people there, I get kind of claustrophobic. Like stayin' up here just fine. Got a bunk in the wrangler's cabin. Half-price food. Sometimes one of the boys has some beer, and we have a little party."

"Just thought we might hook up in Vail sometime."

"We could do that," Gary says, smiling. "I get Sundays off."

"How about this Sunday? I could come and get you, and…"

"Hell, I can drive down. Got my Jeep up here, and… Tell you what, I'll call you Sunday mornin' and let you know when I'll be there. You know that fillin' station right across I-70, right at the turn off to come up here?"

"Sure."

"We'll meet there. How's that sound?"

"Sounds good," Daniel says.

"Okay then." Gary stands and grabs his hat.

Daniel rises too, and they walk back toward the corrals.

"You got a girlfriend?" Gary asks.

"No." Daniel stops himself from saying what he usually does when asked that question: *Just haven't had time to meet many girls.*

"Me either," Gary says and leaves it at that. "So, I'll see you on Sunday." He stops and turns to Daniel, smiles, and holds his hand out.

Daniel shakes his hand and smiles back. "Yeah, I'll be up early, so call as soon as you get there."

"I'll do it." Gary nods, and walks up the steps to the office where a family of four anxiously awaits their time to ride the trails. The daddy and mommy wear red baseball caps reading *Pinecone Lake or Bust*! The kiddies, one boy and one girl, wear cowboy boots that look like they just came out of the box.

///

Had a productive day of writing, Danny. Now, oh, let me tell you that I've dined on crab from a can. Can you believe that! Well, you did bring it to me—the little cans, you know, in the bottom of the box. Yes, candles, Chardonnay, steamed asparagus, a Marlboro afterward. Such a delightful dinner, Danny boy, and all because of you.

Now, let me tell you what I'm writing about. If you liked the demon-cum-priest story, well, I do believe you'll love this one. It's about a clown, a hulking red-nosed clown with tufts of orange hair poking out above his ears. He stalks children and remains in their memory even when they become adults. Wait a minute. Damn! Some hack has already done that?

Actually, I'm writing about an old hairy-assed reprobate, a writer who lures young men into his life with promises they will be preserved for posterity, that he'll write them into a story. Oh, if only it were that easy to...lure.

All I honestly have is words, Danny. But, see, it's not the words themselves that entrance. It's what one experiences when one reads the words. The images, the aromas, the sounds, are not in the words, but in the readers' minds. But, the writer has to, oh, set the stage for the reader. Take, for instance, the word "tree" when it appears in a story without any other description. If I read that word on the page, I see a blue spruce, its boughs spread resplendent against a backdrop of snow-peaked mountains, a sky as blue as skies can ever be. You, on the other hand, might see an ancient maple, struggling to exist while set off a bit from a well-traveled thoroughfare, the sky dull, the air smog-laden, the tree desperate to flourish in that inhospitable place. You see, Danny boy?

Oh, you might tell me that when you read that word, "tree", unless the writer tells you it is a spruce or pine tree, you always see that maple. Always. Without hesitation.

And I might say, "Ah, but what if the story is taking place in, oh, Uzbekistan?" And all I tell you is that the author says there is a tree there, right there in front of you, in Uzbekistan. Would you ask, "But, what kind of trees do they have in Uzbekistan?"

And I would say, "Ah-ha! My point! The author fails! The story is shit!"

Do they have trees in Uzbekistan? I suppose they do. They? Who is they*? And, just exactly where is Uzbekistan?*

I'm getting silly, aren't I? The closeness of my lair does that to me. The walls snuggle closer in every day I don't step from them into the great outdoors, down the path to... To Gary, I suppose, is my usual destination. Or, at least to the lodge where other boys sometimes frolic in the lake, or hike up the mountain, or crawl into their tents along the road well past the lodge's activity, and do what they do within the unseen closeness of their nylon domes. Closeness. When I am alone with the closeness, I never do understand its intent until it's almost too late.

Let me get back to work now, Danny. Still thinking about you and Gary tidying up the trail, your shirts off, your precious parts steaming with your efforts, your back and forth to one another as you do it, the later loll on my floor pillows as all three of us tell stories and lies about the lives we find ourselves living, or have lived so far. Then, well, one thing would lead to another, I have no doubt. No doubt at all. But, yes, if you ain't got them proclivities, Danny boy, I guess we'll play a word game or something. Or, I'll let you and Gary fire up the computer and kill one another with laser-directed accuracy, the dire sound effects booming as Gary yee-haws with his perfect kill, and you... You... Oh, no, it wouldn't be that way at all, would it? Such behavior would not become you, Danny. No. I cannot place you there, even in my imaginings, much less write *you* into *such a...scene.*

///

Daniel opens the door to The Little Diner in Vail and follows Gary into the charming space, adorned with reminders they are in the mountains. Skis, poles, and snowshoes are fastened to the walls, as are pictures of Vail Mountain in winter and spring. It is Sunday morning, and the quaint eatery is hopping with happy-faced tourists, the breakfast aromas wafting about like ambrosia loosed for the gods. They sit down, and the waiter—a fine specimen, a broad smile, his eyes, Daniel notices, lingering on him and Gary as if they are precious oddities within this family-style diner—tells them his name is Brandon, takes their orders for coffee, orange juice, and advises he'll be back to take their breakfast order.

"McDonald's woulda been fine," Gary says, this morning wearing a ball cap reading "Cheyenne Frontier Days," his Wranglers downright blue, his T-shirt white.

"I wanted to take you here," Daniel says, leaving his menu unopened on the table, watching Gary. "They have a great breakfast."

"If it tastes anything like it smells, I guess it'll be good for sure."

They give their orders to the attentive waiter, sip their coffee, and Daniel can't stop wondering what the day ahead will bring. He'd slept poorly in anticipation of this day, waking up again and again with unsettled itineraries flashing across his mind. The only event he'd settled on was what they are doing right now—eating breakfast.

"Mister White wants me to clean up the trail to his cabin," Daniel says, fiddling with his napkin.

"I could help you do that." Gary smiles, leaning across the table as if sharing a confidence. "Bet he'd pay us pretty good. 'Course we'd have to do it on a Sunday when I'm off."

"Okay. I'll give him a call. Maybe I can take his next delivery up in a couple weeks on Sunday, and we can do it then."

Gary leans back as the waiter places food on the table. "How's that, gentlemen? Need anything else? More coffee?" Brandon stands at the side of the table looking as if he would leap a tall building in a single bound for them right now.

"Think we're good," Daniel says.

Brandon nods, stares at them for a moment. "Well, just wave me down if you need anything else." He turns and tends to the table of five just across the aisle.

They dig into their breakfast, deciding as they eat that their next stop will maybe be the Farmer's Market, and then maybe they'll hike up Vail Mountain a ways, and then maybe Daniel will show Gary his family's store, and then maybe on to his house. All maybes. All, in Daniel's mind, tentative destinations according to Gary's whim. If this is a date, and he thinks it is, he wants it to be memorable.

What they do decide to do as they walk out the door of the diner, is head for Daniel's house, his bedroom, where they sit on the bed and flip through the CDs that line the top of Daniel's nightstand. Gary wants to hear Queen, *A Day at the Races*.

"Wow, I haven't heard this for forever," Gary says. "My mom had the album, but she couldn't play it when my dad was in the house. I wonder what happened to all her albums?"

"You didn't have your own music? In your bedroom?"

"Had one of them old portable CD players my mom gave me for Christmas one year. Worked for a week, and then it died. Hell, wasn't much time to spend just hangin' out in my room. Too much work to be done outside—cows, horses, irrigation ditches to dig and clear out, waterin' and feedin' the stock. Nah. I didn't have much time to spend in my room."

"Even in the winter?" Daniel asks as "Somebody to Love," commences its plaintive strains.

Gary listens to the music for a moment before answering. "Oh, winters are the worst. Goddamn cows gettin' lost in blizzards, calves fallin' down in the cold, and dyin' if we don't find 'em in time. Ranchin' ain't somethin' you can set aside to listen to a little music in your bedroom."

"Guess you didn't have much time for friends?"

"Outside of school, no, I didn't. Had a couple best friends. Rode horses mostly. Went campin' and stuff like that. Had fun campin'. Tell me somethin'... Since you ain't got a girlfriend, you ever..." Gary raises his fist and jerks it up and down.

Daniel, who has been *you evering* for quite some time, looks at Gary's hand stroking air. Believes Gary's segue is a little abrupt but not really that disconcerting. He smiles. *Oh yeah...* "I... Yeah. Sure."

"You ever do it with somebody else?"

"I..."

"Wanna do it now? With me?"

And so it goes, Gary's step-by-step deflowering of Daniel. The thought crosses Daniel's mind that this is probably nothing new for Gary, just something he's good at.

"It'll hurt just for a minute," Gary whispers to Daniel. "But, you gotta just relax."

Daniel does relax. Face down, his ass pooched up on a pillow, he can't believe it's actually happening. *Wow! I'm getting fucked!*

Toward evening, after having hiked up Vail Mountain a mile or so, they sit off to the side of the trail sharing intimacies about their natures as a cool breeze sends puffs of fat clouds from the northwest promising the quick-minute, daily rainstorm they're both inured to. They soon hike back down the mountain, and Gary climbs into his Jeep as the rain begins to mist, and then falls with a momentary vengeance. Daniel returns Gary's wave and wonders what will come of this new adventure into the depths of his long-lived yearnings, hidden as a dark secret, but lately bloomed within his bedroom. Maybe he's found somebody to love—a horse wrangler who has showed him the essential ropes for damned sure.

///

Gary stares into the darkness of the room he shares with four others, wincing as Joe farts again in his sleep. When Tyler begins to snore, Gary grits his teeth, stands, grabs his jeans from the foot of his bed, and pulls them on. He puts on his shirt, and then carefully walks through the sleeping quarters, through the office, and steps outside. He sits down in a pine chair, caresses himself against the nighttime chill, and looks up at the ten million stars that spot the blackness of the sky. There is no moon, and he hears the nearly silent rustle from horses, now well-fed, watered, and weary from their endless days of carrying the weight of passenger not attuned to the essential worth of horses.

Daniel had said something there upon the mountain as they spoke their intimacies. Gary had explained he'd always known he was queer, and it'd never bothered him. He's never told his parents. He told Daniel he'd always had a willing partner. "Just for the sex part. None a those boys and me ever thought about dates or fallin' in love."

Daniel had listened, nodded, and then told Gary he too had always known but had always kept it shoved off in a corner of his mind, his heart. He'd thought about acting on it, but just doing something with someone else wasn't possible. He had his education to get through, his friends, the swim team—"God, *they* would not have taken it well!"—but most of all, he was afraid of how his parents would react. "My mom would just die," Daniel had said. "And my dad… I don't even want to think about what he would do."

"But you did it with me," Gary had said.

"Yeah, I did. You were special. You *are* special. I feel good about it with you, Gary. I feel like this huge weight has been lifted from me. It's always been so heavy, so overpowering." Daniel then took Gary's hand in his and stared into his eyes. "Thank you."

Gary hadn't known what to do or say. No one had ever spoken about it the way Daniel had. Even Mister White, with all his experience and smarts—*He writes books, for Christ's sake!*—had always welcomed any opportunity to fool around with him and the boys Gary would take up to the cabin with the same nonchalance Gary had always felt about a good fuck or suck since he'd turned fifteen. *Except for that first time…*

Gary squeezed Daniel's hand, returned his stare, and said, "You're welcome." He kissed Daniel as the sky promised the certainty of rain.

Since that night, Gary has thought about what Daniel said, and what he said to Daniel. He's thought, too, about the ease with which Mister White had lured him into fulfilling his desires. "Life is just a bowl of cherries waiting to be popped," Mister White had said. "And you, Gary, need to learn that lesson before your tits and balls droop, and your ass relocates to your stomach."

Gary had thought that was pretty funny. And though he'd never given it a second thought until Mister White had said it, it was exactly the way he'd begun to think about it not long after the first boy who'd fucked him had told him to stop calling and stop saying hello in the school hallways. "And, keep your fuckin' mouth shut about it!" Fucking had nothing to do with love, and love was overrated anyway. Or so Gary had learned on his own when he was fifteen. He'd thought the world was a shitty place to be as he listened to his mother's Queen album in his bedroom the night he'd tried to talk to that boy for the last time. The boy had been older by a year and had been as nice as could be until he'd pulled it out, wiped himself with Gary's sock, and had left him sitting on the edge of the bed without a nod or a good bye.

Gary looks toward the pasture and sees the slight movement of horses appearing as shadows creeping through the darkness. He shakes his head and whispers, "Jesus Christ! What'd you do to me, Daniel?"

///

Received some suggestions from my editor today, Danny. She sent them Friday, but I've purposefully left the email unopened until today. I've never liked Sundays anyway—thoughts colored darkly with memories of my mother's Roman Church, the two us sharing a niche in a pew every Sunday, Father O'Something or other prancing about with his freckled cherubs—imps in other contexts—following close behind, ringing bells, pouring the rosy-nosed priest's wee libation into a brass goblet. Sure, like penance, I opened the email, downloaded my marked manuscript, saw the right side of it festooned with Track Changes, brightly red in their insistence they be dealt with here and now. Oh, and her comments encapsulated in little bubbles of wisdom, all of which began with, "Perhaps you should think about..." Oh, Danny, yes, my editor is my friend, the singular most conspiratorial presence in my writing life who, and I don't begrudge her this, manages to make my stuff more readable. She deserves a raise. She deserves a new dress, wine with dinner, and a tryst with an Italian stallion hung past his knees, his lips, his tongue gently working her to...um...

Gary called me a day or so ago, Danny. He said he'd be seeing you to reconnoiter your proclivities. Oh, I hope you have them—proclivities, that is. I'd be very disappointed if you didn't. I told him to see what he could see. And, knowing Gary, I'm sure that he will, probably quite straightaway. Just so you know, I didn't teach him that. He picked that up by himself out there on those Wyoming flats where the urgency of the fuck is demanded by the urgency of nature—where the deer and the antelope play and all that—because, hell, the nature Gary knows just doesn't cotton much to delaying any particular scratch upon any particular itch for very long. Got an itch? Well, scratch the damned thing before the arroyo floods, or the wind blows, or the snow falls or, yes, before your red-necked daddy finds you in the barn with your buddy's pants around his ankles. Necessity is the mother of invention, Danny boy. And God knows we all love a good fuck every once in a while.

I have a friend, Danny, who writes in the erotic romance genre. Several years ago, he found a publisher who just adored his boy-meets-boy, boy-fucks-boy, boys-live-happily-ever-after storylines that defy real life scenarios to the point that he is now interjecting shifters, zombies, vampires, dreary dystopian sagas, and Apocalyptic backdrops into his writing. His publisher didn't bat an eye when he lately presented her with one-hundred thousand words about a beaver humping a muskrat, the critter timing his thrusts to the thump, thump, thump of a steam engine that somehow, in some way powers the production of greenery upon a landscape leveled by the unfortunate effects of several hundred thousand kilotons of atomic energy released three hundred years prior. I believe it's called **speculative fiction**. And, oh, it sells, Danny. Sells better than the stuff of real life, I suppose. I guess that's why I write about demons-cum-priests. (Or was it the other way around?) Real life be damned! Except, of course, on the Wyoming flats where that **Old Time Religion** of the fuck persists sans the accouterments of what ifs, an imperative as inevitable as a fart after swallowing a Dairy Queen hot dog. Nothing speculative about that, Danny boy.

Where the hell was I? Never mind. The plan is that you, and Gary will pay me a little visit in the not too distant future. Together. Both of you. What a delight that will be!

///

Daniel listens to Mister White's response: "Of course, Danny, I'd love for you and Gary to come on up and clean the trail. I'll make you both lunch."

"I don't think that's necessary, Mister White," Daniel says, holding his cell slightly away from his ear, Mister White's enthusiasm booming from the phone.

"Oh, it is. It is!"

"Okay. We'll be up there about nine."

"I'll be waiting." Mister White's tone with those last three words strikes Daniel as freaky, or maybe just a tinged with a little too much excitement. When he realizes the connection is severed, Daniel puts his phone in his pocket and continues to fill Mister White's most recent order, putting the requested items in a box. He looks at the list again and wonders why Mister White would need condoms, the same brand Gary had used two Sundays past.

Daniel looks at his watch, hoping Gary remembers he'll be up at the lodge in about an hour. He finishes packing the last of Mister White's order, placing the soft goods in sacks, then putting the sacks in a second box.

Ten minutes later, he crosses I-70 and heads up the hill that will take him to Red Sandstone Road where, eleven miles into the Eagle's Nest wilderness, he'll once again park in the Pinecone Lodge's parking area, hopefully to see Gary waiting for him. As always, he's careful to avoid confrontations with the overgrowth of trees and the ruts in the road, known to rip undercarriages from the most robust vehicles.

Five minutes from his first view of the lodge, the fingers of his left hand find his half-hard dick, teasing it to stiffness through the cotton-synthetic of his cargo shorts. Two weeks since his first fuck, the experience has lingered with an urge to repeat it sans the worry of one of his parents, most likely his mother, opening up his bedroom door and seeing…well… She would have seen he'd been a remarkably successful bottom. *That* she didn't need to know about. Sure, he'd tell his parents eventually about his sexuality, not, he suspected, that they didn't already know. But he certainly didn't want his mother left with the image of somebody's cock shoved up his ass as the initial revelation that he probably wasn't going to give her grandchildren anytime soon. Or ever.

So too, he anticipates seeing Gary again, touching him, speaking words he's never before spoken to another boy. He's relived those moments he spent with Gary a thousand times, each time re-experiencing the joy of it and wanting it to happen again—that feeling of lightness.

As Daniel parks his truck and begins to maneuver the ATV from the trailer, Gary emerges from the aspen grove at the head of the trail that leads to the writer's cabin. Daniel waves and waits for Gary to walk down the slope.

"Hey, Daniel," Gary says, smiling. He, too, is wearing shorts this morning. "I was just up the trail a ways seein' how much we got to do. It ain't that bad…"

Daniel looks at Gary—shorts, tank top, tennis shoes—and believes he'd like to be fucked by that persona too. The wrangler thing two Sundays ago was amazing. But this, well, the angels sing as Gary steps into his space.

"You look like a college kid," Daniel says, wondering if he

should shake Gary's hand or give him a hug.

"Well, we're gonna be sweatin' up there, and I thought I'd dress for it. How you been?"

"Fine," Daniel says, deciding he'll forgo touching Gary. He's new to this after-the-first-fuck encounter, and he'll just follow Gary's lead. For a moment, he watches Gary begin to load the ATV with the supplies from the bed of the truck, and then he grabs a box and asks, "You doing okay?"

"Oh, I'm always okay. You want this trailer unhitched?"

"Yeah, we ought to move it out of the way so it won't block the lot."

And they do move the trailer. Daniel then starts the ATV. Gary sits behind Daniel, their proximity intimate to the point that Daniel catches the scent of something sweet on Gary's skin. Lilac, he thinks, as Gary wraps his arms around his waist.

"I heard you coming," Mister White says from his porch as the ATV comes to a stop. His hair hangs to his shoulders, his right hand on his hip, his left arm raised, holding his cigarette to his side. He wears a caftan, purple silk with gold brocade along the V-neck, and the raised pattern trails down the front of it to the bottom hem. "My trailblazers," he says, flicking his ash with a flourish of this wrist.

"Hi, Mister White," Daniel says as he and Gary slip off the ATV.

"Danny, it's so good to see you. Gary, how's it hanging?"

Gary winks at the writer.

"I guess we can get these things in the cabin," Daniel says, grabbing a box. "Then Gary and I will get to work on the trail."

"Oooo, sounds like a plan to me." Mister White opens the screen door and stands just to the side as Daniel and Gary step into the cabin with their boxes. "In the kitchen," he says.

"Don't look like *you're* dressed to help clear the trail," Gary says, smiling at Mister White as he and Daniel set their boxes on the counter.

"Looks like *you* are," Mister White says, leaning his elbow on the counter, subtly licking his lips.

The interplay is not lost on Daniel. He lowers his head, steps around the writer and stops at the front door. "I didn't bring any tools," he says, turning to Gary and Mister White who are still in the kitchen. "I forgot—"

"I've got all the tools you'll need," Mister White says, flowing from the kitchen. He stops in the parlor, brushes his hair back with his hands, and nods to Gary. "Gary knows where they're kept."

Gary steps from the kitchen and says, "Yeah, they're in the back. C'mon, Daniel." He opens the screen door and steps out of the house.

Daniel follows him, glances back at Mister White, and sees his expression mirror that of the waiter in The Little Diner: *Is there anything else I can get you boys?*

Daniel drives the ATV back toward the head of the trail, down the mountainside toward the lodge. He stops where he's previously determined some work is needed to clear errant dead branches both from the trail and those still precariously attached to rotting trees. "I guess we can start here," he says, stepping off the ATV.

Gary remains seated. "There's somethin' I think we ought to talk about." He stands up and, with the ATV between him and Daniel. "About Mister White, I...ah..."

Daniel watches Gary raise his head and stare off into some unspoken thought. "Okay."

"See, the thing is," Gary says as he grips the handle of a shovel in the ATV's cargo bed, "I...really like you." He looks at Daniel's face, smiles, and tightens his hold on the shovel. "We had a good time in Vail, didn't we?"

"Yes," Daniel says, "we did." Gary looks away again. "Something wrong?"

Gary lets loose of the shovel, and it falls to the ground. Walks to the side of the trail, where he sits down on the felled pine tree trunk. He bows his head slightly, raises his arms and interlaces his fingers behind his head. He sits this way for a moment, then shakes his head, and lowers his hands to his lap. "Mister White and me, we…know each other. I've stayed at his cabin a couple times. I've brought some other guys up there, too, and I'm not proud of what we did."

Daniel steps behind the ATV and also sits on a tree trunk. He doesn't say anything because he doesn't know what to say. He thinks, *Well, okay,* but, at the back of his mind, he knows there's more to this story.

And Gary does continue: "Mister White likes 'em young. Likes to watch, too, and sometimes he likes to get in on the action. You know what I mean?" He looks directly at Daniel.

Daniel sees the question hang on Gary's face. "I get the gist. Mister White's…gay."

Gary stands up and turns his back to Daniel. "Oh, yeah," he says, "Mister White is gay alright." He faces Daniel. "And he *really* likes you, Danny."

"Well—"

"No," Gary says, "let me finish. The whole plan, see, is for you and me to do this trail cleanup thing, and then we'll go back to the cabin, and Mister White, Dick, will give us some lunch with some alcohol, maybe some pills or weed, and then I'm supposed to…well… I'm supposed to get you horny and stuff, and then he'll watch, and maybe wanna join in, and…"

"Wow," Daniel says. He stands up and walks a few steps down the trail. He turns toward Gary and says, "But what about you and me? What we did in Vail? I thought that meant… Something?" He shakes his head, kicks his foot against the dirt. "Are you telling me you and…*Dick* had this planned all along? That you're the…lure, or some damned thing just to get me up here. Wow, Gary," he says, once again turning his back. He begins to walk further down the trail.

Gary whispers, "Shit," as Daniel walks away. He runs toward Daniel. "Daniel, stop. Please," he says. When Daniel doesn't stop, Gary touches his shoulder.

Daniel quickly flicks his hand against Gary's, stops, and faces him. Trying not to cry, he says, "I liked being with you. I thought... I'd never been with another guy, Gary. I thought what we did was... Oh, Jesus, I don't believe this. I don't..." And then he does cry, putting his hands over his eyes.

Gary wraps his arms around Daniel. "Don't do that, Daniel. I like you, too. I really do, man. I'm sorry. I've...never felt so bad before about what I did for Mister White. But now... I'm so sorry. I'm so, so sorry."

Afternoons in these mountains always seem to come earlier than in flatland places where sunshine does not seem to be a caprice of nature, but a daily constant unbounded by forests and rocky peaks. Here, as the afternoon shadows caress the recesses of these mountains, the clouds above them consistently gather to provide what some believe is nature's blessing of another day slipping toward night, a baptism of sorts that is cleansing to some souls and regenerative in its intent.

Caressed on both sides by the thickness of forest and emerging shadows, Daniel and Gary sit for hours, side by side, talking through the mysteries of the lives they've led to this point, including the enigma of the writer up the mountain. They speak about the futures they envision for themselves, but both are careful not to transgress the fragility of their friendship with anything other than that their Sundays will hereafter see them together until the season is over, until school begins again. They don't speak about the *what then?* That will arise upon their inevitable parting. As the rain begins to fall gently and cool, the boys climb back on the ATV and head down the mountain, their task undone, regretting only that nothing much in life is easy to comprehend as to the whys and wherefores of it.

Daniel and Gary will for the next five Sundays meet again, and they will continue to explore those things young men do when they believe they are in love. Gary will take Daniel into the pasture where the concession's horses laze their Sundays, and he will tell Daniel about the worth of horses, that their kindly eyes reflect only what God put there, which is pretty much all that is right with the world. As they pet the critters, stroking their necks and sides, he will tell Daniel about Wyoming sunsets and the spread of land without end where cattle and antelope graze upon nourishing grasses that have grown there for millennia. And as they sit on a hillside above the pasture, Gary will explain that the life he's known forever is a good one, and he will never forsake it for other pursuits. He will tell Daniel he is a cowboy and that's all he knows about his future. What he knows about love is what he's learned from Daniel this summer.

Daniel will tell Gary he understands, and what he knows about love is both a joyful thing and a mystery. He will take Gary once again to Vail Mountain where they will lie on the ground and stare at the sky and the clouds above while holding hands and speaking softly about so many things. Daniel will explain to Gary that someday he wants to be a writer, and he will write about the people he has known or would like to have known, and about the land too, about Colorado, and maybe someday he will write about a Wyoming cowboy who'd been his lover in a place and time of self-discovery. And they will spend their Sunday evenings in a motel room where behind a locked door, the world will not matter, nor the writer, nor the writer's notions about love.

///

I've never picked up a sense of humility, Danny boy. I'm not sure what it is, and if I did know what it is, I believe I would cast it aside as I would a bad wine. I don't need such a thing because it adds little to my enjoyment of the world I've made for myself. And, I'm not sure how one embraces it because it appears to me to be a force for ruin.

But that's just me, Danny.

After talking to Gary—he did call me this morning—I surmise that you and he have... Oh, what should I call it? Coupled? Fallen in love, if there is such a thing? Or, more likely, just fucked the night through, careless in your abandon, con-

cluding before the jism had dried that surely this will last forever. Hah! An unlikely happily ever after, methinks. The Delivery Boy Cometh As the Cowboy Rideth. A Wild West story for sure: The delivery boy all atwitter with the new carnality of it all, the cowboy scratchin' his crotch, and sayin' "Why thank you, ma'am."

I know. Cynicism does not become me. What, then, does?

I started these journal pages since you first stepped over my threshold, Danny. That first time I saw you hefting your loads into my kitchen, smiling as you do, quiet as a dormouse, your voice soft as spring grasses, your body, your hair, your eyes— Oh, those Irish eyes—your…humility… Well, let me tell you, Danny, I was enthralled, and that did become me. Ain't an easy thing to do, considering I haven't been enthralled by much of anything or anybody for a very, very long time.

A thousand years ago, I met a boy when I myself was boy— we're all boys until we're at least forty, Danny—and he and I ventured into the depths of ourselves and each other with the singular purpose of defining a single word—love. He thought he was a poet, but was just a literary day tripper, who thought Garcia Lorca was the boy who watered the flowers. A wee coven of Unitarians was the only audience who truly appreciated his rhymes. I was already quite the successful author by then, but had yet to fuck someone for any reason other than to experience the delightful barely oiled friction of it—the old in-out, you know. But there was just something about him, Danny—his name was Ernesto, a brown boy who smelled of cinnamon and still believed in the Virgin and her blessed son. A boy so different from those I'd had before that he became my obsession for a while. He loved to love. Yes, he defined that word for himself long before I ever did. He loved me, Danny. And, along the rough and tumble road of our short relationship, I suppose I loved him too. A little. But then, well, the bogeyman from anyone's worst nightmare apparently loved him more than I did. Took him away, Danny, covered with purple sores, his lungs awash in an insidious pneumonia. What use, then, is the glory of love?

I guess I've earned my cynicism, Danny boy. Yes, the Good Lord did not work that one in some divinely inspired mysterious way. *The only mystery, Danny, is why Ol' Mister A passed me by. Hah!* The cinnamon boy shrivels as the writer watches and waits; the writer's words, his mere words the only response he can give to such a thing. *(God knows, I shed not one tear...)*

I'll be leaving my lair soon. I've been revealed, I guess, by the cowboy, of all people, who did once loll on my pillows a time or two with others. He appeared to abjure any silly notions of love or commitment, benefiting from our sublime trysts by the libations I provided, the safeness of the seclusion I afforded for him to engage his lusts, (mine, too), and the promise he would become immortal as a character written into one of my books. Oh, and I will put him in a story, Danny, because right now I think he deserves it. Well, as I've told you, my characters are never real people, but only presences who assume the best or worst components of those who actually breathe air. As for Gary, the cowboy, the wrangler of horses whose pert heinie was by far the loveliest assflesh I've ever seen, and whose Wyomin' ways charmed much like the laze of does outside my window on early spring mornings? Well, as for Gary, the cowboy, I believe I'll make of him an imp, a smudged boy much like the throwaway angel who appeared to me in The Pines, who will give another demon-cum-priest a run for his *money. How's that sound, Danny?*

As for you, Danny... No, I still can't write you. You're not formed yet. You're still a mystery. Just another boy delivering groceries—the proverbial pizza boy you are not, Danny—who will someday develop quirks, passions, smudges, failings, and successes. You're whole cloth without stains—as pristine a boy as I've ever met. We of the writing trade have an acronym— HEA, happily ever after. Readers love HEAs, Danny. I hope you have one. Whether you find it with Gary or someone else, I really do hope you experience it sooner rather than later. I think you deserve it. As with most things in life, the simple gifts mean the most. And, oh, how I wish that my cinnamon boy were here now, upon my pillows, gardenias around his neck, hyacinth in his hair. (Did I mention I did not cry for him, Danny? Well, I did. Just a little.)

Oh, and Danny... One last thing. Never become a writer. It's a lonely trudge with an uncertain destination.

The Cow

No moon.

The high plains of north central Colorado indulged the passing of critters haunting the night with the singular purpose of filling their bellies, their craws. The jut of two- and three-hundred foot tall volcanic plugs spotted the plains here and there, rising as fingers pointing to some significance above, blackly witnessing the hoots and yips of the hunt below.

An old cow had wandered purposefully from hay meadow to dense scrub. She had eased down onto her belly, raised her head, studied the night, and felt the flow of her life drain as it seeped from the pulse of pain literally oozing from her legs and chest. She smelled it as an odoriferous thing. Not good or bad. Only an abstraction. She lowered her head, a weakness in her neck begging for release. If she remembered anything, it was that she birthed her children well, sustained them with her milk, and watched them taken from her nurture too soon. If she concluded anything at all, it was that she was ready to sleep. She had served her purpose. She closed her eyes, giving no thought to her vulnerability—the indignity of becoming only a meal for lesser critters intent on serving their purpose. Another abstraction.

///

Jack tied the rope to the ball hitch, looked again at what lay behind. The old Hereford hadn't dropped a calf in two springs. She'd been on the list for auction, probably ending up as some dog's Happy Meal, when she got a notion to try to get to the other side of four strands of prickly wire. Tore her legs and chest up good. Festered to the point she'd just gone off by herself into deep scrub and lay down. Died. Chose her own way, Jack thought. Thought too there was something noble in such a thing. Even for a cow.

Jack fired up the battered Dodge, put it in four-wheel and dragged the cow toward the boneyard, where he and his brothers and his father before had dragged all the critters who'd died of one thing or another over the years. It was a depression up past the hay meadow, unseen from the road, where in time the old cow would leave nothing of herself but bones turned dully white, mixed in with all the others. Coyotes, maggots, some bear maybe, mountain lion, goddamned ravens and crows, owls. All shameless in taking a piece of the rotting pie.

He drove across the hay meadow, felt the tug of the cow—an ungraceful slog over the dip of irrigation ditches that in a few weeks would carry water from Bear Creek to flood the meadow and bring good harvest.

Jack stepped out of the Dodge, tipped his weathered and stained felt hat up a bit from his forehead, and leaned against the side of the pickup. Pulled a cigarette he'd rolled earlier at the kitchen table from his shirt pocket. Cupped his hand over the flame from his daddy's Zippo, the only thing he'd managed to take from his paltry leavings after the son of a bitch had coughed up his lungs. Jack's brothers, older and more conversant with the concept of lineage, had taken their privilege in grabbing what they wanted before Jack was left alone in the bedroom to sort through what was left. Thought it odd his brothers hadn't coveted the lighter.

The forever wind huffed from the north and west, goosing a response from pine, fir, spruce and newly leafed aspens that surrounded the bone yard. Brought with it the aromas and odors of the land, of spring, evergreens, horse and cow shit.

THE COW

Jack turned his head and once again studied the old cow. He'd known this cow. Passed into manhood knowing this cow. She'd dropped some fine calves, fat and sassy. But something else about her, something since he was eighteen had caught his eye, his interest. She was independent, usually kept herself and her calves apart from the herd. Went her own way, he thought. She'd never bawl when they took her calves from her for branding and tagging, castrating if needed. She'd just stand off by herself, listen to her calf scream, and watch the process as though such a thing was an inevitability she could do nothing about.

He had never had to check her ear tag to know who she was. She was known.

Jack finished his smoke, snubbed the thing out on the sole of his boot, breathed deep of the land, sighed, and turned to the cow.

After untying the rope he'd secured around the cow's head and forelegs, he threw it in the pickup's bed, sat to his haunches and took off his glove. Placed his hand on her white face, gently stroked her. "You were a good ol' cow," he said. He pulled his hat back down on his forehead, stood up and drove the Dodge back to the home place.

///

"You get that cow up to the bone yard?" His brother, Bob, twenty-eight, now at the top of the familial male line, said as he sipped coffee at the pine table centered in the kitchen. A new day had begun with gathering for breakfast. The day would end with them sharing supper at the same table.

The kitchen was his mama's space. She'd put her touch to it through the years. Frilly red and blue curtains on the east and south windows, each panel tied in the middle with strips of fine lace. Told her boys to paint the room yellow after her husband had passed. "Make it brighter," she'd said. A red and white checkered cloth covered the table. Porcelain knickknacks, cows mostly but some horses and pigs, sat on the windowsills.

"Got 'er up there yesterday." Jack sat down at the table, let his mama pour him a cup of coffee, lay out his cigarette papers and bag of tobacco. "Funny thing, though, that old cow had no bloat. 'Cept for where she'd tore herself up, wasn't any death signs… maggots, stiffness. Looked as though nothin' was chewin' on 'er either." He licked the lengthwise end of a rolled smoke, gently sealed it.

Hank, Jack's other brother, twenty-five and suffering an itch to leave ranching, go to Denver and do anything not involving cow shit, came in from outside and sat down at the table. "You take care a that cow, Jack?"

"What we been talkin' about." Jack tipped a milk carton over his coffee.

"Jack says she showed no sign of bloat. Nothin' nibblin' on 'er either." Bob sipped his coffee, smiled at Hank. "She's been missin' for a week."

Hank winked at Bob. "Some kinda super cow, I guess. Whadaya think Jack? Or maybe she was just so damned ornery in life she just figured she'd play with us a bit. Just lay down and die, turn her meat sour so she wasn't no good for nothin'… not even Purina."

Jack fiddled with his coffee cup, looked at the tabletop. "She gave us some good calves, Hank. Not much else you could ask of a cow."

"What cow you talkin' about?" Mama Klein bent to the stove, turned on a gas burner, and scooted a skillet over the flame.

"That purposeful old cow we was gonna take to auction. The dried-up one," Bob said.

Jack watched his mama. She had known this cow, too. The greater part of her life on the ranch she had kept the ledgers, the histories of the cattle that had served to pay the mortgage, put food on their table, and keep the electric flowing. She'd sit at a card table at branding time and note the ear tag numbers of the calves, trace the numbers back to the cows who'd dropped them, determine the fate of cows that hadn't given birth for at least two seasons. "I know that cow. She was a loner. Had a distain for mixin' with the herd. That the one?"

THE COW

"That's the one," Jack said, smiling, raising his cup.

Mama Klein broke eggs and let the innards slip into the skillet glazed with bacon grease. "That cow did well by us. Worth her weight."

Hank smiled, traded a glance with Bob. "Worth her weight," he said as the aroma of rising biscuits seeped from the oven.

///

Jack and Hank worked fence north of the home place on the old Reineke spread. Their daddy had bought the land after the Reinekes had given up on it, seeking less constant toil with a promise of greater rewards elsewhere. Reineke now pumped gas in Oak Creek. His wife tended bar at the old Depot Café, where she listened to old men trade lies over longnecks, their butts glued to cracked plastic stool cushions, elbows propped on the oak bartop. The old mens' palms invariably brushed their cheeks, thorny from the sprout of three or four days of growth. Oil and grit-soiled ballcaps pushed up a bit as they stared in silence at satellite-fed ESPN. Missus Reineke wondered through her days, as did her husband, why they'd forsaken the land for this meager toil.

///

"Don't look too bad." Hank grabbed a shovel from the bed of the Dodge, walking to a failed post. "Seen it worse."

Jack pulled pliers from his back pocket and yanked staples from the grayed pine as his brother loosened up the soil around its base.

"Been wantin' to tell you," Hank said, pounding his boot sole on the edge of the shovel. "All that talk about that cow, the one you pulled up to the bone yard? Didn't mean anything by it. Bob just gets me goin' sometimes. Hard not to get all caught up in his... Oh, I guess you'd call it sarcasm. Just like Daddy. Bob's a mean-spirited man."

Jack held the top of the post, watched Hank get to the bottom of the thing where he wedged his shovel against the rotted wood and worked to pry it up. "Didn't take offense."

"Not that I give a shit about some old cow, but I do suppose that particular cow had somethin' special about 'er. Noticed it myself over the years. Bob? Well, Bob ain't never looked at a cow other than somethin' that lives for a while, gives up some calves, dries up, and heads for the auction. But I grant you, that particular cow was notable in a way. Different."

"Notable," Jack said. Remembered the moment he'd spent with the cow, his hand against her face, the words he'd spoken.

The brothers worked the fence, stretching the barbed wire taut, replacing grayed posts with metal. They goddamned the certainty that bull elk had trampled the fence, getting where they needed to go through the winter from high meadow to low, using the hay spread for cattle as sustenance. The fence became a momentary nuisance to an eight-hundred pound ten- or twelve-point bull elk. Fences were easily conquered by elk, bear, and deer. Most jumped over them, many just walked through them. The critters did not share the notions of men who saw a fence line as an intendment, an essential component of a trinity encompassing fat calves, good harvest, and the corral of critters destined for slaughter.

A week of work on the north fence only provided the necessity to work the east and the south fence line where acreage would soon be flooded and hay meadows would once again bloom. The imminent dropping of calves also defined the course of labor required of the brothers, an imperative taught by their daddy who'd inured each of them to the trudge of their days since they'd ceased suckling at their mama's teats.

///

Bob worked on the calving barn, replacing failed slats and plugging holes in the roof. Hollered from up there for Hank and

THE COW

Jack to ride the high meadow to the south and check on the heifers, the two-year-olds who'd soon drop their first calves. "Ride that fence line, too," he'd told them, knowing the hay meadow to the south would soon be flooded.

Jack and Hank saddled horses and felt the joy of the simple gift of such critters that blew from their nostrils, shook their heads, and chewed metal bits as an unsavory necessity, a prelude to get moving, to break the bounds of the stalls to which so much of their lives were confined.

Jack'd taken Rufus, a six-year-old sorrel gelding whose purpose it seemed was to object mightily to the presence of a rider making decisions as to his direction. Out of the barn, Rufus flapped his head, sidestepped, blew, farted, lowered then raised his head in an attempt to free himself from the pull of the reins. Jack gently slapped the gelding on the neck, spoke softly, leaned forward in the saddle, and told the horse he was a good boy. They were moving, would maybe run a little when they got to the meadow. Jack tightened his hold on the reins as Rufus adjusted his spirit to accommodate the nuisance on his back.

Hank had climbed on a paint, a twelve-year-old mare named Lucille who'd long ago come to an understanding of her place in the world. She watched Rufus gyrate through the motions of a less learned critter than herself. Then, as Jack managed control over the gelding and they began a slow walk up to the high scrub, Lucille followed behind without Hank's nudging. She'd been through this exercise before.

As they neared the bone yard, both horses stepped off the trail, intent on distancing themselves from the peculiarity they sensed as something wrong, something not usual amongst the detritus of death.

Jack and Hank reined the horses back on the trail, saw their withers spasm, shaking and raising their heads. They neighed with discomfort.

"Well, goddamn, would you look at that?" Jack stopped Rufus. The horse turned his head away from the sight of the old cow still not bloated, still not chewed up.

"Jesus H.," Hank said, noticing too that Lucille had again

turned away from the sight.

"Jack and Hank sat silently. Stared at the cow.

"She's been up here five, six days, Jack. What the hell?"

"Don't know." Jack worked to keep Rufus steady.

"Maybe we shoulda' set her afire. Appears nature ain't taking its way with her."

Jack shook his head. "No need for that. Critters'll get to her soon enough. Just leave her be."

Hank smiled. "You say so. Kinda your cow, anyway. Come on, let's get up the hill."

Jack continued to stare for a moment. Eased up on the reins. Rufus didn't wait for further guidance. The gelding lurched up the hill.

///

Full moon.

A lambent glow bathed Mama Klein's kitchen. The porcelain critters on the windowsills, stoic, silent as stone, provided a dulled hint of their vibrant colors—reds, blues, yellows. Jack sat at the table. Saw no need for illumination other than what seeped from the moon. He'd quietly slipped from his bed with a sense of something wrong, something that robbed his restful sleep. He brewed coffee, sipped it, folded his hands on the table and looked at them as if they'd provide some solace, some explanation for the wrongness of the night. He rolled a cigarette, lit it with his daddy's Zippo. Watched his exhale slink toward the east-facing window.

The fingers of volcanic plugs, now bathed by a full moon, gave up shadows to the land below as momentary gifts, as safe harbor for critters understanding the worth of remaining unseen by the winged hunters circling above.

Dull gray to black, silent, five hundred feet above, audacious puffs of cumuli eased across the stretch of high prairie. Settled a moment above the bone yard, above the Klein's depository for dead critters left to the caprice of the elements—the critters now bare outlines of themselves, evidence only that they had once existed, alive upon the land. The clouds crept north, an unlikely passage given the blow of the forever wind in the opposite direction.

Jack stood up and looked out the east-facing window. Saw the black jut of Finger Rock three miles away. Saw too the moon shadows, eerie in a way. He sucked his smoke, sighed the result through his nose. Turned toward the south-facing window that opened up to the view of high scrub and the trail leading to the bone yard, pine, fir, and aspen showing shadows of their own substance.

Jack leaned closer to the window. Saw the gray-black presence, a promise of rain suspended above the incline, almost touching the tops of lodgepole pine. Thought it odd the northerly movement of the clouds defied the easterly flow of the wind. The moon glow blinked, and a few seconds of total darkness filled the kitchen as the clouds slipped even farther north. Jack sat back down at the table. Sucked on his smoke, wondered about the old cow, still pristine in the bone yard. The wrongness of the night had passed. He lifted his cup from the saucer, snubbed out the glow of his cigarette upon the china plate, stood up, carried both the cup and saucer to the sink, and rinsed them under the tap. He carefully and quietly slipped past his mother's bedroom and those of his brothers. Entered his bedroom where he eased back into his bed, into sleep comforted with an understanding that whatever it was that had called him from his bed had been assuaged. How? Why? He didn't know. But it had.

///

The Reineke spread, north of the home place and now part of the Klein's ten thousand acres, gave witness to those who had come before the Reinekes. Near the Bear River, upon a small rise fifty yards from the flow of the water, a grayed but sturdy one-room shack snuggled into the rise, its lower half dug into the earth, the earth walls three feet up from the floor, with another three feet of pine logs above that supported the roof. The shack remained intact in spite of a century or more of seasonal wear and tear and the occasional flood of the river. Three windows, one each on the west, south, and east walls, were undersized, utilitarian in a way only to allow sunshine entrance and to disallow the intrusion of the constant wind and troublesome critters. The door to the structure remained intact, a door best suited to dwarfs, barely four feet to the vertical.

Jack, favoring Rufus—the gelding's spirit not so much a challenge, but a wonder—sat astride the sorrel, his legs straddling the horse's barrel. He understood the spasm of the feisty gelding's withers as the essential want of the critter's nature to move, work itself to a sweat. He coaxed Rufus north, up to the yet-to-be flooded hay meadow.

He reined Rufus just short of this ancient shack of folks unknown, folks intent on making a go of it along the Bear River, content to live within the clutch of earthen walls and a ceiling of pine. He dismounted, tied off Rufus to a cottonwood and walked to the old home place of folks who'd left this simple testament to being solidly here upon the land. As children, he and his brothers had played in and around the old shack, had imagined it an impenetrable fortress against raids of White River Utes who'd once valued this land as theirs, given by the Sinawav the Creator.

Feeling a need he could not articulate in words, he walked the perimeter of the half-buried structure, stepped closer, then stooped to look into the interior through a tiny window. Sunlight shone through the east-facing window, painting a square of brilliance on the floor. He stepped back, almost stumbled. Stood for a moment trying to wrap his mind around what he'd just seen.

"No sir," he said, shaking his head and once again walking around the structure, noting it was intact, the door stuck shut, the windows too small for anything except rodents or birds to pass through. He stopped his pace where he'd begun it.

He turned his head, saw Rufus munching new spring grass, saw the dot of black baldies in the distance, a Hereford here and there, a single Charolais large with calf who studied him from just yards away, focusing her stare as if asking a question of weighty import. He turned back to the window and again bent

THE COW

down and peered in. "Christ A'mighty." The purposeful cow lay there, her white head fully framed by the sunlight. *Can't be!*

He stood up, backed away, ran to Rufus, pulled the tie rope from the tree, and mounted. He clicked his tongue against his cheek, gently slapped his heels against the horse's barrel. Stuck his hand atop his hat and pushed it down secure on his head. They galloped south.

Jack slowed Rufus at the foot of the trail. The horse blew, snorted, and shook its head. Nearing the bone yard, he expected the same reaction from Rufus as before, the same intent to shy from the place. But Rufus kept to the trail and seemed to calm himself as they got closer. Once there, he reined Rufus to the depression of land where decades of bones lay scattered by the critters that'd gnawed or picked the meat from them. He halted Rufus, held the reins in his left hand, and dismounted. Stared at the leavings of the dead. The purposeful old cow wasn't there. Her bones, newly stripped, were not atop the others. Knew this revelation, whatever it meant, would not be shared with his brothers, his mama. This thing was his and his alone.

///

In time, Hank's itch to get off the land came to pass. Bob and Jack bought out his share of the ranch. He headed for Denver where he found little gold in the glitter. Quickly burned through the cash he'd arrived with. Worked on cars, did some carpentry, plumbing. Aged himself into a life of lost dreams. Often thought about the land, the ranch. Married twice, divorced once. The second wife just left one day and never returned to the little house crammed in with others in a neighborhood of postage stamp front and back yards that bordered thin streets and skinny alleys.

Mama Klein died on a Sunday in her kitchen as she dusted her knickknacks. Fell to the floor with the punch of a freight train slamming hard into the left side of her body. Bob and Jack buried her ashes next to their daddy's in a high meadow surrounded by aspen.

Bob eventually married, had two children. Girls. Wondered why the Good Lord had done such a thing to him. The girls came to consider cows as shit machines, horses as oddities. Lowered their eyes and giggled at the exposure of penises longer than their forearms. The girls came to value pom-poms and quarterbacks to the exclusion of the land and the critters upon it.

Bob was able to see his girls grow into adulthood. He wasn't able to stop the clot of blood that slowly eased itself to his brain, toppling him to ground on another Sunday morning as he pulled a calf from a heifer that'd not yet quite got the hang of birthing.

///

Oak Creek is a lazy burg near Yampa on the High Plains of north central Colorado, a two-minute wide place in the road for those taking the scenic route to Steamboat Springs where million dollar condos house the seasonal influx of the affluent. Up a side road in Oak Creek is the old train depot, the first floor now a bar frequented by the locals, ranchers and coal diggers, and those servicing the needs of folks ensconced in the comfort of their wealth in Steamboat. The bar offers burgers and fries, other tasty fare, alcohol, cable-fed ESPN.

///

Now older than he ever wanted to be, Jack sits at the bar in the old depot. Has pushed his sweat-soiled hat up on his head, leans over a longneck and smokes a hand-rolled cigarette lit with the gold-colored Zippo. His ass rests on cracked plastic, crisscrossed with gray duct tape. He's bookended by two others, gray-haired, both stubbly-faced from the lack of necessity to shave on a daily basis.

"Your heifers about ready to throw their calves?" one of the men asks Jack.

"About to. Keepin' an eye on 'em," Jack says.

"You short-handed now that Bob is gone?" The rumpled geezer on the other side of Jack says. "I guess I could give you some time with them heifers."

Jack draws on his cigarette, lets the smoke slide from his mouth and nose, puts the cigarette in the little brass ashtray. He tips his longneck to his lips. "Well," he says, placing the bottle back on the bar, "I guess I got it covered. Got some hired help out there."

Jack and the two grizzled presences on either side of him watch the flash of ESPN, smoke their poison, tip their longnecks to their lips. Jack wonders if these old boys also consider their immediate future as a thing undefined, encompassing their slipslide into an age where they each figure their worth as men upon the land is waning. Wonders if their memories encompass their youth, now lost to hired hands, to young men whose commitment to the land and the critters upon it pretty much pales to the worth of a paycheck.

///

Jack Klein never married, never took his yearn for another man's love beyond the yearning stage, as acting on such a thing had been thinkable but impossible. Never saw the need for family other than what the land provided. Now, he sits alone in the kitchen of the home place that had once seen the chatter and nonsense of kin resolute in the singular urge to harden the glue that held them together—the land and everything upon it. Jack sips coffee, smokes his cigarette. Wonders if his hired hands have taken his earlier direction to complete tasks he sees as essential. Hell, he thinks, they probably just while away the hours, not engaged by the urge to do right by me, the land, or the critters. He glances at the delicate caricatures his mama had long ago placed on the kitchen's windowsills, now undusted and unmoved for so many years. Stands and puts his coffee cup in the sink. Turns off the light and walks down the hallway to his bedroom. He pulls off his clothes, tugs the bedclothes to his chest, and stares at the night around him. Thinks it significant that he's slept well, undisturbed for years, ever since that night he'd seen the black billow of cloud creep north, not a drop of rain let loose as it passed. Ever since that day he'd found that old cow still whole in the ancient shack, undisturbed by the want of nature to return her to dust.

///

Come daylight, Jack mounts the six-year-old purely black mare he'd named Mary. Just Mary. She was a gentle soul bought at auction a year before. She'd caught his eye with her own. Seemed to Jack she had seen something of his soul that day of the sale; something deeply personal that he'd never shared with anyone, but damned if she hadn't seen inside him. Corralled amongst many, her black coat shining like silk, her eyes engaged with his own. He'd shaken his head and acknowledged her insight, believed she knew more about him than he did about her. Had seen the worth of taking her home.

"You know the way, Mary." Jack barely reins the mare, the daily routine now known by the horse, their course set for the old Reineke spread and on to the shack by the river.

Mary stops just short of the half-buried structure, lowers her head and begins to munch sprouts of grass. Jack dismounts, knowing he doesn't need to tie Mary off. Knows she will stay close, come when she's called.

He walks to within ten yards of the shack, sits down on the meadow grass, lights up a cigarette, and huffs the smoke to the sky. Looks at the brilliant blue above. He'd long ago stopped checking on the interior of the shack. It was always the same. The old cow still lay there as if sleeping, unspoiled, not ruined by the ravages of nature. He'd ceased to wonder at the mystery of the thing. It was what it was. Hell, he was too damned old to ponder the meaning of it all.

After a half-hour or so, Jack whistles to Mary, waits for the mare to sidle up to him. Ready to mount her, he turns back to the shack. Thinks a moment about what has just crossed his mind. Steps away from the mare, pulls his Zippo from his pocket. Sits to his haunches in front of the tiny east-facing window, fingers

THE COW

the lighter, opening and closing the top with his thumb.

"Yessir, you were a good old cow," he says, staring at the lighter for a moment, thinking something of himself ought to be in there with her. Smiles with the childlike, foolish thought, but nevertheless tosses the Zippo through the little window, into the blackness within. He mounts Mary, pats her softly on the neck, and tells her nothing much of substance other than the simple words of an old man who has come to value quiet conversations with horses. "You go where you want, Mary. Got nothin' but time." As they move on to wherever Mary has a mind to go, Jack looks back at the old homestead, sunk halfway into the earth. Satisfied in accepting the notion that the Good Lord works in mysterious ways, he pulls his hat off and lets the forever wind cool his brow. Laughs at himself, says to Mary, "Good Lord had nothin' to do with it."

///

Jack props pillows against the headboard, raises himself, and glances at his bedroom window. Sees the moon is full, the glow framed as a picture. He reaches to the side table, rolls a cigarette, and lights it with the blue plastic BIC he'd picked up at Reineke's gas station. He watches the smoke lose its substance, fan out and fade to nothing. He smiles. Sees the moon glow blink to black for an instant, then return. Remembers another time, another cloud that had paled the moon. He caresses the thought carried at the back of his mind and within the center of his soul, wishing for the honor to lie next to that purposeful cow, there at the edge of the meadow within the embrace of earthen walls.

///

Jack's bed is empty, the bedclothes still pulled up to the pillow, a BIC lighter, a bag of tobacco, and rolling papers on the side table.

The first light of day turns the meadow golden. The forever

wind has wound down to a kindly breeze, and the rush of Bear Creek is heard as a melody to those men and critters who find it in themselves to listen. Just listen. Mary—no tack, no saddle—munches grass hay stubble in the meadow near the grayed shack half buried in the earth. She has become a purposeful horse, managing to free herself from a corral of pine poles rotted with age. If, at this moment, she remembers anything at all, it is that she had seen in the old man's eyes a hunger for the perfection of the earth. If, at this moment, she concludes anything at all, it is that she has served her purpose, and has come to understand the portent of a dry cloud shoving against the constancy of the forever wind.

An Intended Life

Sam Coyle was alone and apart from the other boys because he felt that way—alone and apart. Sat on the floor where one hallway intersected another, a place where he could hear her before he and the others saw her. The other boys were farther down the hallway where they huddled as conspirators speaking in hushed, adolescent tongues. Sam heard a door close. Then came the whooshing and clicking—a singular nun noise they all knew too well. And there she was, her skirts and veil black as a crow's belly, the purely white wimple, the oversized rosary dangling from her side, broad-heeled old woman shoes, a face carved from granite, eyes the color of and as cold as an artic berg, hands hidden behind the black scapular at her front.

They of the summer catechism lot had gathered in the hallway outside a basement classroom, their conversations those of fourteen-year-old boys more attuned to baseball and bikes than the infinite mysteries of the church. Their parents, or at least their mothers, had insisted on this—two weeks, three hours a day of what they had come to know as interminable contrivances, or, better said, Sister Mary Joseph's attempts to explain the unexplainable.

Sam joined the others whose chatter ceased as she approached. Staring at them for a moment as if they were an oddity beyond description, she pulled her hand palm up from under the scapular and motioned toward the door. She fingered the beads at her side as the twenty of them passed into the classroom.

"Good morning," she said from the front of the room after they had sat at the individual desks lined up in four rows. Many of them glanced at the bright summer day outside the ground-level windows, turned back to Sister Mary Joseph and responded, "Good morning, Sister," said more as sighs than words.

"Today's lesson," she said, folding her hands in front of her, "is the Holy Trinity. Please open your books to the third chapter."

Sam and those who'd remembered to bring their catechisms with them did as they were told. Those who'd not remembered got them from where they were lined up below the windows and returned to their desks.

And, as always, their questions about the content of the day's lesson would invariably be answered with the explanation that reason alone was incapable of understanding the Great Mysteries of the Church. Only faith would eventually lead to the answers they sought, and that eventuality would arrive only after they joined God, who was Jesus, who was the Holy Spirit in heaven.

They of the summer catechism lot either believed what Sister Mary Joseph told them or they didn't. Most of them spent little time thinking about it even though, as the good Sister often said, their immortal souls were at stake. They just had better things to do. In Sam's case, he had always believed without really thinking about it that God, three persons or not, was too large, too complex, too unknowable to be adequately described within the pages of a book or believed through the inadequacies of faith alone. But lately another thought had begun to quietly impose itself upon him. Maybe God was something very basic, something very simple. Maybe God was everything seen and heard, felt, smelled, tasted, and dreamed about. Maybe God was everything, something that even embraced the queer Sam knew he was and always had been.

///

Now, nearly a lifetime behind him, his gait a shuffle more than a walk, Sam stopped about halfway up the dirt road to his house. He pressed his palm against his neck, then took off his once-black felt cowboy hat and drew his arm across his forehead, leaving a wet stain on his shirtsleeve. Felt the cool breeze that shivered itself off the snowpack from Mount Lincoln to the northwest, nodded his thanks to the gracious gentleman, and then studied his hat for a moment. Wondered why the hell he still wore it.

Though it was misshapen and discolored by use, rain, snow, sweat, and more than a thousand days of mountain sunshine that had baked it to near brittleness, he figured it still had worth. At least to him it did. He put it back on as he resumed his ascension toward the house. His boots were scuffed and creased, though the leather was still supple from uncounted hours of care. He glanced down at them and listened to his shuffle across the red-orange sandy ground spotted with pebbles and rocks. Knew the sound bore witness to his passage into an age he didn't want to be but was. Knew, too, his gait had been compromised by the several times he'd been dumped by horses, his pelvis adversely readjusted as a result.

He'd loved those horses in spite of their faults if they were faults at all. Figured the horses had loved him with the same qualification. The old Ute who'd lived up the mountain—called himself Joe Spotted Elk—once told Sam a horse knew more about what was on its back than what was on its back knew about it. Sam thought that was probably right and didn't argue the point. Had always thought horses and dogs knew more about him than he did about them.

He found himself looking down more often, watching where he stepped instead of studying the landscape on either side where he knew critters hid out and searched for sustenance or safety among the pine, fir, and aspen trees, the wild grasses, junipers, boulders, and other recesses. Now that he looked where he was going rather than where he wasn't, he wondered how many critters had escaped his passage unseen. A number of them, he thought.

Even coyotes, with their sly smiles, their golden eyes that

could see to the depth of a man's soul were probably watching him right now from just feet away. Considered the notion time had passed too quickly for him. Smiled with the conclusion time didn't give a shit about him or what he thought about it. Time just was. Pausing again, he looked toward the house he'd built almost forty years ago and affirmed, as he'd lately done over and over again, he was happy he'd done it then because he couldn't do it now. Lots of things he couldn't do now.

Years ago, he'd decided what course his life would take. It was a sweet comfort knowing he'd achieved what he'd intended to do. Were there other roads he could have taken? Of course, but right now it didn't matter. Maybe it had never mattered. When he was a young man, he'd known all along this would be where he'd spend his days until he departed the earth for whatever lay beyond, if anything at all did.

He remembered Sister Mary Joseph's admonition that only faith in the Great Mysteries would save his soul. But he'd long ago found faith in things that had nothing to do with the inexplicable conundrums the good Sister roused. The First Nations people, the Ute in particular, had figured it out a long time before old men from a world away started writing down their God and creation stories that had led to so many unanswered questions. There was no mystery, there were no questions, there was no need to put into printed words what Sam had begun to believe even as a boy—Father Sky and Mother Earth were immediate and explainable.

Hell, Senawahv, the Creator in Ute belief, hadn't even foredoomed humanity with *original sin*. The Creation? Well, all Senawahv did was put some sticks in a bag, intending the sticks to become people to whom he would give the lands he'd created. But Coyote, the sly trickster, upended the bag and the sticks became people who ran away helter-skelter. Senawahv looked into the bag, and at the bottom remained a brave and strong people who would know the sky and the land and the critters upon it as sacred things, all part of the imperative of life he had envisioned and created.

Senawahv gave the Rocky Mountains and the westernmost Colorado prairie to the Ute people. Sam knew he had only borrowed a small piece of that sacred land and was grateful he'd been able to live a good life upon it. Whether he believed the story about Coyote or not, he thought it was a good one, and it made him smile every time he thought about it. It was after all as credible as Adam and Eve and Cain and Abel. Maybe more credible, Sam thought, whenever he wondered where Cain's wife had come from.

Sam resumed his trudge, stopped again, looked to the side of the road at something that had caught his interest. Saw the first assurance spring was easing itself upon the land. Pasque flower shoots had emerged, a bunching of three, and one off by itself. Smiling, he stood over the delicate purple-white sprouts, sat to his haunches and gently touched each of them one at a time. Whispered, "Thank you for coming."

///

Sam Coyle was born and raised in Denver, Colorado, a city bemoaned at the time by politicians, pundits, and the Chamber of Commerce as being a cow town. Or so his daddy had told him one day when he'd taken him downtown.

"Seems folks are never satisfied with what they have, Sam, and always want something better," his daddy said as they watched the demolishment of the Tabor Grand Opera House, once touted as the most spectacular edifice west of the Mississippi.

"Horace Tabor began as a storekeeper in Leadville, grubstaked the owners of the Little Pittsburg Mine, then bought the Matchless Mine, and was soon known as the Bonanza King of Leadville. You might recall from your studies that Tabor kept a consort named Baby Doe?"

"Yes." Sam nodded. Watched the wrecking ball.

"She died a pauper," his daddy said. Both watched the walls come tumbling down.

Sam waited for his daddy to explain what lesson he should take from watching the destruction before them and the little history he'd provided to him. When all his daddy did was turn away and tell him they'd better head for home, Sam made his own conclusions: someday he'd move to the mountains where the only consorts he'd need would be the earth and the sky and the critters who trekked across both. His home would be made from what the earth provided and the things he could touch and fashion with his own hands. And the Chamber of Commerce would be damned.

That was 1964. Sam was sixteen years old, a good student. Swam freestyle for the team, pinned blue and red ribbons on his bedroom wall, read John Updike's *The Centaur* in one sitting, and Dante's *The Inferno* in three. He preferred Crisco to baby oil when his best friend Kirby Dean slept over. "It's just oilier," Sam told Kirby as he'd pull a glob out of the can with two fingers and gently loosen the entry point.

Sam graduated from high school, going directly to the United States Army and finding himself at Fort Polk, Louisiana in the dog days of summer where he was trained to kill gooks in black pajamas. Vietnam was the destination for most young men who'd been sent to Polk at that time, and Sam thought the adventure that lay before him boded possibilities bordering on the epic.

"I don't know why you joined the army," Sam's mother said, nearly sobbing, her eyes wet. "It's not a good place to be right now."

Sam sat in the living room of the only house he'd ever known. Had come home on his last leave before commencing the adventure he'd envisioned for himself, and had known before he'd crossed the threshold that what made his mother his mother, her Italian-ness, would rule the day.

Scooting closer to his mother on the couch that was as old as he was, Sam said, "I'll be fine," as he put his arm around her shoulders. "I'll be okay," he added, knowing what he'd imagined of his future did not include the dark prospect of a maiming or his death. He'd be a soldier and would return to realize the dream he'd fashioned for himself the day he and his father had watched the demise of the grandest edifice west of the Mississippi. He was sure of that.

"I went to war," his father said, sitting in a puffy recliner across from the couch where he sipped scotch and sucked on a fat cigar. "We beat the Japs and Hitler, too. What they got going in Vietnam is child's play compared to that. A goddamned turkey shoot. Sam will do fine, Guistina. He's doing something noble with his life."

"You should be in college." His mother pulled out the handkerchief she'd stuck under the hem of her sleeve. "You could have gotten a deferment. Ah, *Dio abbia pietà di mio bambino.*" She wiped her eyes and dabbed at her nose.

"Dad's right," Sam said. "I'll be fine."

///

Sam went to Vietnam a boy and returned a man who'd killed other men before they'd had a chance to kill him. If he were to describe his experience in Vietnam to anyone—something he never did and would never do—then 'kill or be killed' would constitute the sum total of that story. He could not relate the stories about his friends, his brothers who'd fallen there, or who'd come home without a limb or their minds forever lost to the darkness Vietnam had become. He'd anticipated epic experiences in Nam before he got there, but when he returned home his definition of epic was transmuted into an image that mirrored Charon ferrying dismal souls across the Styx.

When Sam reconnected with his best friend Kirby Dean, he wasn't surprised Kirby was engaged to Betty Collins, a slightly built blonde and giddy girl who, in only three years, had filled out with nice tits, had shed her thick glasses and the silver braces on her teeth. She was working the counter at the U-Gas-Em to support Kirby's matriculation at Metropolitan State College in Denver. Sam visited their one bedroom apartment on Washington Street in the Capitol Hill neighborhood and knew even before he'd sat down on the floor with them—they'd not yet found the wherewithal to buy furniture—that Kirby had grown up, too. They'd known each other as intimately as two boys ever could, but it was only a phase now shrouded in embarrassment and regret for Kirby. And after an hour of senseless gab and uncomfortable silences, after finishing the can of Coors he'd been handed when he first sat down, Sam told them he had to go.

Kirby followed Sam out of the apartment and stopped in the hallway. Looking into Sam's eyes, he said, "That stuff we used to do? You and me? That can stay just between us. Right? We were only kids, Sam. What would Betty say? What would my mother think?"

Sam had left the realm of ordinary people a long time ago, certainly that of his ordinary childhood which he'd shared with Kirby. He'd read a bit of Kierkegaard in boot camp and a line came back to him: "Men's thoughts are thin and flimsy like lace, they are themselves pitiable like the lacemakers."

Sam looked at Kirby and remembered the face of the boy he'd kissed in Nam, conscious but dying of a mortal wound to his stomach. Michael had lain half buried in the black, stinking mire of that detestable jungle, the endless *zzzzzipt* of incoming above and all around them, and he had called out for his mother: "Mama, help me. Where are you, Mama? Please help me."

And Sam had leaned over him, held his face between his palms, leaned down and kissed his lips, saying, "I'm here, Michael. It's all right. I've got you. Mama's here." Michael had then stopped calling out and appeared to die in peace.

"Sure," Sam said, smiling at Kirby. "We were just kids. It didn't *mean* anything."

///

Sam's mother was a Pauldino, her brother Paul, called Fat Pauly, ran the Pauldino business with the quiet strength of a puma ready to pounce, his prey often those who'd miscalculated his calm reserve. When Sam finally finished his three-year enlistment in the Army, Fat Pauly told him to come over to his restaurant where they'd talk about his future. And one Friday afternoon, Sam did that.

"I got somethin' for you, Sammy," Fat Pauly said as he spooned red sauce over the three cheese and sausage-filled ravioli on his plate.

"What's that, Pauly?" Sam sliced a hunk of lasagna with his fork.

"I got a bar downtown, 20th and Broadway. Queer place. The boys tell me the sissies go in there in black leather, cowboy boots, and, you know... Lots a booze, music, foolin' around with each other. You know, *roba macho*. That kinda place."

"Okay."

"Fuckin' manager ain't no good. He's stealin' from me, and I'm gonna fire his ass. Maybe more. He holds the liquor license, though."

"The license isn't in your name?"

"Nah. Hell, some a my past..." Pauly paused. "You know about the business," he said, shoveling mozzarella on top of the red sauce. "I've been in trouble before. No way they're gonna give me a liquor license."

"Sure, Pauly. I know about the business."

"Here's what I got for you. You take over as manager. We'll get the license in your name, and I'll give you twenty percent of the place. You'll do good. Fuckin' queers like their booze, Sammy. Whadaya say?"

"Ah, Uncle Pauly, I don't know. I—"

"You come home from the war a hero in my mind. It's the least I can do for you. And there ain't no funny business goin' on with the bar. It's legit. And if them pansies hit on you, you can take care of yourself. Right? Okay? You can go to college in the daytime if you want."

"Don't want to go to college," Sam said, taking a sip of beer. "Got my own dream, though. I guess I could make some money at the bar, then do what I want to do."

"'Course you can, Sammy. We all got dreams."

Stonewall had set the tone for liberation and excess the year before Sam had come home from the war. When he was discharged two years later, he stepped right into the manifestation of what the Stonewall riots had accomplished. The *Big Party* commenced with robust aplomb and, yes, an aggressive sense of self-worth that demanded all men and women were indeed created equal and must be treated as such.

Sam actually found himself enjoying the work Uncle Pauly had handed to him because it was something to do. He'd learned since coming back from Nam that idle time was spent in dangerous places. The bar thrived, the crowds on Friday and Saturday nights were packed ass to cock, the booze flowed, and the camaraderie of men being men in all facets of their desires and kinks impressed Sam as something as natural as flight to a bird. But during the weekdays, in the daylight hours when the bar became eerily quiet, the place lost its purpose for him. He worked on the books then, ordered product, supervised the cleaning, and hired new staff.

Sam had come home from the Army without an intent to pursue his sexuality to any degree other than his acceptance of it, maybe meet a good man who abjured the ordinariness of passion *sans* love, and to avoid gathering places ironically like the bar where he now worked. If Vietnam had taught him nothing else, it had instilled in him the worth of life where relationships were spiritual, even holy, and that lust might or might not lead to love because it existed in the realm of the ordinary.

He had not avoided the park, though. Cheesman Park had been the nexus for liaisons by men of like minds for decades, even generations. It had never been a secret to anyone that young men skulked the park beginning in the early evening when the sun began its descent behind the purple jut of the Front Range on the Rocky Mountains. Sam often sat in the marble-columned pavilion on the knoll, watching, as many others did, the setting sun give way to the shadows of the evening. And when the mommies and daddies who had come to see the spectacle finally took their children home, the men would begin their prowl with quick glances and subtle smiles. Once the invitation had been accepted, the men paired off and sat down again on the knoll, away from the dimly lit pavilion, traded names—real names or not— and commenced a dialogue to determine, firstly, if their chosen one was homicidally inclined or a cop; and secondly, if they were simpatico. If they were, the rites of the night were pursued, most often in one or the other's house or apartment or the dark recesses behind the clumps of bushes that spotted the perimeter of the park.

Sam met Stephen on a lovely spring evening at Cheesman Park. He'd not intended to meet someone that night. He just wanted to watch the sunset, alone with his thoughts before heading to the bar—to the noise, smoke, the gradually intensifying odor of urine from the bathroom without a door, the sloppiness of the drunks, the egos burning bright and hot, the posers posing, the bar backs slacking off, the pretty Boulder boys slumming, standing huddled in coteries where they giggled and pointed at hairy asscheeks exposed by seatless black chaps. No, he'd only wanted to embrace himself in the calm of the evening, drinking in the charming *oohs* and *ahhs* of neighborhood children who saw the blues, purples, oranges, and reds of the sunset as pretty gifts from Mother Earth and Father Sky given as hopeful signs the world was not really *that* bad. Or, Sam thought, as bad as he'd once thought it to be in a place nearly ten thousand miles away.

He had not even traded a glance or a smile with the dark-haired young man who'd sat down next to him on the knoll and said, "Beautiful evening," his voice as soft as the breeze that had begun to whisper its presence just moments before.

"Yes, it is," Sam said as he turned to look from where such a soothing sound had come. The young man's features were pristine, finely sculpted, so young. A few strands of black hair draped his forehead, and as the man turned his head to look at the mountains, Sam saw the hair around his ear and at the top of his neck was, too, precisely fashioned, sculpted.

"I'm Stephen," the young man said, facing Sam and holding out his hand.

"Sam." He embraced Stephen's hand with his own and looked into blue eyes that appeared to reflect gentleness, perhaps irony, maybe even a hint of amusement.

"You always wear cowboy boots?" Stephen said as he sat down.

"Yes, I do." Sam glanced at Stephen's feet—red tennis shoes with white laces. "Has something to do with where I'd rather be."

"Okay. You'd rather be... Let me see." Stephen paused for a moment, bent down slightly and looked at Sam's face. "I think you'd rather be somewhere where somebody you don't know doesn't ask about your cowboy boots because, well, because they're probably wearing cowboy boots too?"

Sam smiled. "Very perceptive," he said, nodding. The shadows became longer, deeper. "Unfortunately, I have to go to work."

"And where is that?"

Sam told him what he did, the name of the bar, adding, "I'm not that into bars, but it's a job and a person does have to eat. Pay the rent. Put gas in the truck."

"Yeah," Stephen said. "I know. Would you mind if I tagged along? I've never been there, though I've heard about it."

"And what have you heard?"

"Leather, Levis, lots of smoke, poppers, drunks, chickens, chicken hawks, downstairs sex, pool tables, pinball machines, and everybody gets prettier at closing time."

Sam stood up and brushed off his jeans. "That's about it in a nutshell. C'mon." He reached for Stephen's hand. "You can *tag* along with me."

Stephen grabbed Sam's hand, stood up and also brushed off his jeans. "Fair warning, I may not stay long."

"Okay." Sam pulled his keys from his pocket. "Before you leave, though, I'll need your number."

"Of course," Stephen said, following Sam to his truck. "I'll see you there," he said, walking to his car.

The bar was already busy. A beer bust benefiting the Colorado Gay Rodeo organization was underway, and when Sam walked in, his assistant manager rushed to him and explained they had a problem—one of the four taps wasn't working, and they were falling behind. Sam watched the front door a moment to see if Stephen had made it yet. When he didn't see him, he got to work on the tap. After he finally got it working, he looked out into the crowd and saw Stephen step up to the bar and smile at him.

"I'm not staying," Stephen said as Sam leaned his head toward him. "Too many people." He held out a napkin. "There's my number. Call me."

Sam took the napkin and watched Stephen walk out the front door. Stuffed the napkin in his pocket.

///

Sam entered his apartment on Clarkson Street at about three a.m., looked at the napkin on which Stephen had written his number, and laid it next to the phone on the small table that separated his kitchen from his combination living room and bedroom. He opened the refrigerator, pulled out a quart of milk, then grabbed a package of Zingers from the counter, and sat down at the table.

He opened the package, took a bite, washed it down with cold milk, picked up the napkin and studied Stephen's hand. Thought it was precise, readable, and without flourishes. He'd gotten that impression from Stephen himself—except for those red shoes with white laces. He looked at the wall clock to his left and smiled. No, he couldn't call him right now. Wondered for a moment why Stephen hadn't asked for his number. Didn't matter. He'd met some nice men in the park who'd insisted he give them his number, and he had. When they called a second or third time after a one-night encounter, he'd wished he hadn't done that. Decided he was looking for something else besides repeat performances.

"This is Sam," Sam said after punching in the number shortly before noon.

"Sam who?"

"Sam Coyle." Sam knew Stephen was smiling.

"Oh. That Sam."

Sam paused a moment. "You get home okay?"

"Yes, I did. It's Stephen Dunn, by the way."

"Irish?"

"Been told I'm Black Irish. You?"

"And Italian. Fifty fifty."

"Not sure that's a good combination. I'll bet your mother's Italian and your father is Irish."

"How'd you know?"

"Like you said last night, I'm perceptive."

"Okay. I know half the day's gone, but I usually eat breakfast about this time. You want to join me?"

"Sure. I've got a class at three, though."

"We can eat fast. You know where The Kitchen is on Colfax?"

"Everybody knows where The Kitchen is."

"Twenty minutes?"

"Meet you there."

Sam learned that Stephen was studying history at the University of Colorado. He would graduate soon and had already been accepted at the University of Denver, College of Law.

"Going to be a lawyer, then?" Sam sipped coffee, once again looking at those blue eyes.

"Yes, I am. And you're going to be a cowboy somewhere once you decide where you want to plant your boots?"

"Oh, not a cowboy exactly. Just want to make enough money to buy some land in the mountains."

"Colorado mountains?"

Sam nodded. "Of course. Only mountains I know of."

Stephen wadded his napkin into a ball and scooted back a bit in the booth. "You're my age? Twenty-one?"

"Yes." Sam knew he probably looked older.

"You were in Vietnam," Stephen said. It wasn't a question. "In fact," he looked into Sam's eyes, "you graduated from high school, enlisted in the Marines, maybe the Army, went to war and… Well, here you are." Stephen leaned into the table and unfolded the napkin he'd just balled up. "Right?"

"Batting a thousand," Sam said. "It was the Army, though."

"Any regrets?"

Sam folded his hands on table. "'Whether you laugh at the world's follies or weep over them, you will regret both."

Stephen smiled and shook his head. "I neglected to note you've also read Kierkegaard. Nice deflection, but the witness will answer the question?"

"Regrets? No, not really. I regret a lot of what happened over there. But for me? No, I don't."

"You're an interesting man, Sam Coyle, and we've yet to share a bed."

"It's nice we haven't. Not that I don't want to, but…what I've come to expect from guys since I came home is kind of the ordinary way things go nowadays—fuck first, talk later. Not real fond of the ordinary."

Stephen nodded. "Agreed. I've got to get going. When can we spend more than—" he looked at his watch "—forty-seven minutes together?"

"I'm taking Monday off. It's a slow day at the bar. Thought I'd drive up to the mountains. Stay overnight."

"After today, I'm done with classes. I could go with you. To the mountains."

"Okay." Sam grabbed the check and scooted out of the booth. He waited for Stephen to stand. "You can pack a picnic."

"I can do that. What do you like?"

"Anything except raw fish," Sam said as they stopped at the cashier station. "Bring some Zingers—chocolate *and* raspberry."

"Oh. Of course. Zingers." Stephen shook his head as they walked out the door.

Sam followed Stephen to his car and was surprised to see a baby blue BMW roadster.

"Nice car," Sam said.

"It gets me wherever. Shall we take it to the mountains?"

"No." Sam smiled. "We'll take my truck. And bring your toothbrush."

///

Traveling southwest from Denver, catching Colorado Highway 285 from C470, they passed the towns of Conifer, Bailey, Shawnee, Grant, and Jefferson, then climbed to the summit of Kenosha Pass where Sam pulled his truck over. They got out and looked at the spread of the South Park basin below, a thousand square miles of flat grassland nearly ten thousand feet in elevation, where the headwaters of the South Platte River were formed.

"The Ute lived down there," Sam said. "Then the miners and the cavalry came and ended that story in a quick minute."

"It's almost too beautiful to believe," Stephen said.

"C'mon." Sam walked back to the truck. "We've got a ways to go."

"Where we going?"

"You'll see."

Descending from the pass, Sam continued down Colorado 285, turned off at the Fairplay exit, drove through town, and, just after the Alma Junction, turned onto Mosquito Pass Road, a dirt road in poor repair. "It'll get a little bumpy," he said.

"I love bumpy. I've never been up here."

"Well..." Sam shifted to 4L. "I'd like to live around here someday. When we get to the top—*if* we get to the top—we'll be over thirteen thousand feet. This road is called the Highway of the Frozen Death."

"Oh, that's encouraging."

"Yeah. Don't worry. We'll probably run into impassable snow and ice anyway. We'll go as far as we can."

They didn't get far, stopping after about two miles where the road disappeared under a ten-foot barrier of snow and ice.

"We'll have to come back in the middle of summer," Sam said. "Let's get out."

The wind from the northwest carried with it a freeze that belied the springtime fully blossoming in Denver. Sam led the way to the edge of the snowpack, turned around and told Stephen to take a look. Below them, the South Park basin spread out to seeming eternity. Fairplay appeared small and vulnerable.

"Cold as a witch's…" Stephen said, hugging himself. "Great view, though."

"You want to get your coat?"

"Not unless this is where we're going to have our picnic."

"No," Sam said, putting his arm around Stephen's shoulders. "We'll head back over the pass. Rented a cabin for the night. It'll be warmer, too."

As they began to walk back to the car, Sam stopped, let go of Stephen's shoulder, bent down, then sat to his haunches. "Look at this." When Stephen squatted next to him, Sam lightly brushed the light cover of snow off what had caught his attention. "Pasque flowers," he said. "Some people believe they first bloom in late March and early April in celebration of the Ascension."

"Do you believe that?"

"Nah. They bloom when they do because they can, because they just… do."

///

Backdropped by a line of Douglas fir and aspen trees, the cabin—one of four on the property—was a genuine log cabin, well-kept and secluded from the others. It had only two rooms. One included a couch and two chairs, a kitchenette, a queen bed, and a river rock fireplace. The other room was the bathroom. The porch at the back of the cabin had a pine table and two matching chairs.

Sam started a fire inside while Stephen set out the picnic items on the table outside. Once the fire was established, Sam joined Stephen on the porch.

"I hope white is okay," Stephen said, opening the bottle of Chardonnay he'd packed along with two bottles of red. Poured the wine into clear plastic glasses.

Sam looked at the turkey sandwiches on paper plates. "I guess white goes with white."

"Yup." Stephen tore open a bag of potato chips and opened a plastic container with chunks of watermelon, pineapple, and cantaloupe in it. "Fresh fruit, too."

"Zingers?"

"They're in the bag, Sam. Two chocolate, and two raspberry."

"Perfect."

Just as Sam took his first bite of the sandwich, Stephen whispered, "Oh. Look."

Sam turned his head to where Stephen was staring, and there just barely into the tree line stood a mule deer doe with two fawns still spotted on their sides, the whiteness of the spots beginning to fade.

"Cool," Sam said.

"They're watching us."

"Of course they are. They're probably used to being fed from the porch."

"What should I give them?"

"They'll eat that cantaloupe," Sam said.

"Should I?"

"Did you bring it for them or us?"

"Well, us. But..."

"Just eat. If we've got any left, you can give it to them."

Stephen picked three chunks of cantaloupe from the container and threw them out to the deer. "That was my portion," he said as they both watched the deer frantically stot back into the trees, stop, and then ease back toward the fruit.

"Look," Stephen said. "The mama got it all."

"Yeah, and the fawns will be nudging their lips up to her teats in a minute. The babies will get the benefit of your largesse, Stephen."

"Oh, listen to you. *Largesse*."

"C'mon, just eat." Sam smiled. "I'm warming up the cabin for whatever we might want to do in there later."

Stephen nodded. "Okay. It's about time we... Whatevered."

They lay under the sheet, the thick comforter pushed down to the foot of the bed.

Sam had not expected Stephen's passion, the total loss of what Sam had thought defined him—the preciseness, the irony. He'd expected a certain coyness, but when they slipped under the covers, the intensity of Stephen's lovemaking was almost overwhelming, contagious to the point that Sam abandoned the visage that always arose when he made love to another man—the face of that kid, Michael, whom he'd kissed in a place and time he'd thought he would never escape. But he *had* escaped it. Time became only the here and now as Stephen had rolled onto his stomach and said in a nearly frantic whisper, "Fuck me, Sam. Fuck me."

After they cleaned up, Stephen grabbed a bottle of cabernet and plastic cups before they slipped back into the bed. He opened the bottle, poured the wine, and handed a glass to Sam.

"You kiss like an Italian, you fuck like an Irishman," Stephen said.

"Okay." Sam thought the Stephen he'd known before they'd abandoned themselves to their bodies, their lusts, was back.

"You… You're lovely."

"Thank you." Stephen held his cup out to Sam. "You, too. I enjoyed our whatevering."

They touched their cups together, then both sipped.

"You know," Stephen said, "Since I sat down with you in the park, I found myself losing time, actual minutes, just replaying little snapshots of you, even trying to recapture the sound of your voice, the texture of your hair, the color of your eyes, and, yes, your boots. What do you suppose that means?"

"Probably that you live a very boring life."

"Not anymore. Tell me," Stephen scooted slightly away from Sam and turned toward him, "how can you quote Kierkegaard at the drop of a hat."

"I read a lot. Always have."

"Why didn't you go to college?"

"Like I told you, I've got other plans."

"The mountain thing?"

"Yes."

"You could do both."

Sam smiled. "Nah. All the time I was growing up, I always dreamed of getting away somewhere. You know, a place where there's peace. A natural place where you don't have to understand why you're there, only that that's where you belong. Does that make sense?"

"Sure it does."

"And you?" Sam said.

"Where do I belong?"

"Yes."

"I belong…" Stephen hesitated, sipped wine. "I've been bred to fight the good fight in courtrooms. I will be the fourth generation on my father's side to practice law. That's where I belong."

"Are you going to just practice it, or are you actually going to do it?"

"Everyone wants to be a comedian." Stephen pulled the sheet off him and stood up. "Let's eat our Zingers." Put his cup on the floor, grabbed his underwear and pulled them on.

"Good idea." Sam got out of bed. He walked over to the kitchenette and put his cup on the small counter, watching Stephen walk outside to the porch and snatch the bag he'd left out there. Scanned the room for his jeans, saw that he'd dropped them at the side of the bed, walked over there and pulled them on. Realized as he buttoned his fly that he and Stephen had little chance of a future together. They were headed in opposite directions. He regretted that.

"Raspberry or chocolate?" Stephen said coming back into the cabin.

"Raspberry, I guess." Sam wished for a fleeting moment that he'd never met Stephen.

///

Sam attended Stephen's graduation from college, sitting with Stephen's family after having been introduced as an old friend. When Sam was invited to the celebration dinner at Stephen's parents' home—a too-grand-to-believe edifice in Cherry Hills—Sam declined. It was a Friday night, and the bar would be hopping. He needed to be there.

Stephen and Sam continued to see each other during the next three years as Stephen pursued a law degree. Usually they'd meet on Sam's day off and sometimes during the weekdays when Stephen didn't have classes. They spent part of two Christmases together, rushing their little gift exchanges to get back to their families where the traditional dinners were served. They continued to have a late breakfast together whenever possible, and at least twice a year they revisited the rental cabin east of Kenosha Pass, staying the night. And, one day in the middle of August, they finally reached the summit of Mosquito Pass, where the Highway of the Frozen Death was still spotted with snow and ice.

"If you look there," Sam said, pointing northeast from the

summit, "that's where my cabin will be."

"Where?" Stephen said.

"Right there. You see that meadow in the middle of those trees?"

"Oh, yeah. But how do you know you can get that land?"

"Already have it. Well, I'm paying for it. Twenty acres. It'll take a while before I actually get a clear deed, but that's where I'll build."

"Wow. You didn't tell me you'd actually done it."

"Wanted to wait until we finally got up here."

Stephen put his arm around Sam's shoulders and squeezed. "Congratulations."

"Thank you."

They stood a moment more as the wind whipped itself up into a near gale, their shirts flapping like flags, both beginning to shiver with the whisper of the freeze still flowing from the northwest.

///

Stephen graduated law school and entered the firm his great-grandfather had established in Denver in the latter part of the nineteenth century. Though the firm specialized in financial and real estate matters, Stephen favored the criminal law side of the practice and gradually took on cases many thought were unwinnable.

Sam continued to run the bar, his twenty percent stake in it proving more lucrative each year. He kept his small studio on Clarkson Street even though he could now afford a much nicer and larger apartment. He divided his paychecks—a third to living expenses, two-thirds to his dream in the mountains.

Sam and Stephen found their lives rarely connected anymore. Both now moved in different realms, their time becoming more and more precious. The late breakfasts ended after Stephen began to frequently cancel. Their trips to the mountains suffered from the demands of Stephen's schedule and Sam's desire to spend his day and night off on his property, sometimes taking Tuesday off as well, to clear the land where he would someday build. They occasionally spoke on the phone, and would spend a night together about once a month. Stephen never ventured into the bar anymore, perhaps because of the vice raids that had begun to sporadically occur, sometimes resulting in arrests, other times in a two- or three-day suspension of Sam's liquor license. So too, Stephen had learned who Sam's uncle was.

"Not *the* Fat Pauly?" Stephen asked as Sam and he shared a rare dinner out.

"Yes. *The* Fat Pauly."

"God, Sam. Why didn't you ever tell me? I mean… That family has… killed people."

"He's my mother's brother. I only know he's had some trouble with the law in the past, but what he does now is pretty tame."

"But he actually owns the bar?"

"Unofficially, yes."

"Wow. With the raids and… I can't go in there again, Sam. I could be disbarred."

"That's fine. You haven't been there forever anyway. No one ever put a gun to your head—"

"Jesus! That's a nice way to put it. Why didn't you tell me?"

Sam shook his head. "I'm sorry. I didn't think you were so uptight about stuff like that."

"If it's my livelihood. Yes, I'm uptight."

"Your livelihood is in at least two trust funds you've told me about."

Stephen stared at Sam. "Let me rephrase then. My life's work is at stake."

"Whatever," Sam said, understanding exactly what Stephen was concerned about, but knowing, too, that their relationship had just been compromised. "The fruit of the poisoned tree, and all that, huh?"

Stephen didn't answer immediately. He placed his napkin on the table and drank the last of his wine. "Yeah, maybe that's it. You know what? You belong in the forest with the rest of the stumps."

They'd planned to spend the night together, but Sam asked Stephen to just take him home. Stephen drove across town, let Sam out, and pulled away from the curb without either saying good night.

After he'd gone inside his apartment, Sam sat down at his kitchen table, sipped bourbon, and wondered if he'd misread Stephen from the very beginning. Ordinary people had a way of devaluing the preciousness of life's little gifts—love, for example. In his mind he traveled a bit over the time and space Stephen and he had shared. Had he loved Stephen? Yes, he thought he had. Maybe he still did. But Stephen had managed to make those moments ordinary. Remembered the conclusion he'd made the first time they'd stayed at the cabin. There was little chance they were destined to be together. They were moving in separate directions.

A year of silence between them soon stretched to two, then three. Both of them sleeping with men they'd choose not to see a second time.

///

"You're doing a good job."

Sam looked toward the tree line from where the voice had come. Saw the dark-faced man standing there, his black hair in braids, a leather vest over his red and white flannel shirt. His jeans were the color of ash.

"Thank you." Sam dropped the adze and walked toward the man.

"Been watching you for a long time." The man raised his hand and swept it back and forth. "Your house is a good one."

Sam stopped a few feet away and offered his hand. "I'm Sam Coyle."

The man shook his hand. "Joe Spotted Elk. I live up the mountain a ways. Couple times I was gonna offer to help, but you figured it out."

"Yeah. I'd always thought I could make my own lumber, but realized pretty quickly I wouldn't have a house built for another ten years."

"Store-bought lumber works just as good." Joe walked closer to the house, ran his palm against the cedar siding. "You gonna stain it?"

"Yes. That's on my list."

"You want a puppy?"

Sam waited a moment for the *non sequitur* to sink in and for Joe to smile. When he didn't, Sam did. "I've been thinking a while about getting a dog. Just haven't gotten around to looking."

"Okay. I still got two. Malamutes. Mountain dogs. I'll bring them down here tomorrow. You can pick one."

"Okay."

"You meet your neighbor yet?" Joe pointed south.

Sam looked that way. "Yeah. He came up here a couple weeks ago. Had a Glock strapped on his hip and a Marine ballcap on his head. Seemed like he was conducting an inspection rather than being friendly."

"I call him Colonel. He's an asshole."

Sam smiled and looked at Joe's still serious face. "Got that impression myself."

Joe turned and walked toward the tree line. "I'll bring the puppies tomorrow," he said over his shoulder. He stopped and turned back to Sam. "Want to ride a horse?"

Sam was liking this guy more every second. "Yes, I would."

"I've got three. I'll take you up to my place, and you can ride."

"Okay."

Joe again turned and walked toward what Sam now saw was a barely discernable path up the mountain.

///

Sam had given the bar keys to Fat Pauly a year ago, a few days after his thirtieth birthday. Pauly had thanked him for running the place for nearly ten years, and, as a parting gift, gave him a check for ten thousand dollars.

"It ain't much, Sammy, but it might help a little to get you situated up there."

"Pauly, I can't take this. I don't need this. I—"

Pauly put his hands on Sam's shoulders and looked directly into his eyes as they stood outside the bar's front door. "Listen to me, Sammy. You take this and go do what you want to do. Get up there in the mountains and don't look back."

"I will, Pauly, but—"

"No buts. And I wanna tell you I don't care about… Guistina told me what you told them. The gay thing. Said your papa don't like it. Said—"

"Ah, Pauly, I—"

"Listen to me, Sammy. You only got one life. You go live it. You be happy. You hear me? You go live your life and you find somebody to love. You hear me?"

"Sure, Pauly." Sam nodded. "I'll try my best."

"Good. Now let's go have some lunch."

After that lunch, Sam left Denver for the last time, his few accumulated possessions packed in the bed of his pickup. He thought about stopping by to see his mother and father before he went up the mountain but decided against it. His father wouldn't acknowledge him, and his mother would just sob, tugging at her handkerchief, speaking in Italian. He'd told them he was gay two weeks before—a kind of tying up loose ends before he moved to the mountains. He'd anticipated their reaction but not the intensity of it.

AN INTENDED LIFE

As he drove up Highway 285, the tarp over the truck's bed flapping with the intense winds riled by the weather patterns created by the tallest mountains ahead, he remembered most of what he was leaving behind. Stephen came to mind, intertwined with the bar crowds, the visits to the Highway of the Frozen Death, the overnight stays at the rental cabin, the dozen or so men he'd slept with and seen as ordinary, the visits to Cheesman Park. All of it seemed balled up in a conflated mishmash of uncertainties creating questions to which he'd found no reasonable answers. He remembered the kiss he'd given to Michael, who'd called for his mother from the inestimable horrors of a war that begged the question why for which there'd never been and probably never would be a reasonable answer. Sister Mary Joseph had insisted faith alone would point in the right direction, where all questions could and would eventually be answered. Sam didn't think so. And if an answer ever came, he knew it wouldn't assuage the pain of that moment with Michael, the kiss to his lips.

During the years Sam ran the bar he'd managed to pay off the note on his mountain property, enlist professionals to lay a foundation for his house, drill a well, put in septic. He'd framed the structure himself, a little bit at a time. Once he'd finished that, he again called on professionals to string electrical, put in the plumbing he'd not been able to do. The decision he'd made as a child to depend only on what the earth provided to build a house had butted up against the requisites of twentieth century building codes, besides his own lack of practical skills. Now, after a year of work, the house was built, and he began to concentrate on furnishings.

And the puppies. Joe Spotted Elk had said he would bring them down the mountain today.

Sam sat on a patio chair in his bare kitchen waiting for the butane-fueled hotplate to heat his coffee. Looking out the window at the dirt road connecting him to the county road a mile away, he saw a black bear amble across it and disappear into the tree line. Now he knew why he'd not seen any mule deer that morning. He lifted the small tin pot off the hotplate and poured the steaming coffee into a cup sitting on the collapsible card table that served as his dining table, desk, and catchall. Raised the cup to his lips and again looked out the window. Staring back at him was what he at first thought was a wolf, but he knew that was unlikely. Wolves had been killed off in Colorado in the 1940s. He affirmed that when he saw two miniatures of itself scrambling around, nipping at one another. And Joe Spotted Elk was coming around the side of the house carrying a sack.

"Good morning," Sam said as he opened the door, only taking a few steps before the huge female Malamute nudged her nose into his crotch. Got to his knees when the puppies scampered to him, the mother now sniffing his ear.

"That's Chipeta. I call the little ones He and She," Joe said.

"Wow." Sam stood. Watched the puppies follow their mama to the side of the house. "So, a male and female?"

"Yeah. Had six to start with. These two are left. Nearly ten weeks old."

"Maybe we ought to bring them in the house. Saw a bear just a few minutes ago."

"Saw it, too. Told it to go away."

"Chipeta didn't chase it?"

"Nah. She told it to come back later."

"I had dogs when I was a kid. My mother would only let me have little ones."

"The little ones are good for sitting on your lap. Malamutes are good for talking to bears and lions." Joe looked inside the house. Turned to Sam. "You need some furniture in there."

"Yes, I do. I'm going to have to go down the mountain and shop for some."

Joe stepped away from the door and whistled—a single, high-pitched shriek. Chipeta and the pups immediately rushed from the side of the house, and all three sat down at Joe's feet.

"They already learned to do that?" Sam smiled. All three tails brushed against the dirt.

"Yeah. Chipeta is a good teacher. You want one?"

"Yes, of course. But...how would I choose?"

"Take them both. Gotta get them into good homes. I told the Colonel they were already spoken for."

"He wants one?"

"Yeah. But I don't want him to have one. He'll make it mean. Teach it to do things it shouldn't. Make it forget things it already knows. You take them both, and me and Chipeta will help you raise them. Brought some food." Joe raised the bag. "Besides, you need them. Maybe serve a purpose you never thought of."

Sam looked at the pups still sitting next to their mother. Wondered what Joe had meant. ...*serve a purpose you never thought of*? Couldn't think of any reason why he shouldn't have two dogs. He had the time. He wanted them. Better to interact with something besides the four walls of his house. "But when I'm gone? When I go down the mountain? I can't leave them alone in the house."

"Sure you can. Put them in a room. Close the door. They'll sleep while you're gone."

"They'll need a vet."

"There's a good one up here. She already saw them once. Gave them shots."

Joe clicked his tongue and the dogs stood up. Sam kneeled and was once again surrounded.

///

The first winter was pretty bad, though Sam had prepared for it. He'd furnished the house and bought an ATV with a plow on the front. He'd cut what seemed like a mountain of wood into lengths small enough to fit into the stove he'd installed in the small living room. Had stocked up on canned food, toilet paper, and bottled water. The power had gone off four times, once for seventeen hours. He hadn't thought he'd need a generator, but he was determined he'd buy one come next spring. Or sooner. Joe told him spring up here came on May 1st, summer came on July

4th, and fall began to move in on July 5th. Joe wasn't half wrong about that.

He'd named the male dog Michael and the female Mary. Joe commented on that, saying, "I could have given you some good names. Native names, maybe."

"Named after a kid in Vietnam and my favorite aunt."

"Okay. I named Chipeta after Chief Ouray's second wife. He was a great Ute chief. She was a Kiowa Apache."

"Well—"

"It's okay. They'll still talk to the bear, though the bear might not listen."

Sam realized Joe had probably given him the dogs because he knew they would indeed serve a purpose Sam had never thought of. The dogs had become his life, defining love in the simplest equation—unconditional.

By the time spring arrived, Sam had visited Joe's house up the mountain several times, Mike and Mary always with him, each time Chipeta and her children reuniting with yips and howls, running here and there as if discovering joy for the first time.

When the snow finally melted, Joe introduced Sam to his horses. "The pinto is Mariposa. Means butterfly in Spanish. She's a good horse. The bay is Mi-hi. Means beautiful joy in Korean. Met my wife in Korea. That was her name. The Appaloosa is Crazy Horse."

"The Sioux war chief?" Sam asked.

"Nah. He's just a little crazy horse. He's the youngest. You can ride him. I don't think he likes me."

"I haven't ridden since I was a kid."

"That's okay. You and him can figure it out together."

Joe had a round pen on his property where he gave Sam pointers on riding and the nature of horses. Once Sam was comfortable atop a horse, he and Joe rode the trails Joe, his wife, and the horses had carved out over the years. Crazy Horse dumped Sam three times on those trail rides, and Mariposa did it once. Sam came away from two of those falls with the certainty his back and hips would never be the same. Joe drove him down the mountain after the last accident where x-rays revealed he'd fractured three vertebrae and two ribs. Took a month for Sam to fully recover, but over the years he still climbed on a horse whenever he could, Joe urging him on, the dogs scampering over the trails and the countryside behind them.

///

Sam's forays into Denver were short and eventful only to the extent that gradually his mother and father seemed to come to terms with their distaste. Figured they believed if he was up there alone, then loving the sinner but hating the sin was a reasonable approach for them, that celibacy was the next best thing to a wife and children. What they didn't know was Sam always ended his visit to the city with a stop at Cheesman Park where he spent some time with a few different men in a few different small Capitol Hill apartments, and once in a lovely Queen Anne home with towers and turrets and satin sheets on the bed. The man asked him when they could do it again. "Soon," Sam lied.

As he drove back up the mountain after each of those lustful encounters, he wondered why he'd done that, acknowledging once again that the ordinariness of those men and their passions devalued what he had come to know about himself, what he had determined his life would become when he'd watched the grandest edifice west of Mississippi come tumbling down.

///

The first winter led to the second, the second to the third, and the ensuing spring brought with it an urge to rejoin just a smidgen of civilization. Besides that, Sam's bank account was looking thin—money going out, but none coming in.

The nearest town, Fairplay, was about ten miles south, and, in the late spring and summer, it blossomed with tourists seeking a Western experience. It had one relatively fancy restaurant and two less fancy but more authentic establishments, all with a need for seasonal employees. Sam's experience running a bar in Denver proved valuable when he approached Cathy, the proprietor of Cathy's Café, the most authentic eatery and saloon at the edge of town.

"What bar was that?" she asked, as they sat at a pine table next to a window with a view of the Mosquito Range of the Rocky Mountains. Sam told her, and she smiled. "You gay?"

He knew he'd read her correctly when he first walked into the café. She was a stocky woman in cargo shorts, and she wore her blonde hair short, sporting a T-shirt reading *Mama Bear*—the image of a fanged grizzly holding a cub. Wore hiking boots. Her handshake had been impressive.

"Yeah," Sam said, "I am."

"When can you start?"

"Tomorrow."

"Okay. It'll be a little slow for a while. You'll be my assistant manager, tending bar most of the time, helping out on the floor when we start to get the flatlanders coming in. I've got the kitchen covered, so you won't have to worry about that. Long days from open to close. You'll get Mondays off. How's that sound?"

"Fine. Like four months' work?"

"Five. It starts slow and ends slow. I don't close for the winter, but probably won't need you past September."

"That's perfect."

They once again shook hands upon parting. Sam drove back home cataloging the things he'd need to do in order to successfully navigate this urge to dip his toe into life as others knew it. Had picked up a copy of the *Rocky Mountain News* from a blue box outside the café. Thought he'd catch up on things since he'd abjured media once he had moved up the mountain.

Mike, who had grown into a standoffish boy, stood at the gate of the half-acre yard Sam had fenced for him and Mary after that first winter. He barely wagged his arced tail when Sam got out of his pickup, while Mary woo-wooed with excitement, scratching at the metal netting. Sam grabbed his newspaper from the seat and walked toward the gate.

"Hey, you two," he said as he opened the gate. Mary ran to him and raised herself up, placing her front paws on his chest. Sam kissed her nose and scratched her head as Mike sniffed the truck's tires. "C'mon, let's go inside."

Sam gave them cookies, and they took them into the second bedroom, which Sam had furnished with matching dogs beds, and food and water bowls. He grabbed a beer from the fridge, sat down at his small dining table and opened up the *News*. It didn't surprise him that the world was still a dangerous place where politicians and pundits jockeyed for attention, told their lies with impunity. Turning to page four, he saw a small headline that read: **Rare cancer seen in 41 homosexuals.** It was a reprint of a story from the *New York Times*. Kaposi's Sarcoma was the culprit, a rare cancer known to affect men over fifty. But, the story read, it was seen in young men in New York and San Francisco, all of whom admitted to having multiple sexual encounters with different men on a frequent basis. The doctors didn't know why this rare cancer was happening.

Sam closed the paper and finished his beer. He sat on the floor, calling the dogs. Mary came from the bedroom first, Mike following behind. Mary plopped down and lay her head on his lap. Mike sat next to them. Sam put his arm around the boy's neck and stroked Mary's head. Wondered what was going on with young men of like mind dying too soon.

He later took the dogs almost a mile up the mountain to Joe's house. A hundred yards before they got there, Chipeta's howls echoed off the mountainside, and she was soon amongst them, greeting Sam and her children with delightful exuberance. Sam saw Joe standing on his porch and returned his wave.

"I don't know how to ask this of you," Sam said once he and Joe had sat on the picnic bench off Joe's porch. "I need someone to check on Mike and Mary. I took a job down at Cathy's Café, and she said the hours are long. Don't want to leave then outside all day. They've got their yard, but... I'd worry about them, Joe."

"Sure. I can check on them. I'll drive the Jeep down. Won't take but a couple minutes. Why'd you take a job?"

Sam shook his head. "Need the money, Joe."

"Good answer."

"How do you make ends meet?"

"Got my pension. Social Security."

Sam had always assumed Joe Spotted Elk just existed like Native Americans had when they roamed these mountains before the white man showed up. Now, he realized how absurd that assumption had been.

"Twenty years in the Marine Corps," Joe continued. "Was in the Pacific. 28th Marines. Knew Ira Haynes—the Pima who raised the flag on Iwo Jima."

"Wow."

"After the war, they put me in the engineers. Learned how to weld and taught others to do it, too. Went to Korea. Came back. Retired as a master sergeant. I make ends meet. Don't need much. My wife died a few years ago. So just me and Chipeta."

"I was in Vietnam. The Army."

"Yeah, I thought so. You got the look in your eyes of someone who's seen bad things."

"I did, Joe. Probably not any more than you did."

"Probably not."

Sam worked three weeks at Cathy's Café, mostly ten-hour days where he was doing exactly what Cathy had described—tending bar, clearing tables, dealing with the flatlanders who came in with their cameras, kids, and attitudes. Was comforted Joe was looking after Mike and Mary. Came home each evening exhausted, but rallied when he saw the dogs—their enthusiasm, their love.

Sam had not pulled a *News* out of the blue box in front of

the restaurant for a month. Actually avoided looking at the front page showing through the box's plastic window. But at the end of a particularly busy day, as he and Cathy sat at one of the pine tables, she asked him if he had been reading about the gay cancer and pneumonia showing up in cities on the East and West coasts.

"Saw an article about the cancer. There's pneumonia now?"

"Yeah, it's called… Let me get it." She stood and walked over to the cashier counter, stepped behind it, bent down, and came back with a paper. She opened it up. "Pneumocystis carinii it's called. Lots of cases showing up, besides the cancer."

"They know what's causing it yet?"

"All sorts of theories. They mostly hone in on the multiple sex partners. Like it's spread from one person to another through sex." She looked at Sam, at his eyes. "I know you don't have time to get down the mountain much, but you're not, um—"

"No, I'm not, Cathy. I never was very… prolific that way."

"Good." She patted his hand. "Gotta keep you safe. Here—" she shoved the paper over to him "—you take this home. There's a couple articles in there."

Sam did take the paper home. Laid it on the small dining table. And, after feeding Mike and Mary, after his own dinner, he sat and read one of the articles that reported two hundred and thirty four men had already died from the exotic diseases. Left the second article for later. But after a few days, he threw the paper away. Those maladies had come to be known as Gay Cancer and Gay Pneumonia—a queer kind of death, Sam thought. Began thinking about mothers and sons. Wondered if some of those mothers didn't know their sons were gay until they pondered the reason for their child's death. Thought too about that boy in Nam. Wondered if the boys dying on either coast had called for their mothers, and if their mothers were there when the time came.

///

Through the winter of 1981, Sam kept busy. Had not seen the need for a furnace when the time had come to consider if he should put one in, and now he knew he'd made the right decision. The wood stove was doing just fine, though he'd wake to the creeping freeze on the coldest nights and have to get up and feed the fire. After each heavy snowfall, he'd dig out the accumulation at his front door, then get up on his roof and shovel off what he could. Mike and Mary would get out there with him, both more swimming through the drifts rather than trekking through them. Joe would come down the mountain on his Ski-Doo with Chipeta riding on the homemade sled he pulled behind. They'd leave the dogs outside in the yard, and sit before the fire on the couch, both bracing hot coffee cups between their palms.

"Fifteen inches, maybe," Joe said as he pulled off his parka.

"At least," Sam said, watching the fire through the stove's grate.

"You get lonely here?" Joe asked.

"Ah…" Sam smiled, glanced at Joe. "No. I've got the dogs. I keep myself busy."

"Human companionship?"

Sam felt an involuntary tightening of every muscle in his body. "I, ah… I really haven't given it much thought, Joe."

"Need somebody to hug. You got the dogs, but… Well." Joe sipped his coffee. "You know what I mean."

"Joe, I…" Sam stopped himself. Wanted to be honest with Joe, but in the instant before doing it, he thought better of it. "I'm okay."

"You need a girlfriend or a boyfriend." When Sam didn't respond, Joe looked at him. "Human beings need human beings. Bears need other bears. Elk needs—"

"Joe," Sam said, still not believing Joe had said *boyfriend*. "You're my best friend. Since I came up here you've been… You're kind of my rock. Every day when I'm trying to figure out what needs to be done, what I need to do to fix some damned thing or another, I ask myself what would Joe do. Ever since I was a kid, I wanted this kind of life for myself. And now that I've got it, now that I've…" Sam knew he was trying to tell Joe about himself, something that just moments before he'd thought better of. "Joe, I've got to tell you, I've got to be honest with you. I've—"

"I can't be your boyfriend, Sam. I'm too old."

Sam was trying to find some reasonably cogent way to tell Joe who he was, what he had been since he'd envisioned a God capable of embracing even queers because God was everything great and small, every breath that he took, every exhale he gave back. And now? Now Joe had taken everything down to the most common denominator—humor. Sam shook his head, smiled. Shook his head again.

"Had a few boys come through the engineers," Joe said. "They were different. Quiet. Learned quickly. Didn't fit in with the other grunts. I wondered why not. Got to know them before they left for permanent duty somewhere. Just like you, I figured them out. I gotta go."

When Joe stood, Sam did too, now used to Joe's abrupt comings and goings. Joe pulled on his jacket, and Sam walked him to the door.

"Thank—" Sam wanted to thank him.

"Dogs will love you," Joe said, "no matter what you do. Human beings take a little more work than that. Sometimes it's worth it. Sometimes it isn't."

Joe opened the gate and let Chipeta out. Sam watched from the porch as Chipeta climbed on the sled. Joe revved the Ski-Doo and turned it back up the mountain.

///

Another spring, and then another passed, and when the flatlanders had gradually petered out with the early freezes of fall, Sam once again left the little taste of civilization—sometimes sweet, sometimes sour—Cathy's Café provided to him. He stored up on needful things for the coming winter, Mike and Mary accompanying him to edge of the greater civilization down the mountain where Costco offered the quantities he sought. Often recalled his childish determination to live off the land and wondered why it'd occurred to him only after returning from Vietnam he'd need to kill critters for sustenance to survive. Though he'd purchased a rifle shortly after moving to the mountains, he knew its only use would be for protection against the willfulness of bears and mountain lions pursuing their natural imperatives, and then probably only a shot aimed at the sky to scare them away.

He kept in contact with his parents by walking down to the county road where one bar would appear on his phone, and he'd engage in conversations, mostly with his mother, that consisted of pleasantries always shrouded in the unsaid resentments of a mother who wanted grandchildren, and a father who wanted nothing to do with the vagaries of his son's sexuality. Or so Sam interpreted the conversations. He always invited them to take a drive up the mountain to see his place. But, as yet, they hadn't done that.

Sam opened his truck's door and Mike and Mary leapt up on the seat, then climbed over it to the extended area behind. Cathy had Sam's last paycheck of the season waiting for him, and he thought he'd better pick it up before the predicted early snow began to fall. He opened the two back windows for the dogs and turned on the heater as he headed for the county road.

Turning into the café's small parking lot, Sam noticed only two cars. One was Cathy's, the other one he didn't recognize. Off season was a slow time for Cathy, but she persisted in keeping the café open regardless. Thought it was her civic duty, though she lost money doing it.

"Hey, Sam," Cathy hollered from the kitchen when he walked in.

Sam walked behind the counter and leaned his arms on the window to the kitchen. "You by yourself?"

She shoved a spatula under eggs cooking in butter. "Yeah. Beth was here but I told her to go home. Your check is in the office."

Sam nodded. "Okay. Thanks, Cathy." He turned and walked toward the hallway that led to the office and the two restrooms—the Buck and the Doe. The Buck door opened and Sam swerved too late to avoid the collision.

"I'm sorry," Sam said, backing up, realizing he was looking into blue eyes that had once captured a piece of his heart, maybe his soul, blue eyes staring back at him with a question.

"Sam?"

"Stephen."

"Jesus."

"No, just Sam."

Stephen smiled. "I'm sorry. I—"

"How are you?" Sam said, holding out his hand.

"Good. Good." Stephen shook his hand. "We, um, my friend and I took the long way from Breckenridge over Boreas pass and stopped for some lunch. Went skiing for a few days, and... I told him an old friend of mine lived around here. Didn't expect to actually see you."

"Nor me you."

"Well... Here we are then. Come and meet my friend." Stephen took a couple steps back toward the dining room.

"I've got to get something from the office. You go ahead. I'll stop at your table."

"Good," Stephen said, nodding.

Sam closed the office door behind him, then sat in Cathy's chair behind the desk. Stephen. After all these years. After all this time. Stephen looked good. His hair was shorter, though trimmed precisely as Sam remembered it. *I told him an old friend of mine lived around here.* Wow. The rhythm his life had eased into over the past several years seemed to have broken apart in just the last five minutes, shards of memories, thoughts, feelings that had been at rest now revived, firing on cylinders he didn't even know he still had. "Humph." He huffed out something that probably defined what he was feeling. He grabbed his check from the desk.

"Sam, this in my friend William," Stephen said when Sam approached them.

Stephen and William stood. Sam walked over to them and shook William's hand. "Nice to meet you." Thought William was a handsome man, a blond with brown eyes, whose handshake was affectedly firm.

"He's the friend I told you about," Stephen said to William. "The one who lives up here."

"Yeah," William said. "The mountain man."

"Well, not exactly that," Sam said, smiling, wondering what else Stephen had told him.

"Can you sit with us?" Stephen asked.

"Ah, I've got the dogs in the truck outside." Sam looked out the window. "I better not."

Stephen turned and also looked. "Where?"

"Can't see them from here."

"I want to see them," Stephen said. "I'll walk you out. C'mon, William."

"I'll finish my coffee," William said. "You go ahead."

When they got outside, Mike and Mary were sticking their heads out the side window.

"God. Big guys," Stephen said, following Sam to the truck. "Huskies?"

"No, they're Malamutes. This is Mary." Sam ruffled the top of Mary's head "And this is Mike. Brother and sister."

Stephen reached out his hands, letting the dogs sniff him. "Beautiful animals, Sam."

"Yeah. You ought to see their mother. She lives just up a ways from us."

"So, you built that house you were always talking about?"

"Yes, I did. North of here about ten miles."

"I'd love to see it."

"Sure. Any time," Sam said. Wondered if Stephen was sincere or just saying it to be saying it. Being polite.

"We've got to get back to Denver, but I'd love to come up some other time."

"You and William?"

"Oh…" Stephen looked off into what Sam thought was a place of uncertainty, as if he was attempting to find an adequate response. "William isn't one to…" He looked back at Sam. "No, probably just me."

"Okay. Spring would be better. There's a storm coming in, you know."

"Yeah, I know. Here." He tugged his wallet out, pulled a business card from it, and handed it to Sam. "That's got my home number on it. Give me a call when it would be convenient."

Sam looked at the card. "Sure. I'll do that."

Stephen put his hand on Sam's arm. "The last time we saw each other… We didn't, um, part well, Sam. I've always regretted that."

Sam nodded. "No, we didn't."

Stephen squeezed his arm. "You'll call me?"

"Yes. Yes I will. Next spring."

"Promise."

Sam smiled as Stephen let go of his arm. "Promise."

///

On the final day of Sam's last summer enduring the catechism of the Catholic Church—the rite of Confirmation ahead when he turned sixteen—Sister Mary Joseph handed out awards for what she saw as achievements amongst the twenty boys who'd managed to finish the sessions, either by choice or parental duress. Sam received a small, plastic representation of the birth of Jesus in the manger. It was a bluish-gray sculpture from a mold and had a little tab on the back that allowed it to sit upright on a shelf. The selling point of this award, as Sister Mary Joseph pointed out, was that it glowed in the dark. "As you sleep," she told Sam, "the miracle of the virgin birth will watch over you." Sam didn't know what worth such an expectation—*It will watch over me?*—would have outside the basement classroom where he accepted it with a smile and a thank you, but thought the glow in the dark aspect of it was cool as could be.

The special event of that last day was a visit by Father Schmidt, the pastor of the parish, a tall, stern, white-haired man who favored the top-of-the-shoe-length black cassock attire over the black trousers the assistant pastor wore. The assistant pastor, Father Bob, was about thirty years younger than Father Schmidt, and ran the Catholic Youth Recreation Association program at the parish where he diligently presided over the changing room after swim lessons, assuring the boys dried themselves well before they put their clothes back on.

Sister Mary Joseph bowed her head slightly as she stepped away from the desk when Father Schmidt entered the classroom, flapping her hands, saying, "Let's stand, children, Father is here."

Father Schmidt watched the boys stand, glared a moment at their faces. "You may be seated," he said, his voice befitting his demeanor. "As you leave us today…"

Sam didn't really listen to what Father Schmidt had to say, but did perk up a bit when he mentioned *unnatural and sinful* play between two boys, or even one boy by himself. "You may want to touch yourself," he said, "or your best friend might want to touch you where they shouldn't because it is unnatural and sinful to do it."

Sam's first thought was his butt, or Kirby Dean's butt which he'd already touched many times, and Kirby had reciprocated. So too, they'd become hands-on intimate with each other's hardons. They called it wrestling, but both knew it was something else altogether.

"Soon," Father Schmidt continued, "if it hasn't already happened, you may swell in that place sometimes and it is especially at that time when you must not touch yourself, or let your friend touch you there. It is unnatural and sinful to do so. If you die with unconfessed sins on your souls, you will not go to heaven. You will not meet Jesus Christ, our Lord and Savior. Do you understand?"

"Yes Father," the boys said in unison, some probably wondering what the hell he was talking about, while others, like Sam, knew exactly what the topic was. Sister Mary Joseph fiddled with the beads hanging at her side.

"The devil wants you to sin. The devil wants you in Hell. Do you understand?"

"Yes, Father."

Sam bowed his head as Father Schmidt gave them his blessing. Watched Sister Mary Joseph cross herself, her face now colored crimson.

When Sam got home, he placed the award on the small desk in his bedroom, flipped the tab down, and turned the face of it toward his bed. Couldn't wait for nightfall to see if it really did glow in the dark. Remembered Sister Mary Joseph's words, "As you sleep," she'd told him, "the miracle of the virgin birth will watch over you."

He wondered how the cheap hunk of plastic would do that. As he'd thought when he received the thing in the basement classroom, Sister Mary Joseph's words had meaning only in that room, in that place where he and the other boys were urged to understand that only blind faith could reveal truths from interminable contrivances. By that time, Sam had moved on from what he thought was the silliness of it all. It wasn't that difficult to get to the meaning of life. Life just was. Anyone's God just was. You didn't need to read a book or believe in *mysterious ways* to figure that out. His life, his God would be the earth and the sky, and the critters that tarried there, the air that he breathed, the needles and leaves on the trees, every flower, every blade of grass, every coyote's yip as day faded to night, or dawn crept up a mountain.

///

Sam slowly rose from his haunches, the pain in his knees expected. Took another look at the Pasque flowers and smiled. Saw a blur of something farther up the hill, turned, and Chief Ouray was running from the house toward him. The four-year-old Malamute was the great-great-grandson of Chipeta, long ago lost to time and this place where another spring was rising from the earth and glowing from the sky. Sam braced himself for the nudge the dog gave him, bending down to stroke the boy's ears and take the wet kiss from his tongue.

"You'd think I'd gone to Alaska," Sam said, bending down to pick up the mail Chief had managed to dislodge from behind Sam's belt where he'd stuck it after pulling it from the box that sat a half-mile down the county road. He stuffed the envelopes back in at his waist and looked toward the house. Waved at the Stephen who stood on the porch. Stephen caught his hand in the tangle of oxygen tubes at his side when he waved back. Sam wondered if Stephen had managed to get his meds down without choking again. Or maybe he was waiting for him to get back.

"C'mon, Chief," Sam said, resuming his trek up the hill. Thought again, for about the thousandth time, that he should have called Stephen after he'd seen him at Cathy's Café so many years ago. If he had called him, things might have taken a better turn. He didn't know why he hadn't done that except at the time he hadn't been ready to become involved again with anyone. He'd been doing just fine with the consorts he'd found on the mountain. Twelve years later, he did call after Cathy had told him a guy named Stephen had called her, asking if she would pass his number along to his old friend Sam. It wasn't exactly an emergency, the guy had said, but he did have to talk to him.

When Sam called, Stephen explained he was sick. "I've got it, Sam. I've had it for a while. William left, and my family... They don't understand. I haven't worked in two years. I don't know what to do, Sam."

When Sam got to the porch, he again took off his hat and wiped his brow. Looked at Stephen who had sat down on one of the lawn chairs. "You okay? Take your meds?"

"Thought I better wait."

"Good idea. Pasque flowers have come out."

"So spring has sprung," Stephen said, gulping for air after he said it.

Sam nodded. "Yes, it has." He saw Stephen shiver, and he noticed he hadn't tied the white laces on his red tennis shoes, the fifth or sixth pair Stephen had purchased since Sam had first noticed them forty or more years before. Those silly red shoes. Stephen had put his robe on inside out, too. Sam didn't say anything about it. Stephen was losing his mind. Some days better than others. The last time he was checked, his viral load was okay, but somewhere along the line of dealing with the disease his brain had been irretrievably affected. His lungs, too. Over the past twenty years, Sam never regretted Stephen's presence, only the sickness. Only that. Sam put his hat back on, stepped on the porch, whistled for Chief, and grasped Stephen's arm. "Let's get you inside, sit you down in front of the window. I'll make a fire. Maybe the doe will bring her fawns by later. You'd like that, wouldn't you?"

"Yes, I would, Sam. Do you think she will?"

"I have faith she will, Stephen. Either today or tomorrow." Sam knew the fawns wouldn't appear for another month, maybe two, but it didn't matter. Stephen needed to hope for something.

"It means something, doesn't it, Sam? The fawns coming to see us?"

"Yes, it does, Stephen. It *means* a lot. Life does go on." Sam eased Stephen onto the couch facing the stove, the window-lined wall just beyond. Grabbed a blanket from the side chair and draped it over Stephen, then opened the stove's grate. He snatched a long match from the coffee table, struck it, and then lit the newspaper under the pile of sticks he'd fashioned there last evening.

"Life does go on." Stephen repeated it as if in awe of the words themselves.

"Yes, it does." Sam closed the grate after placing a larger log onto the burning kindling. "You okay?"

"Yes."

"I'll get your pills."

"Thank you."

Sam looked at the faraway gaze in Stephen's eyes as he stared at the fire. What did he see? What was he thinking? Watched as Chief climbed up on the couch with Stephen and lay down beside him. Stephen absently placed his hand upon the dog's head.

Sam walked into the kitchen and opened the plastic container of pills grouped in sevens, the required doses for each day of the week. Placed his hands on the counter, bowed his head, and thought about Joe.

Nearly fifteen years ago, Joe Spotted Elk had asked Sam to call his family, some in Utah, and some in southern Colorado.

It had been about this same time in the spring when Sam had gone up the mountain to check on Joe. Stephen never wanted to go with him. For some reason, he didn't like Joe and always found something else to do when Sam told him he was going up there. Joe had been failing for a while, his legs mostly, and Sam made sure Joe had food to eat, and that he was still getting around okay. He'd bought Joe a walker. Even though Joe had said he'd never use it, Sam had insisted and Joe finally saw the worth of it. But that day in the spring when Sam walked up the mountain, Joe asked him to call his family. "Here's the list," Joe said, handing Sam a piece of paper where he'd written down the names and numbers. "Not sure if they're still around," Joe said. "If they are, tell them I'm going to die soon."

Sam didn't argue the point. He'd come to know Joe well over the years, and if he knew anything at all about him, he knew he used words carefully, as if every one he spoke revealed a piece of his soul. Sam drove down to Cathy's and used her landline to contact Joe's family members, reaching four on the list of six. They all took the news with few words in response. In the next week, seven strangers, all Native people, came up the mountain to be with Joe.

The last time Sam spoke to Joe, he was sitting in the fabric Laz-E-Boy chair he'd had for as long as Sam had known him. Joe asked his family to step outside, and then he told Sam to pull up a chair next to him.

"Want to tell you that my family will bury me. Back in that little meadow, behind the house. The county can't know about that. Okay?"

"Sure, Joe. Of course."

"Okay. Want to tell you that you have been a good friend. We lived pretty good up here. Us and the dogs. The animals. Had some deep snow, some bears, some lions. But we did okay."

"We did, Joe."

"We know the earth. And the sky."

"Yes, we do."

"The couple times I spoke to Stephen?"

Sam nodded.

"He doesn't know these things. I don't think he ever learned what we know."

Sam smiled. Of course Stephen hadn't. "He's... ill, Joe."

"Yeah." Joe closed his eyes and grimaced with pain.

"You all right?"

"Yes," Joe said, opening his eyes. He smiled at Sam. "You try to teach him what we know. You give him that gift."

"I will try."

"Okay." Joe reached his hand out to Sam.

Sam grasped Joe's hand, felt his eyes fill up as his throat clenched. "I will miss you, Joe."

"Nah. I'll be here. You come and visit. My family will put rocks over me. You come up and touch the rocks every once in a while. We'll talk about things."

Sam squeezed Joe's hand. "I will, Joe. I will."

Joe died the next day. His family buried him in the meadow behind his house. Put rocks over the grave, as was their custom.

Sam brought the pills into the living room with a glass of water. Told Stephen to just take one at a time. "Slowly, Stephen," he said. "Lots of water." When Stephen managed to get all the pills down, Sam set the glass on the coffee table. "Will you be okay for a while?"

"I'll just watch for the fawns."

"Good." Sam put two more logs on the fire. "C'mon, Chief," he said, "let's take a walk."

Chief Ouray climbed off the couch, and followed Sam as he walked to the front door.

"Let's go see Joe."

Sam opened the door. Let Chief precede him outside. As he walked up the mountain, he listened to his shuffle, felt the sun's glow from above, smelled the freshness of the breeze as it swept from snowpack yet to succumb to the inevitable. Thought he'd tell Joe about the Pasque flowers he'd seen earlier, maybe describe the breeze, or maybe just sit and listen to what Joe had to say.

The Flies of August

Lamentings heard i' the air; strange screams of death…
William Shakespeare - "Macbeth"

The summer Felix flew off to do God's work in the elevator shafts of the tallest buildings in New York City, I stayed in Denver and praised God for beautiful boys with beautiful eyes. It was a good summer. It was 1978, and I was living next door to Joe then, who was still drinking heavily and raising hell three or four nights a week at the bar. He was *into* leather and motorcycles and vast quantities of booze that, along with his treasured collection of Nazi paraphernalia, had earned him the nickname "Kraut" amongst that esoteric group of black-booted hell-raisers with whom he hung around. I had no particular qualms about tagging along with him on his excursions to the bar where a fabulous time was always had by all—especially Joe, who would drink himself halfway to eternity every time we went out. It didn't occur to me then that Joe was subconsciously, or consciously, engineering his own little cannonball express to oblivion with only one scheduled inevitable stop: the last stop—death.

I'd moved in next door to Joe upon my return from what had become three increasingly gloomy years of what they euphemistically call "life" in Los Angeles. Having left a lover—"ex" by this time—and any commitment of fidelity to that lover in the City of Angels, I was ready to take an active role in the Big Party in Denver, which, at times, was emceed by none other than my next-door neighbor, Joe. He was then about thirty-five. I was eleven years younger. Joe was jaded beyond salvage. I was getting there.

Although I had been out for four years, I had spent three of those years with a lover in a relationship that was ostensibly monogamous, but was for both of us stifling. I had not participated to any degree in the Big Party by then, and upon my return to my lifelong home of Denver and after a brief interrogation by Joe that revealed my relative innocence, Joe latched on to me like a dog on that proverbial bone. Whether he was out to corrupt the innocent or just tired of his old compadres is unsure. What is sure is that there was urgency to our lives back then. The Big Party's allure was overpowering. We were having fun…most of us, that is, except Felix.

It was one terribly hot night in August when Felix knocked on my door. I remember it was August because the flies were loud and aggressive. Unafraid. Strength in numbers, I suppose. And as Felix and I sat cross-legged on the carpet in front of the air conditioner, he told me about the journey he was about to take. He stared at me with those large, dark, intense eyes, alive with the effects of cannabis and his Cuban heritage. As I stared back, knowing without doubt that he was hearing his voices and seeing his visions again, he told me that God had directed him to go to Manhattan and spread His message to the masses of ungodly hoards who roamed that great but evil city. And he told me that the flies, the flies of August were a presage of something, just *something* that had yet to be revealed to him.

I had known Felix pre-Los Angeles, and had seen him cross that delicate line that separates rational from *extra*-rational thought at least twice prior to that August night. The doctors called it paranoid schizophrenia. I called it experiencing, with the implicit understanding that I was making no comment on whether the clinical definition of paranoid schizophrenia applied to Felix or not. All I meant when I said experiencing was that Felix was hearing what he alone heard, and seeing the visions the he alone saw that would invariably catapult him off on another journey from which he would eventually return after having completed the work God had sent him there, wherever, to do.

So after listening to his explanation, interspersed with biblical quotations, for undertaking his journey, I told him to be careful, write if he could, and come back safe and sound. Prior to embarking on his previous journeys, I had always attempted to talk him out of them, citing quite rational reasons why he shouldn't go. But reasoning with someone who believes they have direct dial privileges with the Almighty is like trying to argue the worth of bacon to a pig. So when I told him to be careful, write if he could, and come back safe and sound, he cocked his head to one side and studied me for a moment with a little grin on his otherwise serious face. He rose from the carpet and said, "God bless you." He then walked out the door.

I followed him out, and before he descended the stairs to the ground floor he walked to Joe, who was sitting on a little redwood bench outside the door to his apartment.

"Peace be with you," Felix said, extending his thumb to Joe's forehead where he made the sign of the cross.

"And also with you," Joe said, remembering the response from the Catholic mass, realizing that Felix was probably loopy again.

I leaned on the rail, and watched Felix navigate the stairs, then walk to the alley where he turned once and waved. I waved back as he proceeded on his way to fulfill his holy mission in New York City.

"Crazy again," Joe said, and it was not a question, just a statement, just Joe's perception of the situation. Joe rose from the bench and stretched his arms over his head. "Beer bust in half an hour," he said as he yawned.

"Yeah," I said, wishing Felix was not going away, wishing He would cut a little slack for Felix, and wishing that Felix had not said the flies were an omen of something coming, something he was not able to articulate until the *Truth* was revealed to him by his Master.

///

Then there was the Big Party. Since Stonewall, since 1969 when the patrons of a small New York gay bar responded to the degrading harassment inflicted by New York's finest by standing up to the cops and refusing to be intimidated any longer (*Oh, sweet Jesus, who was the first to say no, I will not take this any longer? Who? Who placed his Vodka Collins back on the bar and snubbed out his cigarette and said, "Sonofabitch, I will not take this any longer," with the S's elongated, accented, sounding something like the dangerous hiss of a gas burner ready to ignite, needing only a puny spark to set it off? Oh, sweet Jesus, who?*).

Yes, since Stonewall, the Big Party had surged unabated, frantically compounding itself in vengeful convolutions borne of the frustrations of men and women suddenly let loose from the strictures of those damnable, horrible closets. Yes, day after day after night after night. It was ethereal for just so long, and then a fuck by any other name... Do you know that one had to struggle to assure that the intimacies of the sex did not become banal, boring, blasé? Do you know that after having fucked five different men in five consecutive days, I decided enough was definitely enough, and I stayed home on the sixth day, but only long enough for Joe to knock on my door, and then I was at it again, at the bar, in the basement of the bar where a hundred men were packed with only their breath between them in an area the size of my dining room. And, on the sixth day, it became eight men in six days?

Jesus, let me tell you that the basement of the bar was a phantasmagoria of mansmell and mansex, a lustful camaraderie of men adoring men, manfingers exploring manbodies, each touch electric and somehow new, and it was as if each feel, each caress of assmeat or cock was a sublime discovery of precious worth revealing the Truth, indeed, documenting the Truth that there were so, so many men who loved other men. And the baths... Beginning in Los Angeles, there was the 8709 and the Hollywood Spa, the Club Baths in Phoenix, Dallas and San Francisco, the Empire and the Ballpark in Denver. Oh, let me tell you that my primordial essence was spread amongst the kindness of strangers in one city after another. The poppers, the grease, the steam hissing from unseen outlets clouding the dimly lit silhouettes of manbodies; steam-streaked, slick manbodies pursuing the satisfaction of the urge to communicate, to share the revelation of the Truth of ourselves. "The love that dare not speak its name?" Hah! We spoke its name often, and more often ignored the implicitness of that single word, love. The Big Party saw little value in the emotional entanglements of love. And few of us paused long enough to consider the consequences of our new, Truth-laden, post-Stonewall selves.

With perfect hindsight, those of us who lived through the Big Party and who are still healthy can regret our callousness. But for me and for so many others, the Big Party remains a fantastic, almost unbelievably sensuous part of our lives. We were having fun then, buckaroos. What else can I or anyone else say?

///

In mid-September of '78, Ron and Jason, two black-booted giants whom I had befriended over that summer, helped me drag Joe from his apartment where he had closeted himself for seventeen days with as many gallons of wine to assuage the pain or grief or whatever it was that made him drink. I would learn that it was his fourth time in detox. It would be his last.

It must have been early-October before I saw Felix again. Like his appearance in August, he knocked on my door one night, his eyes alive with the kind of truths only cannabis and experiencing can reveal. He sat down on the couch and lit a cigarette.

"I spray painted His message in elevator shafts. All over New York. Black spray paint. Almost got arrested. He protected me. My Master protected me. Got laid, too. It was wonderful."

"The flies?" I asked. "What about the flies."

"Death," was all he said, a slight tremor in his voice.

///

By late 1981 and through '82, the writing on the wall that would eventually spell "AIDS" loomed dangerously, and persisted as a particular potentially deadly nuisance. Why us? Why now? Those of us who were able to glean the message in that writing adjusted quickly.

It must have been November or December of 1982, when David, who became my lover and my friend that same year, and I lay on the carpet in our living room, listening to Rossini's *The Siege of Corinth*. Beverly Sills sings the role of Pamira, who within the catacombs of Corinth is preparing to kill herself, as are many of the Greek countrywomen who also huddle in the caves. Their men, their lovers, have gone to battle with the Turks, and face certain defeat and death. In her mind, Pamira sees her lover dying: *"Parmi verderlo, ahi misero, vicino a morte orrible."* "Alas, I seem to see a poor man near a horrible death," she sang. There were goose bumps on David's arm, and his entire body twitched when the word *orrible* was sung. I held David tight to my body then. I smelled his hair, his blond hair, and I kissed the back of his neck. If I had not already turned my back on the Big Party, then that single kiss, there on the floor of our living room, affirmed my choice. I had opted for life, for love.

///

I have told David—who is twelve years younger than I—about the Big Party of the '70s. He believes he missed something essential in the history of ourselves, our brotherhood. "I was born too late," he has said more than once. And I cannot lie to him. The Big Party was, well, a party of unequaled delight. The Big Party was so much fun, that few of us who experienced it ever paused long enough to consider that it would end. *Had* to end. And it did.

THE FLIES OF AUGUST

///

Felix, who is now "sane" with the help of modern drugs, will occasionally meet me at the bar where the memories of the Big Party persist. We will usually drink too much and talk about the old times while prefacing most sentences with "Do you remember…?" We will laugh like hell, and there are always the inevitable moments of silence when we each bring up the private memories that cannot be shared; memories that neither of us can do justice to with a retelling. Felix, after the silences, will begin to sob, and I will grab his shoulders and remind him that we are alive; we lived through it. And he will look at me, his voice shaking, and say, "Yes, but I should have warned them. I should have… The flies. The flies of August." And we will part then, he to his lover and me to David, whose eyes, whose beautiful eyes that reveal the essence of his soul and perhaps reflect upon my own, are all that I ever truly wanted from the Big Party anyway.

The White Buck

When I was sixteen, the truths imparted to me as a child were revealed as impermanent and, as a consequence, I began to believe in magic. Or, more precisely, I began to believe in more robust truths that did not come from my parents, teachers, priests, or pundits, but from the world around me and the cosmos inside of me. I was beginning to know myself, and to understand I was magical and attuned to the magic of the world around me.

That was when I saw the white buck for the first time. It was springtime, and that first sighting was just dumb luck or, I'd like to believe, a manifestation of the magic I'd just discovered. I'd taken a moment from my chores to look at the stands of fir, pine, and aspen trees that surrounded my family's home, and the white buck appeared, standing not twenty yards from me, staring at me as if to ask, *Yes? May I help you?* I whispered something then, probably just an *ah*, and the white buck turned and disappeared down the mountainside. Ghostlike. An apparition I wasn't sure had been there at all.

When I was seventeen, I saw the white buck for the second time from my bedroom window. It was an autumn dawn; the sky painted in broad strokes of orange, gray, and blue, and the aspens' leaves were holding on in a last desperate grasp for life, all quaking as if pleading for something they knew they could not have. Just beyond the aspens, almost beyond my sight, the white buck stood staring at me intently and, as I smiled out my bedroom window, I knew—and I was sure of this—that the white buck knew we had done this once before.

I promised myself if I ever saw the white buck again, I would be ready. And the winter of my eighteenth year, the white buck appeared.

I saw him only because his brown-gray antlers gave him away. Otherwise, he would have been invisible against the layer upon layer of snow that had begun falling in late October and by now, in December, spread as an immense, forever whiteness.

I had him in my sights. I wanted the clean shot I'd promised myself at a moment's notice; something that would later show the full spread of him in all of his beauty, his nobility. Knee deep in snow, I sank to my haunches, watched the buck amble through a copse of aspens, the trees mere ghosts of themselves, stretching their thin, delicate limbs toward the uncaring white sky above. The buck stopped at the base of a thick-trunked aspen, cocked his head to the side, then lowered it and began rubbing that part of his head at the base of his antlers against the tree's bark, leaving his scent as a warning or a welcome. He then nibbled at the bark he had scraped off. I adjusted my aim. Sighted right between the buck's eyes, then slowly fixed my aim to the middle of his chest. I applied pressure with my finger, held my breath, and saw the perfect moment.

The buck raised his head when the camera clicked, and in that place where noise was measured in pin drops, the click sounded like a gunshot. The buck jerked to the right, stood rigid for a moment, stared at me still hovering near the ground nearly buried in the snow, and then he shook his head in a spiral motion as if scolding me for ruining the magic of the moment. He turned, stotting away.

That was fifty years ago, and I never saw the white buck again.

The picture came out well, I framed it and hung it on my bedroom wall. I took it to college with me, then to law school, and then to Virginia, which was the first stop on the four-year commitment I'd made to the United States Army. I gave the picture to the woman I married when I was twenty-four. Churchmouse poor at the time, it had been the only valued treasure I'd had to give her.

Over the years, I've tried to find the negative for that picture. But like so much of the odds and ends people collect during their lives, it's been lost to time or circumstance.

The marriage didn't last long, and that was okay for my wife and me. Most men who find themselves in the military necessarily discover what they're capable of and what they're not capable of fairly quickly. My wife understood that as well as I did. Not long after she had joined me in Virginia, we parted without tears or recrimination, and, just like the white buck, I never saw her again.

///

Sam and I met in a dark bar in downtown Denver one night in 1982. I don't think either one of us knew at the time we'd spend the rest of our lives together. And it's not a stretch to believe we saved each other's lives that night. An insidious disease, the bogeyman from anyone's worst nightmare, had begun to slither toward Denver that year, and I believe we escaped its wrath with our decision to commit to domesticity rather than continue to participate in the *Big Party* that had been ongoing since 1969 when the Stonewall Inn signaled a double-edged liberation for men like us.

Not long ago, I told Sam that during the thirty-three years we've been together, I've held no secrets from him, nor ever wanted to. Sam appeared to accept that, smiling as he does, but he didn't tell me the same thing. I've thought about that for a while. In fact, I've examined those thirty-three years in my mind and stopped at several of the most likely places Sam might have wandered off the path we'd made for ourselves, and I've not been able to pin down a time or location where I suspected he had gone astray. What if he had? I suppose it doesn't matter. We're now old men. Well, I'm old, and Sam is getting there.

THE WHITE BUCK

My mother died ten years ago, and Sam and I moved into my childhood home in the Colorado mountains; the place where I'd seen the white buck. We're at 9,235 feet, and besides the wild critters who make this place their home, we have some neighbors whom we seldom see except in passing. The locals up here have a saying that goes something like this: *You live in the mountains until it's time to move closer to a hospital.*

That's what my parents did. They moved from the mountains to Denver, and my father didn't last long after that. My mother hung on for two more years, and when she went, I got the deed to the cabin as well as the rest of her estate. It wasn't much, but by that time Sam and I had the means to live out the rest of our lives as comfortably as we cared to do.

///

I follow Sam into the eatery about seven miles from our home. It's called Cathy's Café, owned by a single woman, Cathy, who wears cargo shorts year-round, sturdy boots, and T-shirts in the summer boldly declaring her perspective on life—OF WOLVES AND WOMEN is one of my favorites, and another one is IF I WANTED YOUR ATTITUDE I'D ASK FOR IT. In the winter, she wears long-sleeved flannel shirts that don't provide reading material. She's what you would call *no nonsense*, and that's fine by me. Her café is a homey place, all pine fixtures with a warm fire in the river-rock fireplace. The clientele is homey, too, mountain folks who long ago ceased to care about flatlanders' affectations or fancy cuisine.

I nod when Sam points to an empty booth, and we slide in facing each other. I feel the duct tape Cathy uses to patch holes in the red vinyl snag on my back pocket. I reach down and press the tape back on the seat's slick fabric. It's happened before, and I always check when I stand up to see if the tape hasn't decided to come home with me. It did once, and Sam got a kick out of that.

The waitress, Mary, hovers over us before we're able to grab menus from the side of the table. We order drinks. She's somewhere in her mid- or late-thirties, with a pretty face, and a smile that offers more empathy than it does happiness. Her hair's tied back in a ponytail, and her white sweatshirt says she's the PROUD MOTHER OF A MARINE—the eagle, globe, and anchor emblem prominent in red and black in the middle of the shirt. Like always, she wears jeans that may have flattered her five years ago, but now stretch to reveal all the extra baggage she carries underneath. She's worked for Cathy for only about two months and has become our regular server when Sam and I show up at least once a week.

Cathy put a jukebox in last winter. She used to play cassette tapes of her favorite music, amplified by the four speakers that hang from the ceiling. The repeated taped repertoire was Melissa Etheridge, Mary Chapin Carpenter, k.d. lang, and a few other female singers of vigorous and soulful songs. Although Sam and I didn't mind the repetition—I did, after all, learn the words to most of the songs—some other customers did. And now I tap my foot to a song I've enjoyed for a long time. It flows from the multi-colored domed box in the corner framed by snakes of light that dance to the beat. It's "Lonely People" by America. I glance at the regulars sitting on barstools and believe it's an apt song about now.

When Mary returns with our drinks—my PBR in a glass, and Sam's merlot—I ask her about her shirt.

"He's twenty-one and just graduated from boot camp," she says, a tinge of sadness in her smile.

"What's he going to do for them?" I say.

"Oh." She loses her smile completely. "He's infantry."

I know she knows as well as I do what that might mean, and I'm momentarily at a loss for words. "Well," I finally say, "growing up here, I'm sure he knows how to take care of himself with a weapon."

"He does. Deer and elk don't shoot back, though." She turns her head when the little bell in the kitchen dings. "I'll come back for your food orders," she says, excusing herself.

Sam and I look at each other. Sam shakes his head, and I look down on the table top and refold the napkin I'd just unfolded.

"There are other places he could go besides the Middle East," I say.

Sam, still wearing his stocking cap because he'd just cut what little hair he still has, nods, says, "Yeah. But he's a Marine, Harley. A fighting machine. Is it cold in here?" He pulls his cap a little farther down on his head.

"No. Not really."

I have on my U.S. Army ballcap, and both Sam and I have not taken off our puffy parkas, just pulled the zippers down. I wear a gray coat, Sam's is red—the colors indicative of our personalities. I tend toward the quiet side, and Sam is a talker. I'm thankful for that when we're entertaining company or happen to be amidst a group of people we don't know that well.

Mary returns for our meal orders. I have never seen her write anything down, and she doesn't this time. She nods when we tell her what we want. "It'll be just a minute," she says, heading for the half-wall between the dining room and the kitchen where she tells Cathy and her helper what we want.

Sam checks his phone. He's pushed his glasses up on his forehead, holds the cell inches from his eyes and flicks his index finger on the screen, scrolling through posts from his Facebook friends and checking his emails. He's still got a lot of family, mostly in Washington state, and many friends he keeps in touch with. I've got a few family members left, only a couple of whom waste their time on social media. My Facebook friends are only acquaintances from cyberspace. Most have friended me because after fifty years I still take photographs of the critters and the scenery up here, which I upload for folks to enjoy.

"Derek, the oldest nephew," Sam says, turning the face of his phone toward me, "posted these of his twins."

It's a picture of two infant girls wrapped in pink blankets with red ribbons around their heads. They're only a few weeks old, and they're still in that ugly phase; their squinched faces appear old, and I wonder if that's what they'll look like when they're my age. "Well, look at that," I say, smiling. "Beautiful little girls."

Sam turns the phone back, takes another look, smiles, and says, "They are pretty. They look like their mother."

I look out the window to my right and see it's snowing again. There's no breeze right now, and thick flakes float downward as if they're in no hurry to end their journey. The view is a treeline of snow-laden Douglas fir that covers the rise behind the cafe. Their limbs sag a little with the accumulation of snow and, if the wind happens to pick up, they'll shed that burden and wait for another.

Waylon Jennings is now telling us all about a waltz to heaven, his outlaw croon as beautiful as any song I've ever heard, and I've come to appreciate its simplicity. I look back at the folks sitting at the bar and the old guy wearing a deep red almost burgundy Stetson is leaning a little closer to a woman with long, gray hair that hangs like a horsetail down her back sitting next to him. I know that hat. It's our nearest neighbor, Hank.

"You ever wonder where we'd be if we hadn't met each other?" Sam says.

I look at Sam and consider what he just said. "Well, I guess I'd still be looking for love in all the wrong places. Or maybe I'd be dust in the wind by now. Hell, I don't know. Why'd you ask?"

"It's a reasonable question," he says, laying his phone on the table. "Don't you ever ask yourself the same thing?"

"At my age, I try to avoid the irrelevant and impossible."

Mary approaches with our food, and Sam scoots his phone to the side of the table and picks up his napkin. "Here you go," She places my club sandwich and Sam's guacamole burger on the table. "What else can I get you?"

"Think we're fine right now, Mary," I say. "Wanted to ask what your husband thinks of your boy going into the infantry?"

She closes her eyes for a moment and cocks her head a little to the side. "My husband died in Iraq. He was a Marine, too."

"Oh. So, your boy just wants to follow in his daddy's—" I realize I've said this wrong and correct myself. "He wants to be a Marine just like his daddy?"

"Exactly. He went to school to be a diesel mechanic, but he's always had the idea there's something, um, noble about being a Marine."

"There is," Sam says, nodding, lifting his bun and squirting ketchup on his burger.

"Are you a veteran, Harley?" Mary says.

"Feel funny wearing this hat if I wasn't."

"Sorry. I'm asking because we're having a silent auction next week to support homeless veterans. You two ought to come. We'll have free drinks for those who served in the military, and you might be interested in some of the items people are donating for the auction."

"Sure," I say. "We'll come. Won't we, Sam?"

"Of course. What day is that?"

"Next Friday. It'll start at seven p.m. and go until we're done."

"Good deal," I say. "You think we could bring some things to put in the auction?"

Mary smiles. "Of course, you can. So, you're okay for now?"

"Yes, we are," I say. "Thank you."

///

When we get back home, Jack, the Alaskan Malamute we rescued two years ago greets us at the door, and we let him go outside to do his numbers. He hurriedly takes care of of his business because he's hungry. If he weren't, Sam and I would be standing out in the cold for a half-hour, urging him to hurry it up as he reads the daily news from the multitude of critters that have passed this way. We always go out there with him because there are coyotes around, and maybe bobcats, too. Jack has seen coyotes before, and either Sam or I have had to hold him back from running after them. We've tried to explain to him that if he sees one coyote, probably six or seven more are waiting just out of sight ready to pounce on him. We don't think he believes us, but we believe it, and our watchfulness has so far paid off.

We return inside. I feed Jack, wait the fourteen seconds it takes him to empty his bowl, and then give him a cookie. Sam has gone upstairs to his music room, the place where he keeps his collection of classical and Christmas music.

Six thousand CDs fill the shelves in Sam's music room, each one filed according to specific criteria Sam has devised, but which I don't understand. Though Sam's Christmas music occupies only part of two shelves, he's got it filed so that on the day after Thanksgiving, he starts the annual rotation, bringing it downstairs to play on our main system, and the merry tunes don't end until New Year's Day. I suffer through this annual rite. I really do. But now that it's mid-February, Sam is back to classical, sometimes listening through earphones and sometimes on the downstairs system.

Sam was a musician and teacher during his working years. He plays the piano and every woodwind instrument there is. He taught music for twenty-five years, both in the classroom and privately, and taught more than a few church choirs the meaning of harmonization, besides gently dissuading the older, blue-haired sopranos from coveting the solo parts.

My little study is on the first floor, in what used to be my childhood bedroom. I was a criminal defense attorney for thirty years, but keep only a few mementos to remind me of that. Instead, I have my photography equipment, shelves of fiction and history books, a desk, and a computer. I don't file my books by anything other than the author's last name.

As I sit down in my black leather chair, I think about young men, boys really, joining the military, some of whom will end their lives in a place I perceive as hell incarnate. But, then, what field of battle has ever been anything but the devil's playground?

Although I was happy to let Uncle Sam pay for my college education and law school, I never sought nor saw combat up close, but did see the effect it had had on young men and women, and even the seasoned lifers.

I had to give four years of my life to the military, working as a JAG—Judge Advocate General—lawyer, where I applied the principles and mandates of the UCMJ—Uniform Code of Military Justice—to situations mostly involving boys who'd yet to become men. And, yes, just as Clemenceau observed, I wasted no time in affirming that military justice is to justice as military music is to music.

As always, my musings about my army past brings to my mind Rob Steinmann, a Navy JAG officer I befriended in Virginia and served with for almost two years. Yes, I've lied to Sam about sharing all my secrets with him. Sometimes treasured experiences, feelings, and thoughts become ordinary and less magical if they are shared, even with loved ones. Some secrets we must take with us to our graves.

Rob and I were the same age when we met, and we had followed the same educational path, finding ourselves at a Navy base in Virginia, teeming with soldiers, sailors, and Marines. We lived down the hall from each other in the unmarried officers' quarters, and we sat across the hall from each other in the JAG Office.

Rob and I found that we were simpatico in the sense that... Well, for example, we went to see *A Separate Peace* when it first came out in 1972 and then returned to see it two more times. It was a good movie based on a novel by John Knowles, where the protagonist, Gene, goes back to the American boarding school he'd attended as a teenager during WWII, and recalls the time he spent there. Gene's best friend is Finny, a devil-may-care boy who provides a stark contrast to the serious and introverted Gene. Rob and I were that way. Rob was Finny, blue-eyed and fair. I was Gene, a mixture of Irish and Italian.

While some read a homoerotic component into those characters, I see the story as portraying the deepest sense of companionship that two boys can achieve without actually becoming sexually physical with one another. Rob and I mirrored the relationship Gene and Finny portrayed in the narrative, and I think that's why it struck a chord with us. The darker motif in the story, though, places the serious and studious Gene, internally in conflict with the seemingly indomitable Finny. Finny is the consummate athlete, a bright student who never studies, and who is completely at ease with himself. Finny defies seriousness. Gene wrongly assumes he and Finny are in competition with each other, both jealous of each other's talents. I ignored that darkness, and I believe Rob did, too. Rob and I were better than that.

Rob and I spent all of our free time together, neither one of us interested in the particular delights that Norfolk had to offer young and perpetually horny military boys. Rob had stayed true to his girlfriend since his junior year in college and never had any doubt he would eventually marry her. My disinterest in women had more to do with the ambiguousness I felt about them, and my gut hunch that I was queer as could be. And, of course, our positions as JAG officers precluded any liaisons with easy women, and in my case, other men.

Almost every day, with Rob always in the lead, we'd jog from our quarters to Chesapeake Bay, along the beach for a mile or two, and finally back to our quarters. Rob ran like a gazelle while I plodded along in the steady but slow pace reminiscent of a pack animal. On weekends, we'd ride bicycles for miles, sometimes play eighteen holes of golf, then swim laps in the base pool—the only endeavor where I could best Rob. On weekends, we'd have picnics, too, and sit on the sand or the grass, usually within view of the Chesapeake Bay Bridge and Tunnel. At the end of our workday, we'd usually sit in Rob's or my room and bullshit for hours. And, yes, a few times as we sat at the little table in my room, sipping bourbon—which neither of us were that fond of, but *What the hell*, we'd say, sipping it anyway—and Rob would look at the picture of the white buck I'd hung on the wall and remark on its beauty and nobility, the two things I'd most wanted to capture when I'd taken the picture so may years before.

About six months into my posting in Virginia, I realized my *queer as could be* hunch had better be nipped in the bud before it got me in trouble. I returned to Denver on Christmas leave, gave the young woman I'd known as a good friend a ring with a tiny diamond, and told her to come out to Virginia. We got married in the Prince George County, Virginia municipal building. The ceremony cost twenty dollars, and the motel afterward set me back about three times that for two nights. We consummated the marriage in that motel room, and she left after spending two days with me. I'd arranged to live off base in light of her impending return to Virginia and rented a small cottage in Chesapeake Beach with a view of the bay. She returned in two weeks with her clothes and other items she needed to make our cottage a home.

Again, most men who find themselves in the army necessarily discover the truth of themselves fairly quickly. That was as true for me as for anyone else. After three months together, I told her it wouldn't work, and she agreed. Whether she knew why I'd come to that conclusion, she never said, and I never admitted to it. The day she left, I packed the only two things she wanted from me—the bicycle I'd bought for her, and the picture of the white buck that she'd hung in our little parlor. I didn't argue about letting her take the picture when she left the cottage for the last time. Though it meant a great deal to me, I'd given it to her and figured I owed her at least that much.

Rob had made himself scarce during the three months I lived with my wife, and our only contact was during working hours. We still ate lunch together when I didn't head for the cottage at noon, but the subject of my marriage and it's failing didn't come up in conversation except for a few words here and there. I appreciated Rob for that. And I often wondered at the time if Rob hadn't known me better than I'd known myself.

The day before the Navy sent Rob to his next duty station at the Great Lakes Naval Base in Illinois, we took some salami and cheese and a bottle of wine to a spot overlooking the Chesapeake Bay. Below us, in a pond, white Great egrets frolicked, often pausing their antics, as if to display their beauty for Rob's and my pleasure. Once we returned to the cottage, we opened another bottle of wine. Half way into that bottle, Rob told me he'd had too much to drink and asked if he could stay the night.

We slept together that night, naked in my failed marriage bed, and held each other, skin on skin. It was a loving experience, and it remains one of the most precious moments of my life. I'd never before touched another man in such a loving and caring way. I had never envisioned a sexual relationship with Rob. And we didn't have one that night. But I have often thought, what we did that night was Rob's final gift to me—something Finny might have done for Gene.

Before Rob left the next day, we agreed to keep in touch. Neither of us was embarrassed by what we'd done the night before. We'd consummated our friendship in the only way we knew would persist as the memory it became. We wrote to each other, promising we'd get together somewhere, sometime in the future. But we never did. Eventually, we ended our correspondence. I stopped writing first, knowing our lives had diverged—certainly mine more than Rob's—and, as I have often told myself, sometimes memories are best left as just that—memories.

Although I knew I couldn't sustain a marriage with a woman without pushing our relationship to a place of darkness and regret, I'd yet to find the courage to admit to myself who exactly I was. Yes, I'd discovered the magic of myself in the mountains when I was sixteen. But it would be a while before I finally understood the implications of that magic and what it portended.

///

Sam is three inches taller than me and every morning, he reaches for the birdfeeder that hangs from the aspen limb right outside our living room window. I'd used a ladder to install the damned thing, tied it too high for my reach, and now it's a two-man job to refill it because my right hip seems to be veering south, and I don't climb that ladder anymore. I've thought about telling Sam to lower it a few inches, but as much as I've thought about it, I haven't yet done it. We've established the daily ritual now, and we're both happy with it. Sam hands the feeder down to me, I refill it, and then Sam hooks it back onto the wire that hangs from the limb.

This morning I tell Sam that's why I married him: "Every man needs a hand every once in a while, preferably someone with a longer reach."

"We got married two years ago," Sam replies. "I've been reaching high for you for thirty-three years. I've often thought," he says as he follows me back into the house, "you had some ulterior motive for keeping me on for the last three decades. Able to reach higher than you wasn't something that ever came to mind."

I put the seed bucket in the laundry room, then step into the kitchen. "Would you hand me the water pitcher?"

"Hah!" Sam says, opening the cupboard and reaching to the top shelf where we keep the pitcher. "I guess we were made for each other."

"Yes, I guess we were." I take the pitcher from him and fill it with water. I carry it outside and tip it over the heated birdbath. This time of year, the birds still take a drink, but mule deer and pine squirrels are the major users, emptying it twice a day.

Back in the house, I find Sam on the loveseat, sorting through yesterday's mail. His head is tilted forward as he opens the envelopes spread on the top of the coffee table. He's shaved his head again because I think he thinks it's better to have nothing rather than the monastic crown he sports if he lets it grow very long. I prefer to let my hair grow until Sam reaches his hands to the back of my neck when we're watching cable and starts to braid it. He never gets very far, but it is his way of telling me I need a haircut.

I sit down in my recliner, turn my head to watch the mule deer eat the sunflower seeds I throw out there every day, and then turn back to Sam. "The silent auction Mary told us about?"

"Yes," Sam says, not raising his eyes from whatever he's studying on the coffee table.

"What should we donate?"

"Well." He pauses and looks at me. "Don't you have some pictures you could contribute? I've got a few CDs I could give them."

"That's what I was thinking. Do we still have those frames we've never used?"

"Harley, those are your frames."

"I know, but you're in charge of keeping track of where we put them."

Sam shakes his head. "They're in a box out in the shed."

"Would you kindly find that box and bring it in the house?"

"Of course, dear," Sam says, and then gets back to what he's laid out on the coffee table.

"When do you think you might do that?"

Sam slowly raises his head, gives me that look of his I know so well, sighs, stands up and walks across the parlor to the mud room, puts on his coat and walks out the front door.

///

It's snowed for two days and nights. Jack is ecstatic, more swimming in the snow than prancing through it. Over a foot of it is on the ground, and I have the ATV idling as Sam fiddles with the plow blade mechanism on the front end. I tell him it's all going to melt before he's done with whatever he's doing, and he gives me *that look* again. It's my job to clear our lane down to the county tar top, providing a reasonably clear path for our SUV to navigate from the house to the road and back. The county maintains their road when they get around to it, and they've yet to do that. Tonight is the big event at Cathy's, and we've loaded up a box with framed photographs of critters and vistas, and Sam has chosen about fifteen CDs he can live without. I haven't checked to see if Sam put any of his Christmas CDs in there, and I suspect he hasn't. The silent auction is a worthy cause, but Sam's largesse only goes so far.

"Okay," Sam says. "Try it now."

I pull the lever back, the hydraulics hum, and the plow blade inches up. I push the lever down, and the blade goes down.

"Good to go," I say, advancing the gas button and slowly commencing the chore. I've never shared with Sam that I've taken on this chore because I think it's fun. I also think using the chainsaw is fun. Sam isn't fond of power tools or equipment, and he's happy to let me operate the ones we've found to be essential up here.

"Watch the rocks," Sam says over the noise of the engine.

I don't answer because Sam knows I've memorized the location of the rocks in our lane. I keep an eye on the blade level when I approach them, now buried under a foot or more of snow. When I get to the end of our lane, I see the little family of four does, the twin fawns, a young buck, and the big buck we've named Calvin standing off in the distance, their intense stares following my every move. They're used to this, and I'm sure they'll get back to foraging as soon as I turn the ATV around.

Just as I'm about to reach the road, I hear the county plow truck coming up the hill. I stop the ATV and wait for the behemoth to pass. I wave at the driver, and he waves back. The huge blade creates a two-foot ridge of snow right in front of the end of our lane. I get to work clearing that out of the way, then turn around and head back toward the house. After three more trips to the road and back, I've finished the job.

I stop the ATV just outside the garage and watch Sam shovel snow from our porch, while Jack searches for something in the snow ridges off to the side of the house and down the hill. I don't think I ever envisioned this scene for my life, especially now that I've got fewer years ahead of me than behind. But it's okay. It's a nice scene. It's what I've made of my life, and I don't regret a moment of it. It's made of magic.

///

Though March is just around the corner, Cathy has yet to take the Christmas lights off the outside of the café, and she's turned them on tonight, their green, red, and blue glow reflecting off the accumulated snow along the edge of the roof. That, along with the blue and green neon beer signs in the windows, gives the place a… Well, as I've said before, it's a homey place that beckons a smile. Sam parks our SUV, a decade old Dodge with less than fifty thousand miles on it, and we step out, our feet crunching on the hardened snow below the newest layer that has lately fallen.

"You go on in," Sam says. "I'll bring in the box."

When I open the front door, I hear chatter inside and Faith Hill is singing about a kiss that's perpetual bliss. I hold open the door for Sam, who carries our box of auction items.

"Hey, you two," Cathy says, wiping her hands on a towel she carries with her. She's wearing a red and blue checkered flannel shirt, khaki cargo shorts, and hiking boots. "There's a booth right over there." She points to the other side of the room. "I'll take your box. You have any minimums on anything?"

"You can give them away if we don't get any bids," I say, as she takes the box from Sam.

"Oh, I think you'll get some bids. I'll send Mary over to your booth."

Cathy totes the box to a corner table piled with auction items.

I follow Sam across the room, both of us stepping around folks gabbing and laughing in the walkway. We slide into the booth and unzip our coats.

"About as crowded as I've ever seen it," I say.

"Yeah." Sam appraises the crowd. "There's got to be somebody in here who'll take that Jimmy Swaggart box set I never opened."

Sam has groused for three years about that box set taking up valuable space on his shelves. I've been kind and suggested Sam's sister meant well when she gave it to him several birthdays ago. However, Sam took it as a message from his family back in Eastern Washington that, after thirty-three years, his dalliance with abominable behavior might still be just a phase.

"Maybe so," I say, smiling at Mary as she comes to our table.

"Harley, Sam," she says. "Glad you showed up. What can I get you?"

"Just my usual," I say. "PBR in a glass."

"How about an orange slice martini?" Sam says.

Both Mary and I look at Sam as if he's lost his mind.

"What?" Sam says.

"Sorry," Mary says. "I was expecting you to say merlot. I'm not sure anybody knows how to make— Did you say an orange slice martini?"

"Just some vodka and orange juice, a squeeze of lemon, and throw in a little vermouth. Do you have a shaker?"

"I think we do."

"Good. Shake it all up with some ice, and we'll be good to go."

"Okay," Mary says. "Are you going to want something to eat tonight?"

I look at Sam. We'd decided we wouldn't stay long and would try to get back home before more snow falls. "We'll see how it goes."

"All right. I'll be right back." Mary stops at the next booth in line, takes their drink orders and then heads to the bar.

"Living dangerously tonight?" I say.

Before Sam can answer, Hank, our nearest neighbor, sets his tall mug of dark beer on our table, sits down next to me, and tips his red Stetson up a bit on his head. "What the hell are you two old farts doing out on a night like this?" he says, staring at Sam and then turning toward me.

"Hank." I glance into his tiny gray eyes, then confirm again that his overgrown horseshoe mustache does look like frazzled steel wool. "I've missed you, too."

"Saw you got your lane plowed," he says, turning his head to look at the crowd. "Drove the front loader up your way, but you'd already done it."

"You don't do it right," I say.

"Yeah, I know." Hank takes a sip of beer. "Ever since I took out those little trees you replanted in the wrong place. Hey." He taps his index finger on the table. "This is a goddamned good turnout for a fucking good cause. Semper Fi!"

I raise my fist, knowing Hank will do the same.

Hank fist bumps me and says with a little too much enthusiasm, "Oorah!" He served in Nam when he was only eighteen, and once a Marine always a Marine. Or so he's reminded us about a thousand times.

Mary brings our drinks. They've put Sam's martini in a tumbler, and there's an orange slice hanging on the side of the glass. "I hope Suzy did it okay, Sam." She stands there waiting for Sam's reaction.

"It'll be fine."

Hank stares at the tumbler. "The fuck is that?"

"A martini." Sam lifts the tumbler up and takes a sip.

"Shirley Temple is more like it," Hank says.

Sam puckers a little. "It's vodka and ice actually."

"But it's okay?" Mary says, a concerned look on her face.

"It's fine, Mary."

"Good. You need a refill, Hank?"

"Sure," Hank says. He downs what's left of his beer and holds the mug out to her.

"Be right back," she says, taking the mug and turning away from our table.

Hank shakes his head. "Sad case there," he says. "You know her story?"

"That her son is going infantry?" I say.

"Oh, that and everything else," Hank says. "You know her husband was killed in Iraq?"

"Yes, Mary told us the last time we came in," Sam says.

"Yeah, well… I knew her when she worked down in the Junction. Believe she still lives there. The thing is, her husband was adopted. When he got killed, the kid—his name is Joe, after his daddy—was only nine years old. All they told Mary about her husband was that he was killed by hostile fire. Anbar Province in 2004. Helluva thing. Anyway, Mary's parents were nowhere to be found when that happened—they'd divorced by then, and went their separate ways—and Joe senior's adoptive parents had died in a car crash somewhere several years before. Mary had to raise that boy by herself. She worked two jobs all those years. And now. Hell, I never discouraged any kid from becoming a Marine, but… That boy is all she's got. He has a good trade, too. But damned if he didn't get a bug up his ass to be a Marine."

Hank looks at the front door when it opens and waves his hand. "There's my date." He slaps his hands on the table top and scoots out of the booth. "You enjoy your night." He walks toward the woman with the horsetail hair we saw him with before. He embraces her, gives her a kiss on the cheek, and they head for the bar.

"Sad story," Sam says, squeezing his orange slice over his drink.

"Yeah. Losing his parents, too."

Sam takes another sip and once again puckers.

"That bad?" I say.

"Oh, Sam." Mary stops at our booth. "Maybe Suzy ought to try that again."

"No. She did fine, Mary. It's just a little heavy on the vodka."

"You want me to pour some orange juice in there?"

"That might help a bit." Sam hands her the tumbler.

"They've got the auction items all spread out. You ought to take a look."

I look at the two tables in the corner. Several folks are hovering over them, holding items up and pointing at other items still on the table. I ask, "Anything worth looking at?"

"I think your pictures are the hit of the night, Harley. But, yeah, there's a few things that are really nice. I put in a picture myself—well, it's only a copy—but it's something my husband—" Mary turns toward the man who has just put his hand on her shoulder.

"Hon, I think our food is ready over there," the man says, and we all look toward the half-wall where the kitchen is. Three plates are sitting on the counter.

"I'm sorry," Mary says. "I'll get it right now." She turns back to Sam. "I'll get Suzy to make you a new one, Sam. I'll tell her to put in more juice this time."

"Thank you," Sam says, and Mary hustles toward the bar.

I watch Mary lean over the bar and tell Suzy something, and then she heads toward the kitchen. "Let's take a look at the stuff on the tables."

Sam nods and we walk over to the display tables. I see my pictures spread out on the tables, and Sam's CDs are there, too. Somebody has taped a bid sheet on each, and I notice a couple of my pictures have already collected bids.

An old guy with a VFW hat on decorated with tiny brass and silver pins is standing behind the tables. He's a big man, and his smile comes from his entire face. "Come on now," he says, "it's all for a good cause. You sir," he says, looking directly at Sam. "You look like a man who'd appreciate some of these CDs. Lookey here." He picks up the Jimmy Swaggert box set. "Some of the most beautiful sacred songs ever recorded. And it hasn't even been opened."

"Think I'll pass on that," Sam says.

Sam nudges me, and we move around a couple studying a shiny-new Craftsman socket set, and get to the other side of the table away from the VFW guy's line of sight. There are books over here, a couple of pairs of knitted mittens and stocking caps, some flashlights, and other miscellaneous items that appear as though they might have been yard sale rejects.

"You see anything?" Sam asks.

"No. We already have enough clutter."

Sam heads back to our table.

I begin to turn away when I realize what I've just seen. I squeeze myself between the wall and the table. Right there, behind a small vase with multi-colored daisies painted on it is a picture, no, *my* picture of the white buck. I pick it up. It's nicely framed but obviously a copy; the printer ink used to create it is slightly discolored. I'm aware the VFW guy is saying something to me, but my total concentration is on the picture I'd captured fifty years ago. *How in the hell did this get here? Who? What?*

"Just put down your offer and name on that piece of paper."

I finally process what the VFW guy is saying as he leans over the table and points at the picture with a ballpoint pen.

"Right there," he says like I'm feebleminded.

"Yes," I say. "Okay. I know what to do."

"In about an hour, you'll know if you're the highest bidder." He holds the ballpoint out to me.

I take the pen, place the picture on the table and fill out the tag.

THE WHITE BUCK

My hand is shaking, and I can barely write my own name. I want to tell the VFW guy the picture is mine; it's priceless, and no amount of money can equal what it means to me. I glance at him, and he's watching me as if he thinks I might bolt and run. I write down one hundred dollars. Think about adding another hundred to the number and decide I'll come back and check if anyone offers more. I give the pen back and put the picture back behind the flowered vase where I'd found it. Before I inch my way back out from between the wall and the table, I grab a pair of knitted mittens and absently drape them over the picture.

When I get back to the booth, Sam is reading a menu.

"You decided to have dinner?"

"Thinking about it," Sam says. He looks over the top of the menu at me. "Find something you like over there?"

"Yes, I... There's a nice picture of a white buck. It's a copy of an original, but it's... I put a bid in on it."

"How much?"

"Enough."

Sam holds my gaze. I grab a menu from the side of the table, but the words and pictures have no meaning. *How did it get here?* It strikes me there's one possibility, and I envision my ex-wife staring at me from the across the room. I study the happy crowd, searching for a woman about my age who might be glaring at me with a sly smile on her lips. What I see is Mary coming toward us.

"You've picked up menus," she says. "You want some supper after all?"

"Harley's put a bid on something," Sam says, "so I guess we have to wait and see if he gets it."

"Really? What'd you find, Harley?"

"Just a picture of a buck."

"The white buck?"

"Yes."

"Oh, good," she says. "That's my contribution. I think it's so pretty. So unusual."

I clear my throat. I want to ask her how the hell she got that picture, but instead, I say, "Yes, it is. I notice it's a copy. Do you have the original?"

"Yes, I do. But I can't sell that. There's a story behind it."

"How are the fish and chips tonight?" Sam asks.

I look at Sam and wonder how on earth he can be thinking about food at a time like this. *It's the white buck for Christ's sake!*

"Not too greasy. Cathy's cooking tonight, and she takes care not to send them out sopping."

"Okay. I'll have that."

"And for you, Harley?"

"The same." I'm not hungry and want Mary to sit down so we can talk about the white buck. "That a long story about that picture?" I ask her before she turns away.

"Yeah," she says, losing her smile. "It was my husband's. If you get it, I'll tell you all about it. Now, let me get your order in."

I watch her walk away and then look at the auction table. It doesn't appear as though anyone has their hands on the picture, but I can't take that chance. "I'll be right back." I get out of the booth and walk back to the table. The VFW guy sees me coming.

"Can't hide the merchandise," he says a little too sternly.

I glance at the picture and see the mitten I'd put over it isn't there anymore.

"Nobody's bid on it except you," the VFW guy says, his tone and expression patronizing me.

I nod. "Thanks." I square my shoulders in an attempt to appear not as feebleminded as the VFW guy apparently thinks I am. I walk back to the booth and slide in. Sam has finished his drink and is scrolling through his messages on his phone.

"You really want that picture, don't you?" Sam says, keeping his eyes on his phone.

"Are you going to have another martini?"

"No. Just water for now."

I reach for my beer but think better of it. I look outside. Still snowing. As I always do when we leave Jack alone, I wonder what he's doing about now? Probably sleeping like I expect he always does when we're not there, and most of the time when we are.

Mary returns with two plastic trays, both heaped with fried fish pieces and french fries. "I didn't ask you if you wanted cole slaw instead of fries," she says, placing the trays in front of us.

"Fries are good," Sam says.

"That's fine, Mary," I say. "Don't you get a break pretty soon?"

She reaches for the bottle of ketchup on our table. "Should have had one earlier, but it's so busy. I'll get you a new bottle," she says, stepping away from the table too quickly for me to ask her to sit down a minute and… *Tell me about the picture.*

"Here yah go." Mary returns with a fresh bottle of ketchup.

"Mary," I say, "if you get a break can you sit with us? Tell me about that picture?"

She looks toward the kitchen, then looks at the line of booths she's been serving. "Maybe, Harley. Give me a few minutes, and I'll be back."

Sam dips his fish into tartar sauce. "Why's the story about the picture so important?"

"I…" No, I can't tell Sam about the white buck now. I don't know why I haven't ever mentioned it to him, except that… Hell, it was only a picture I'd taken when I was a kid and gave away a long time ago. What would be the point of telling him now? Yes, Sam knows I was married to a woman for a quick minute in the Army, but not that I'd given her the evidence of the magic I'd discovered about the world on that mountainside fifty years ago. "She said there's a story behind it," I say. "The dead husband. Her boy in the Marines. What Hank told us about her. You know?"

"Okay." Sam dumps ketchup into a corner of his food basket.

"Just a curiosity, then?"

"Yeah." I look at the auction tables and can just barely see the top edge of the picture where I'd put it. The VFW guy is sipping from a beer mug; his eyes are still intently focused on the folks hovering around the tables, watching, I suspect, for any pilfering, especially from addle-minded oldsters. Laced through the dull din of the crowd's chatter, I hear someone's odd selection of Dr. Hook's rendition of "Sylvia's Mother" coming from the jukebox. And, there's Hank leaning over to give his date a kiss on her lips, the brim of his Stetson resting on the top of her head. This all becomes surreal for a moment: the white buck, the dead husband, the VFW man ready to pounce, Hank and his girlfriend, "Sylvia's Mother" for Christ's sake!

"I've got just a few minutes," Mary sits down next to Sam and places a glass of what appears to be a Coke on the table.

I didn't see her coming, and I'm immediately brought back to the present. "Good," I say. "Tell us about the picture."

And she does.

Her husband, Joe, had the picture when she met him. It had come from his birth mother whom he never knew. His adoptive mother had told him the white buck had magical powers and it would protect him his entire life. When Mary and Joe met, she was only eighteen, and he was twenty. But, as she says, it was love at first sight. He'd been in the Marines for two years already, had an income, and—I conclude, remembering Faith Hill's words when Sam and I first came in tonight—perpetual bliss had ruled the day they met. That was 1993.

Yes, I suspect a coincidence and do a quick calculation and know that Joe was born in 1973. By the time Mary and Joe had their baby, Joe Junior, Joe was rising through the ranks. He was an E-5 sergeant then, working on his staff sergeant requirements. Mary says Joe was upset he'd missed the First Gulf War in 1990, but she thinks to this day the white buck had done his duty by keeping Joe home safe and sound even though he was only seventeen at the time, and his adoptive parents wouldn't consent to his enlistment. The Marines moved Joe to Twentynine Palms, California, the major pre-deployment center for Marines going to war, where he earned his staff sergeant stripes and was anxious to complete the requirements for gunnery sergeant. Mary and Joe Junior lived on base, the apartment small but adequate, the white buck hanging on the living room wall.

"He made one mistake in the Marines," Mary says, picking up her drink and taking a sip. "Some of his buddies took him to the base in San Diego to celebrate his promotion. The second night they were there, Joe didn't like something some Navy guy said about the Marines, and Joe hit him. Guess he broke the guy's nose. I really ought to get back on the floor," she says, glancing toward the kitchen.

I want to reach over the table and hold her down. "No, Mary," I want to say, "I need to know about this." But I just tell her that she can surely take just a few more minutes. "And," I add, "what does the white buck have to do with Joe getting into trouble in San Diego?"

"Okay. Just a minute more." She folds her hands on the table and continues. "They kept Joe overnight at the Navy base, and in the morning they took him in before a military judge; an arraignment, I guess you call it. The judge was nice. He asked about Joe's family and his service in the Marines. And, after talking to Joe for a few minutes—and I don't know how the judge did this or why—he told Joe to get back to Twentynine Palms and to stay out of trouble. Joe did have to talk to his commander about what had happened, but Joe was a good Marine, and I guess they gave him a little slack about the whole thing. Anyway, Joe wanted to do something nice for the judge, and about the only thing he could think of was to make a copy of the white buck—he did so love that picture. The next time he had some leave, he took the copy to that judge. So, in the entire world, there're only two copies of it and, of course, the original. And I hope you get one of them."

"Mary, we need some help out here," Cathy impatiently says when she stops at our table.

"Sorry," Mary says, quickly standing up and grabbing her glass. She and Cathy head back toward the kitchen.

He jounced the limb.

The context of the end of Mary's story—Joe's mistake, the military judge—sends me off into the Tidewater region of Virginia. Rob and I often declared our intentions to flee the military at the first opportunity.

"Everything has to evolve, or else it perishes," either Rob or I would say, repeating one of the lines from *A Separate Peace*, and we'd both nod, agreeing what Knowles had given to us had wisdom, and the military was no place to evolve. We'd seen the movie three times and had memorized quite a few of the lines, including, "I jounced the limb," which was Gene's confession that he caused Finny to fall from a tall tree, the injury eventually leading to Finny's death. But Rob and I would say those words mostly in jest whenever Rob or I would do something stupid or clumsy or anything that had the merest tinge of mendacity to it. Sometimes, too, we'd discuss the cases we were working on, mostly the ones where a young sailor, soldier, or marine had fucked up in one way or another, and who'd offered excuses or defenses that were lame as hell. We'd characterize those cases as just another *jouncing the limb* scenario. More than a few times, though, either Rob or I would argue for leniency if our client struck us as having potential in the military, as someone who deserved a second chance.

Had Joe's "mistake" in San Diego been just another *jouncing the limb* offense in the eyes of the judge who'd told Joe to go home and behave?

There's an eeriness to what I'm remembering. I look at Sam, and Sam's staring at me with his *I've got a question for you* face.

"What?" I say.

"Do you know what that all means?"

"No, I don't. Except..." *Except what?* "Except that the picture has a past."

"Well," Sam picks up the remaining piece of fish, "if you do get the picture, I hope it isn't hexed or something."

Static and feedback erupt as Cathy hooks up a microphone to the sound system. She stands in front of the auction tables and says, "I want to welcome everybody to our third silent auction for homeless vets."

Some clapping ensues, and Hank hollers, "Oorah!" from the bar.

"We had a good turnout," Cathy says, "and I want to thank all the donors and everybody who bid on something. And, a big thank you to Bert Mason, who handled the auction for us."

The VFW guy waves his hand from behind the tables.

"You all remember Bert when he was a deputy sheriff up here."

I nod. *Figures.*

When the applause ends for Bert, some guy in the booth next to us says into the momentary quiet, "Got me a few times after I'd had a few."

There's laughter from the crowd as Bert reaches for the microphone. "I'll getcha again, Gary, if you stumble outta here." There's more laughter, and Bert hands the microphone back to Cathy.

"Thank you, Bert," Cathy says. "Well, the auction is over, and everybody who bid on something can come on up and see if you won. If you did, Bert will take your money. And now, drinks are on the house for everybody who served our great country in the armed forces."

I wait for Hank to grunt *Oorah* again, but he doesn't. I look at the bar and see he and his date are wrapped up together on their bar stools, oblivious to what's going on around them.

"Why don't you get your picture?" Sam says. "We ought to go home. Jack'll be waiting."

I slip out of the booth. As I approach the auction tables, Bert, the VFW guy sees me, reaches for the picture and hands it to me. "You got it," he says. "No other bids."

I take it from him, study it for a second, and then look back at him. "You'll take a check?"

"Yes, indeed. Just make it out to The Veterans' Assistance League," he says, handing me a pen.

I tug my wallet out of my back pocket. "Thank you." I write out the check and hand it to him, pick up the picture, and start back to the booth when Mary stops me.

"I'm so happy you got it, Harley."

"Me, too. It's a lovely picture."

"Yes," she says. "Joe thought it was magical, and that it would protect him. Where are you going to hang it?"

"In my study where I can see it every day."

"That's wonderful. Don't you want a free drink?"

"No thanks. We've got to get back home." I give her a hug.

Sam's on his feet, coat zipped. He drops two twenties on our table to settle our tab.

"I see you got it," Sam says.

"Yeah. I was the only bidder."

"You going to tell me how much you bid?"

"No, I'm not."

"Okay then," he says, and we head toward the front door.

I take one last look at the auction table, and there's Bert, opening up Sam's box set of *Jimmy Swaggart's Greatest Hits*, studying the list of song titles on the insert.

As we walk to our car, the weight of the picture seems as enormous as the possibility that I may have had a son. And a grandson who's alive and well, but may be headed for the same fate as his father. I sit down on the passenger side and hold the picture in my lap, my palms atop it. I don't hear Sam start the car, and I can barely see the road ahead.

///

The sun has finally emerged, and today the sky is as blue as the Caribbean with errant puffs of clouds here and there, white as the snow they'd given up days ago. The snow has begun to deflate in upon itself; the foot or more high ridges and drifts here yesterday are now sagging to the imperatives of the sunny day. It's still cold, though, as Sam and I step off the back porch to refill the bird feeders and spread sunflower seeds on the ground. Jack follows us out and takes note of all the interlopers that have passed through his territory during the night, sticking his nose into paw or hoofprints, and sniffing at the waste the critters have left behind.

As Sam hands the feeder down to me, I grab it and quickly turn my head toward the dense treeline that surrounds us. Sam has heard it too, just a slight cracking of something within the dark recess to our left. We both listen for a moment, knowing critters often watch us from where they cannot be seen. We say nothing and get back to the task at hand.

///

Sam stands in the doorway to my study and looks at the picture of the white buck I've hung on the wall to the side of my desk. "It *is* a great picture. Something you might hope to see up here."

"Yeah." I turn and look at the picture even though I'd been staring at it for half hour before Sam came in. I'd averted my eyes when I heard Sam approach my door. I didn't want to him to think that I was *that* obsessed with the picture and didn't want to give him cause to ask more questions than he already has. "I think it could have happened up here," I say. "I mean… A white buck could appear up here as well as anywhere else."

"Maybe. We're having dinner at Cathy's tonight? Right?"

"Yes. We break that habit, and they'll have a search party looking for us."

"Isn't that the truth?" he says as he shuts my door. I hear him climb the stairs to his music room.

I turn back to the picture. Ever since I put two and two together that I had a son, the realization glares like a goddamned strobe light at the back of my brain. But the evidence is circumstantial, and God knows I spent a good part of my professional life turning circumstantial evidence on its head.

A son.

Wow. No, it's just too…Magical? No, not that. But what? A son I never knew? A son killed in a war that should never have happened? A son who dearly loved the white buck and its magic, neither turning out to be a match for the reality of war? And a grandson?

I turn to my desktop and fire up iTunes. I made a playlist two years ago I've listened to probably a hundred or more times. It begins with Bob Seger's "Still the Same," and ends with John Prine's "Lake Marie." I click on the last song and listen to Prine's story about life, lost love, and death. Some songs tell stories better than most novels do. *Ah, baby…*

About an hour ago, Sam let Jack out into the side yard we erected a year ago just off the front porch. It's about a half-acre, fenced, and its got some small boulders in it, some trees, and wild grasses. We put gates on the porch so Jack can come up there from the yard if he wants to and let us know if he wants to come in the house. As I turn off iTunes, I hear Jack's scratch on the front door. From above, I hear Sam immediately react to that sound, scrambling to get downstairs to let in Jack. I also stand up with the same intent. Sam and I are that way with Jack; he's our child, and we're indulgent parents. When Sam hears me open my study door, he reverses himself and goes back upstairs. I let Jack in, and he follows me into the living room where he makes himself comfortable on the couch.

Through the living room windows, I see a family of eight mule deer digging into the sunflower seeds. Calvin, the patriarch, steps under the lowest hanging bird feeder and laps the seeds until the feeder tips and they all spill out.

I sit in my recliner, grab the camera I always keep on the side table and snap a few pictures. I've got hundreds of pictures of these guys, but I never tire of shooting just a few more. Right now, a couple of does are shooing away the fawns, lifting their forelegs to butt them out of the way. I watch the fawns who Sam and I decided were twins when we first saw them together when they still had their spots. and Calvin, the alpha buck who likely sired all the younger deer around him. The smallest ones are probably his grandchildren. *A grandchild.* No. That's not— Possible?

///

"You have something on your mind?" Sam says as I turn the SUV onto the county road at the bottom of our lane.

"No. Why?" I know why, but I ask the expected question anyway.

"You've just been in your distant mode lately."

"You know me. I clam up sometimes."

"Yes, you do."

Usually, this kind of question and answer period lasts for only as long it takes me to confirm that I have indeed clammed up for a while. For thirty-three years, Sam has patiently endured my quiet moods, having learned a long time ago that inquiries about them rarely leads to anything but more silence. Sometimes I just want to take some time off from the world, pull down the shades, close the doors, and reflect inward for a while.

We pass by Hank's property where his house sits about a hundred yards up his lane. There's a little red car parked outside. "Looks like Hank has some company tonight," I say.

Sam looks up Hank's lane, nods, and says, "Probably that woman he's been hanging all over at Cathy's."

"Probably so." I envision Hank and the horsetail woman sitting before a fire, trading lies about their fidelity to each other while putting a big dent in a case of cold Coors. I start to follow them into the bedroom and quickly turn off that vision when the woman tugs on Hank's belt buckle. I do wonder, though, if Hank ever takes off that Stetson.

The county road isn't bad, but the dropping temperature creates icy patches I avoid.

Sam pulls out his phone and starts tapping on it.

"You emailing somebody?"

"Yes," Sam says. "Thought I'd tell Cathy to keep the stove hot, because we've been delayed by some old woman driver."

"Yeah, well. We fly off the side of the road, and you'll eat those words."

"Rather have the guacamole burger again at Cathy's. But, by the time we get there, she'll probably have taken it off the menu."

"You oughtta be in the circus. You could be the clown."

"And you'd be…"

And, so it goes, as it has gone for so many years, as Sam and I fill the dead space of yet another drive somewhere with well-practiced inanities. Then, again, sometimes we ride in silence. And, if my hip has quieted down, sometimes during our two mile walks up and down the county road or along the hiking paths around our property, we say not a word to each other. I guess after thirty-three years together, we just don't have much to say anymore. A comfortable silence, an affirmation of unwavering love that doesn't need to sustain itself with lustful passion.

Cathy's place is still lit up like it's Christmastime, but as we walk in the front door, the crowd is sparse and the festiveness of auction night is absent. The regulars cluster along the bar except for Hank and his girlfriend. We sit down to Willie crooning about blue eyes crying in the rain.

Suzy, who usually tends bar, walks to our booth and greets us.

"Mary out tonight?" I ask.

"Yeah, her son is flying into DIA tonight. He got leave, and she's picking him up. I think they're staying in Denver until tomorrow."

"Good deal," Sam says.

My grandson. My stomach does a backflip, and I catch myself shaking my head. "You think she'll bring him here?"

"Oh, I know she will. She's proud as hell of that boy. He got his Rifle Expert badge, you know?"

"No, I didn't know that," I say. *His daddy's footsteps.*

"So, what can I get you to drink?"

I order my usual, and Sam is back to his merlot. Suzy heads for the bar, and there's Cathy standing behind it. She waves and I wave back.

"Wonder who's cooking tonight."

Sam looks toward the bar. "Maybe Cathy's doing double duty. Her kitchen helper? What's his name?"

"Believe it's Jimmy or something like that."

"Yeah. Jimmy. Cute kid. Too skinny for me, but…"

The retort I usually give Sam—*Dream on!*—when he says something like this is lost to the thousand things going through my mind right now. *A grandson.* Yes, the white buck is *my* picture. Mary's story pointed in *my* direction. But, goddamnit, a thousand years have passed since— Hell, I barely remember what my wife looked like, for Christ's sake. It's just too unlikely. But if Sam and I are sitting here next Thursday, and Mary walks in with her son, and he's got my eyes, or nose, or…

"Here you go," Suzy says, placing our drinks on the table.

A son, and now a grandson. I think about that, and I get angry. I don't know who I'm angry at or why. I look at my beer, and there's no fizz in it; the tiny bubbles that float up from the bottom aren't there, nor does it have a head. "Why don't they fix the goddamned beer delivery system. Look at that. It doesn't even have a head."

"Beer delivery system?" Sam asks, "What's up, Harley?"

"I've got to get out of here." I slide out of the booth and head for the front door.

"Whoa," Sam says as he slides out and follows me.

I hustle outside and around the building and continue walking toward the treeline of Douglas fir, my hip screaming discontent. It's dark enough that the trees appear black, dangerous as nightmares. I stop when I hear Sam call out to me.

Sam comes up from behind me and puts his hand on my shoulder. "You want to go home?"

"Yes." I nod and turn toward him. "Let's go home."

///

After two days, Sam hasn't mentioned my behavior at Cathy's. That's Sam's way. He won't bring it up unless I do.

The morning is bright; not a single cloud obscures the sun. It's only sixteen degrees but seems warmer. We have refilled the bird feeders, and I have spread sunflower seeds in the places I know will get the attention of the usual critters. We've decided we'll spend this Sunday outside, repairing the sagging portions and holes in Jack's sideyard fence that mule deer and elk have made. Jack lies on a snow-covered boulder in the middle of the yard and supervises our activities.

I pull taut a section of fence. "Sorry, I got weird the other night."

Sam is on his knees, ready to pound a nail into the post that will hold the fencing secure. He looks up at me. "That's okay. You want to tell me what that was all about?"

I brace the post against Sam's pounding. "Sorry, I seemed angry, too," I say after Sam stops pounding.

"You're just full of regrets today, aren't you?"

"I was thinking about my past."

"You miss the halcyon days?"

I pull hard on the fencing, as Sam repositions himself to pound in another nail. "No. I think I'm living those now. I was angry because…"

Sam again looks up at me. "Because?"

I'm not ready to explain everything to Sam. I should have just kept my mouth shut. When I don't say anything more, he gets back to his task.

Jack leaps off the boulder and runs to the porch, his tail wagging, making sounds that are between a bark and a growl.

We look toward where Jack directs his attention, and see an older, green SUV coming up our lane. Sam drops his hammer, and I let go of the fence.

"Who is that?" Sam says.

I know who it is. I've been expecting them. For a moment I cannot move, but feel my heart pounding, and blood rushes to my head. In an instant, I envision everything that's led up to this moment: the picture, Rob, my wife and I together and then so quickly apart, Sam in that bar thirty-three years ago, standing there as if his presence were an inevitability. I see my son--*My son! for Christ's sake!*--dying or dead in a wink of the devil's eye. I lower my hands from the fence, glance at Sam, then look back at the car. "It's Mary and her son."

"Oh. Good," Sam says, walking to the porch and opening up the gate.

Jack scrambles out to meet the car, and Sam and I follow.

Mary gets out of the car, and a young man steps out from the passenger side. "Harley, Sam, I want you to meet my son, Joe," Mary says.

The young man takes off his stocking cap. His hair is burr cut, and he shows big white teeth as he smiles and holds his hand out to Sam. "Very nice to meet you," he says.

Sam grabs his hand and says, "It's my pleasure. This is Harley."

I take Joe's hand and shake it. I'm touching my son's child, my grandson whose hand is warm, his grip tight.

"You look like a Marine," I say, noticing Joe's eyes are green, and his face is handsome. *This is what my son looked like.*

"I certainly hope so," Joe says, kneeling down to give Jack a hug.

"Can you come in?" Sam asks. "We'll have some coffee or something."

"Sure," Mary says. "We've got some other stops to make, but we can stay a minute."

We all go into the house and after we've shed our coats and hats, I ask Mary and Joe to have a seat in the living room. Sam steps into the kitchen to make coffee, and I sit in my recliner. Mary settles onto the loveseat, and Joe steps to the windows to look upon the snow-covered landscape.

"Wow," Joe says. "I could live up here."

Mary stands up and joins Joe at the window. "Oh, it is beautiful," she says. She steps back to the loveseat and again sits down. "I want to thank you, Harley, for bidding on the picture."

Joe sits on the loveseat beside Mary. "Mom said you really wanted it."

"Yes, I did. It… It spoke to me."

"I wish we would have come up here years ago when Joe was growing up," Mary says, looking out the windows. "We live down the mountain by the Junction and don't have anything at all like this down there."

"This is where I grew up," I say, smiling at Joe and trying not to see myself sitting there as a young man, but I do admit there's a resemblance. *He's got my eyes.*

"Oh," Mary says, reaching into her pocket. "There's something I wanted to show you, Harley." She pulls out an envelope. "It was in Joe's things when I went through them after he passed. Like I told you, Joe wanted to do something nice for that judge who let him go after he made his mistake, and Joe gave him a copy of the buck picture. The judge wrote him a nice thank you note." She stands up and hands the envelope to me.

I take the envelope, supposing that whatever the judge had to say is the last part of the story. I open the envelope and pull out the folded piece of paper inside, and open it up. It's handwritten:

Dear SSgt. Potter,

Thank you for the great shot of this magnificently noble animal. It will hang in a prominent place in my home. My wife asked me to express her thanks to you for giving it to me. My youngest daughter thinks it's awesome. A long time ago I memorized some good words that came back to me as I looked closely at the picture. "Everything has to evolve or else it perishes." That probably won't mean anything to you, but it did to me and someone I knew years ago. We all grow into ourselves, hopefully for the best, and I sincerely hope you saw the opportunity I gave you in San Diego as contributing to your growth, both as a person and a Marine.

Sincerely,
Capt. Robert Steinmann

I read it a second time and take another look at the signature. *You stayed in, Rob. Why? And you remembered.* Sam brings in the coffee, and Mary, Joe, and he start gabbing about some damned thing that I cannot focus on. When he hands me a cup, I nod a thank you and set the cup on the window sill to my left. I think about the inevitability of things coming full circle.

As Sam keeps the conversation going, I envision grabbing Joe and taking him outside to the precise point where I lingered in the snow and raised my camera to get the shot of the white buck. I see myself pointing to where the white buck stood, asking Joe what he sees. Joe answers: "That's where the buck was. Look," he says. "There's the thick aspen and the smaller trees to the side. And there," he looks farther, "is the mountain in the background." I see him turning to me and asking, "How? How can this be?" And I don't answer him, but tell him to follow me to the thick-trunked aspen, and I say, "Look there." I point to a black scar on the trunk. "If you look very closely at the picture," I tell him, "you can see bark shavings at the base of the buck's antlers. That scar on the tree is where he scraped it. There are initials and a date carved above the scar, but it's all now grown together." Again, I see him standing there, looking at me with only questions in his eyes. And all I can think to say him is, "Magic abounds. It persists."

"Harley."

I look at Sam who has just called out my name.

"Harley. Mary and Joe have to leave," Sam says, frowning.

"Oh," I say, shaking off my reverie. "I'm sorry. I was just… You're leaving so soon?"

Mary stands up and steps to the side of the loveseat. "Yes, we've got to see a few more people before Joe leaves tomorrow. That was a nice letter, wasn't it?"

I realize I've still got the letter in my lap. "Oh. Yes, it was very nice. It was good of the captain to do it." I put the letter back in the envelope, stand and walk over to Mary. "Your husband must have been a good man," I say handing her the letter.

She puts the letter back in her purse. "Yes," she says, "he was the best."

Joe holds his hand out to me. "Very nice to have met you, Harley."

I shake his hand and look at his eyes, his face. "You'll come home safe and sound one day?"

"Yes," he says. "That's my plan." He walks over to Sam, who is standing in the mud room. "Thanks for the coffee, Sam."

"My pleasure," Sam says as he takes Mary's coat from the tree and holds it so she can slip it on.

I watch Joe pull on his jacket and stocking cap and realize I haven't taken any pictures. "Wait," I say, going back into the living room and grabbing my camera. "I've got to get some shots. Put on your coat, Sam. I've got the perfect spot."

I lead them to the *perfect spot*, apologizing that I've made them traipse so far through the snow. I keep their attention focused away from the view, and line them up next to the thick aspen with the mountain in the distance. I take a shot of all three of them, then just Mary and Joe, and then one of Joe by himself. I ask him to take off his stocking cap, and he does.

Sam and I then walk them to their car and watch them go down our lane. *Please return Joe*, I say a silent prayer. *Come up to the mountain. There's magic here.*

///

I've put the picture of Joe, bareheaded and smiling, on the wall next to the white buck. Someday Sam will come in here and note the obvious about those two pictures. And I will probably tell him the story from beginning to end, hoping he won't mind too much that I hadn't shared *all* my secrets with him. He might want me to share the story with Mary and Joe, though. But who would benefit from that? *What we don't know...* Right?

I sit here in my black chair listening to my iTunes playlist and look at those two pictures. I'm reminded of the darker theme of *A Separate Peace*, where Knowles tells us: "Nothing endures. Not a tree. Not love. Not even death by violence." And, I suppose, not even a person's past endures beyond what they wish to reveal of it. I don't know. Magic endures, though. I'm sure of that. Yes, certainly *that*.

Clowns Never Cry

Now

Here is Lester Fogg, paunch-burdened, feeling old at sixty-seven, bad hip, bad skin, but nevertheless determined to just get on with it. He sits at his makeup table in the upstairs bedroom of the 1893 Victorian he'd settled into thirty years ago. Applies spirit gum on the appropriate places, then gently presses the red bulbous honker over his nose. He'd earlier daubed on whiteface, then red and blue paint to accentuate his features, especially his mouth where he gave himself a happy smile. Pulls on a skullcap with orange hair spikes sticking out from it. Leans in closer to the mirror surrounded with a string of clear miniature Christmas bulbs, grabs a tissue, and carefully exposes the single tear tattoo below his left eye that he'd paid to have inked there shortly after returning from Vietnam in 1968. He didn't know at the time why he'd done that, except it was something he had to do.

He sits back, studies what he sees, nods, turns off the Christmas lights, and stands. Stepping in front of the mirror on the back of the bedroom door, he looks at himself—the bulky red, white, and blue silk jumpsuit, red shoes, orange hair, ruffled cuffs, powder puff buttons—the whole shebang that is Lester the Clown.

CLOWNS NEVER CRY

Though Stephen King's Pennywise has soured many to the delightful presence of clowns, Fogg persists. His clients are mostly mommies, who, Fogg surmises, remember their own fascination with circus clowns and want their children to have the same memories, albeit sadly without the smell of canvas, the enormity of the big top. Who can forget the unicycles, tiny cars, silly antics, the buckets of water thrown at the crowd who realized a moment too late it wasn't water at all, but brightly-colored confetti, or the fat lady wearing a broad hoop skirt who wasn't really a fat lady at all, but three tiny clowns, two under the skirt, and one standing on their shoulders. Fogg smiles with the memories. Understands a clown's job is to fool the world into believing something that isn't real, sly tricksters who make you laugh at your own gullibility.

Children's birthday parties and other happy events are Fogg's specialty, though he sometimes agrees to add something special to adult gatherings such as retirements, promotions, and wedding receptions. He always provides his services *gratis* to nursing homes, especially the ones where seniors are losing or have already lost their minds.

With children, he pulls a quarter from behind their ears, shows it to them and then makes it disappear. At first some of the younger children are frightened by him. But his gentleness, his colorful attire, his smile, and those magic quarters always reassures them there is no harm in this clown who speaks in near whispers. He delights the children who always gather in a semi-circle before him. Mommies and daddies hover, smile, and hug themselves with the simple joy from the scene before them.

As Fogg walks out of the bedroom, he stops in the hallway at the top of the stairs. Looks behind him and nods. "Yes," he says. "Thank you."

The benign spirits who live within the walls and flutter across the rooms in his old house have wished him well. They always do that. Fogg hopes they always will. He doesn't care if the spirits are real or imagined, he values them anyway. They've been a comfort for a long time, standing up to demons who were and remain very real indeed.

1967

Lester Fogg's left arm was crooked and resting on the window frame, a Lucky Strike devouring itself between his fingers. His right wrist was gently pressed against the top of the steering wheel. Merle Haggard crooned from a station in Ponca City, just a hop-skip from the Kansas border. Clicked his brights off for an on-coming semi as a train's lonesome wail was carried on the no-moon Oklahoma midnight. .

Glanced at Tucker Beene slouched down on the passenger side, his head against the seatback and window, his hands folded in his lap as though contentment had arrived. Fogg smiled as he looked back to the road ahead. *Let's get the hell out of Oklahoma.* He reached his Lucky outside the window, pinched off the cherry, and field-stripped the rest of it between his thumb and forefinger. Closed his window and gave the 287 V8 under the 1955 Pontiac Chieftain's hood enough gas to bring the speedometer needle up to about 105 miles per hour in no time at all.

They'd left Fort Polk, Louisiana nearly eight hours before, the Chieftain purring at no less than eighty except for slowdowns in Shreveport, Dallas, Oklahoma City, and four-way flashing yellows at the only intersections in two-bit towns in between. They'd stopped in Edmond, Oklahoma for a bite, then gassed up. Tucker said he'd drive whenever Fogg got tired, then proceeded to sip from the pint of Wild Turkey he'd brought with him, his intentions lost to the haze the whiskey evoked.

Fogg had seen the Chieftain for the first time when he donned his Class As and shared a taxi to Leesville, the town north of the base. As they rode into town, there she was, her front grill shining from a half a block down a side street, parked in a skinny driveway beside a small pink house. When the taxi driver pulled over in front of the Chez Paree—the boys had told the driver they were looking for a good time—Sam told them he'd catch up with them later. "Want to go look at something," he said as he glanced back toward that side street and started walking.

"What you see there, soldier-boy?" a firm and steady woman's voice came from the front porch.

Fogg had found the pink house, circled the Chieftain, peeked in the windows, and stepped back into the street a bit just to take in the beauty of it plus the sign on the windshield that read *For Sale*. He looked at the porch when he heard the voice. The large, brown-skinned woman sat in a rocking chair, her black hair with white strands was pulled back and coiled in a bun. Held a needle in her right hand, her left hand resting upon a small wooden hoop in her lap atop what looked like a table cloth spread across her legs. She peered over the top of tiny wire-framed glasses.

"I'm looking at this Chieftain," Fogg said. "It's a beauty."

"It's for sale."

"I see that."

"You want to buy it?"

Fogg again glanced at the Chieftain, then walked toward the woman. "How much you asking?"

"Three hundred dollars." She put her embroidery down on a second rocking chair next to her, stood up, tugged at her waist and then fluffed her cotton flower-printed dress out from behind.

Fogg put his hands on the porch rail. "That a firm price?"

"Yes it is. You want to take a look inside?"

"I guess."

"I'm Mrs. Qualls." Held her hand out over the porch rail.

"Lester Fogg." He clutched her hand and she squeezed.

"Got the key just inside," Mrs. Qualls said as she let go of his hand and opened the screen door. "That car is near to new," she hollered from inside.

"I was thinking that." Fogg turned and again gazed at the Chieftain. Thought it looked noble sitting there, obviously recently washed and waxed, quietly waiting for someone to feed it gas to get it doing what it was meant to do.

"Sergeant Jefferson Qualls, my son, bought it in 1960," she said, stepping back onto the porch. "Mister Bowers was the original owner in 1955. Bought it when it first came out. He lived just down the street before he died of pancreatic cancer. He drank a bit, you know." She walked down the three steps, her arm outstretched with the keys dangling from her hand. "His wife sold it to my son five years almost to the day after that."

Fogg grabbed the keys. "Looks like it wasn't driven very much."

Mrs. Qualls followed Fogg across the tiny square of lawn. "No, it wasn't. Been parked where you see it since August of 1961. A couple times a month, I drive it down to the Texaco and get everything checked—hoses, water, oil, put gas in it if needed. I get a neighbor boy to wash and wax it every other month."

Fogg unlocked the driver side door and sat behind the wheel. Grasped it with both hands, noticed the still lingering new car aroma, and studied the dashboard. He turned his head to Mrs. Qualls who had rested her arm on top of the door. "You called your son Sergeant. Was he military?"

"Of course he was. Staff Sergeant with the Green Berets. One of the first soldiers to go to Vietnam. Worked with the Montagnards—Vietnamese Indians, you might say—until he was killed in battle in October of 1961. That was two months after he parked the car where you find it today."

"Wow. Didn't know the war had been going on that long. Me and the boys I came to town with are headed there pretty soon."

"Why you want to buy a car then?"

"Gonna drive me and my best friend, Tucker Beene, to Oakland, California. That's where we'll get on a plane to Vietnam. We're in Basic Training at Fort Polk."

"Guessed that. You got family along the way?"

"We both do. In Wyoming. We're going there on the way to California."

///

CLOWNS NEVER CRY

They hadn't noticed each other that first day because that first day was a frenzied blur of hovering Drill Sergeants almost convincing them they were worth less than pond scum, and they'd better get their heads out of their Alpha Sierra Sierras. The whole bunch of them had recently been made bald by thirty seconds in a barber's chair. During their short stay in the reception area, they'd been assigned uniforms, combat boots, and made to lug duffel bags from here to there, double-timing to the croon of obscenities from Drill Sergeants at their backs telling them their fat asses were obscenities in themselves. Their meals were eaten in minutes, their egos taken down one step at a time.

Through the frenzy of those first days, Fogg studied the young men with whom he'd live for the next eight or so weeks of his life, maybe even accompany some of them to their ultimate destination ten thousand miles away. There were some crotchscratchers for sure, the ilk of which he'd grown up with outside of Laramie. Black, white, and brown young men, even some he thought we're probably Native, maybe Sioux, maybe Cherokee. Some had yet to sprout hair on their chins, some still suffered red and purple acne on their faces, some bug-eyed with all the hubbub, some calmly taking it all in as just another day in the life. Blue, brown, black, gray, and green eyes—a veritable mixture of hues born of ancestry Fogg didn't even try to imagine.

Their first night in their permanent barracks, they had a moment to catch their breath before lights out. Fogg sat on his bed, lowered his head and caressed it between his palms. Closed his eyes. When he felt a warm and comforting presence before him, he raised his head and looked to the other side of the barracks. And there sat Tucker Beene on his own bunk, staring at him with a smile and then a slight nod as they acknowledged each other, and in their acknowledgment was the conclusion they'd both had a tough day.

Before the sun was up, an enormous clamor sent them from their bunks to their feet not knowing if the end of the world was riding on the oppressive humidity of the Louisiana darkness. The lights popped on, and the Drill Sergeants were banging on garbage can lids. Told them to stand at attention at the foot of their bunks, so they did that, many still with their morning hardons poking against their Army-issue boxers, their eyes yet to adjust to the light that surrounded them.

Fogg stared across the room and saw the kid in the morning light, smiling as he had the night before.

The biggest, blackest Drill Sergeant of them all told them they had one half hour to piss, shit, shave, dress, make their bunks, and then assemble outside. He then stepped in front of the boy across the room, his back to Fogg. "You gonna eat shit with that grin, Beene?"

"No, Drill Sergeant!"

"Looks like you want one of your fellow trainees to sit on your goddamned face and take a big shit in your mouth. Is that what you want, trainee?"

"No, Drill Sergeant!"

"Then I suggest you get rid of that grin, trainee."

"Yes, Drill Sergeant."

The Drill Sergeant turned, stepped to the middle of the walkway that separated the rows of bunks. "Any one of you girls wanna eat shit, then keep on grinnin'. I'll make it happen." He looked at his watch. "You sorry assholes now have twenty-three minutes to assemble outside. You hear me?"

"Yes, Drill Sergeant!" came the emphatic reply.

"I can't hear you! A sissy girl has bigger balls, and a louder voice than all of you put together. Do you hear me?"

"Yes, Drill Sergeant!"

"Any sissy girls here?"

"No, Drill Sergeant!"

"You sure?"

"Yes, Drill Sergeant!"

"Now you've got twenty minutes to get your sorry asses to formation! MOVE! MOVE! MOVE!"

They did move, and once the outside formation was over, they ran three miles then stopped in front of the mess hall where *breakfast awaited. Fogg waited for the kid with whom he'd shared a smile from across the room and walked into the mess hall with him. Said hi when they grabbed trays and stepped to the chow line. The boy turned, and Fogg saw that his nametag read BEENE, just as the Drill Sergeant had said. They shook hands. Both simultaneously asked the inevitable question most asked upon first meeting in that place where the proverbial melting pot boiled over—Where you from? They shared a laugh and discovered they were both from Wyoming, Fogg from Laramie, and Tucker from Greybull, not far from Cody.*

///

"Jefferson always wanted to go to Wyoming," Mrs. Qualls said as if to herself, as if whatever dreams she'd cherished had long ago been stifled by circumstance. "Well," she smiled, perked up. "I guess we ought to go for a test drive."

"That'd be great."

Mrs. Qualls walked around the front end and sat down on the passenger seat. "It's got a lot of power, Lester. Just take it easy. Turn right on the next street."

Fogg did take it easy. "Hasn't somebody wanted to buy this before I showed up?" he asked as he turned right.

"Oh, many have wanted to. But I knew some day the right one would come along. Owed it to my son to wait for the right person to show up. Turn left here at the stop sign."

"So, I'm the right one?"

"You and your friend. Yes. The day you drive it away, I'll just sit on my porch and go along with you in my mind. Wyoming, for goodness sake! And you'll be in my mind after that as well. Vietnam is a hellish place, Lester. Sergeant Qualls found that out. You'll be in my prayers. Maybe someday you'll drive the Chieftain back here to see me."

Fogg glanced to his right as Mrs. Qualls dabbed her eyes with a lace handkerchief. "Thank you. I've got two hundred dollars on me. Have to wait 'til payday for the rest."

"That's fine. You can get on 171 right there. See how it handles on the highway."

Mrs. Qualls invited Fogg into her pink house after Fogg had driven the Chieftain, taking it up to eighty-five on 171. They sat at her little kitchen table and drank lemonade.

"How long have you lived here?" Fogg asked.

"All my life."

"Sergeant Saunders's daddy, too?"

"Oh," she said, closing her eyes for a moment. "He came to Polk in August, 1941, just after the base was first opened. World War Two was startin' up, and it seemed like this quiet little town just erupted with people and excitement after the base opened. Sergeant Qualls's daddy was a nineteen-year-old boy from Detroit. Handsome, too. I was eighteen when I met him on the one time he took leave and came to town." She fiddled with a cloth napkin, the embroidery showing two pigs touching noses. "He said he loved me and would come back for me. That never happened. So, I raised Jefferson myself. Right here."

"How'd Jefferson get the money to buy the Chieftain?"

"Saved all the time. When he got to be thirteen, he started workin' for a negro man, you know, helpin' clean out the white folks's cesspools. *Shovelin' shit*, he'd call it. Ha! He'd come home smellin' like shit himself."

"Wow."

"Yeah. Had to make sure he cleaned himself up before goin' to school. It was the negro school, you see. 'Course we're still separated—white from black. Leesville was built on an old plantation. In those days, the white school would send all their old ratty books to the negro school—pages torn out, scribblin' all over them. But, Jefferson learned about things just the same. Learned about Wyoming, too. Geography class. Said someday he wanted to go see all them cowboys and Indians in Wyoming. Lord, think of that! And you takin' the Chieftain there! He took up the clarinet at one time and got in the marching band. White school sent over all their old uniforms one time, but donjaknow he was proud of that uniform. Strutted all over the house in it. Was proud of his Army uniform, too. Wore it every day on leave before he left for Vietnam. You want some more lemonade?"

"No, I probably ought to get going. My buddies'll be wondering where I'm at. You said you're still separated. Whites from black?"

"Yes, though President Johnson says that ain't right. Jim Crow has done outlived his welcome here. At least for the negroes he has."

Fogg thought about that. Maybe the first time he'd ever thought about that at all. Hell, it wasn't an issue in Wyoming. Negroes were few and far between. He'd heard the epithets though—nigger this, nigger that. Wondered about Sergeant Jefferson Qualls dying in battle, his country allowing him that but denying him his dignity. No, that wasn't it. From what Mrs. Qualls had told him, Jefferson had his dignity in spite of everything. Maybe it was respect they denied him.

"Well…" Fogg stood. "I gotta go." He reached into his back pocket and pulled out his wallet. "Here's the two hundred. Payday is next week, and I've got a little bit stashed away. I'll get the rest to you then."

Mrs. Qualls stood, took the money, and stepped from behind the table. "You can take the Chieftain now, if you like. I trust you."

"Oh, that's the other thing. We might be headed for AIT in a couple weeks. Maybe another eight or nine weeks of training. Was wondering if you could keep the car here 'til we're ready to leave on our trip?"

"Of course I can. Have it all cleaned up and ready to go for you. You give me the rest of the money when you come to get it." She walked through her parlor and out to the porch.

"Thank you," Fogg said, holding the car keys out to her.

"I'll hold 'em for you," she said, taking the keys. "Chieftain is yours now. Lord Jesus, goin' to Wyoming. Thank you for showin' up. Answered prayers, I'd say."

Fogg didn't know what to say to that. "Okay then… I'll be

back." He stepped off the porch, took one last look at the car, and headed for the Chez Paree where he knew his buddies were mostly likely drunk, broke, and ready to head back to the base.

///

When their Basic Combat Training ended, Fogg and Tucker were given their MOS, Military Occupational Specialty—11 Bravo, light weapons infantry. Found themselves in a deuce and a half headed to Tiger Land in North Fort Polk for nine weeks where they would be inculcated with the knowledge men had been learning since the beginning to time—kill or be killed.

A certain civility ensued between the trainees and Drill Sergeants that hadn't been the case during Basic. "I won't yell at you," Drill Sergeant Amos told the platoon. "I won't curse at you. And I'll expect the same from you." Fogg thought the Drill Sergeants had found a kindness in themselves because they knew where their wards were going—an unkind place, a destiny of horror. That and the sense the young men in their charge had become closer to encompassing what they were—soldiers.

Required to growl like tigers, to always wear their helmets outside with camouflage covers affixed, to run everywhere they went, to get the notion out of their heads they were going anywhere except Vietnam—their days were devoted to learning how to protect themselves and their fellow soldiers, and how to kill the enemy. They were given M16 rifles to replace the M14s they'd trained with in Basic. They were schooled on the use of the M72 anti-tank rocket, .50 and .60 caliber machine guns, the M79 grenade launcher, how to avoid trip wires, how to apply a compress against a wound, how to breathe silently, and how to fight man-to-man. They practiced tactics that had been perfected in Korea which they'd learn were useless in Vietnam. All of it in the thick undergrowth of North Fort Polk, Louisiana, within the oppressive wet heat that only hinted at what they'd find ten thousand miles away. Drill Sergeant Amos reminded them over and over that there are only two kind of soldiers, the quick and the dead. "And what kind of soldiers are you?" he'd scream.

"*The quick, Drill Sergeant,*" *they'd scream back.* "*The what?*" *he'd yell.* "*The quick!*"

Fogg and Tucker Beene endured Tiger Land together, each relying on the other to correct their mistakes, to keep them going, to understand what it all meant, what it would mean once they stepped off the plane that would take them to war—Tucker's grin a persistent leveler whenever the going seemed to get too tough. They talked about their trip to Wyoming in quiet moments offered mostly during chow and before lights out.

///

Tucker stirred, opened his eyes. Shoved himself up in the seat. "Where we at?"

"Wichita ahead. We're in Kansas." Fogg pointed at the flatlands ahead.

"Goddamn, Lester, you musta been flyin' through Oklahoma."

"A little. You get a good nap?"

Tucker rubbed his eyes. "Yes, I did. I can drive whenever you're ready."

"Let's wait 'til we get to Wichita. Get some breakfast, gas up, take a piss."

"Should be daylight by then." Tucker reached for the bag of potato chips between them. "Been wantin' to ask you about somethin' we already talked a little about." He dug into the sack, grabbed a handful of chips with his left hand and picked one out with his right.

"What's that?"

"Girlfriends. We both know neither one of us has got one back home. Nobody to write to when we get to Vietnam."

"And?"

"I was wonderin' if you ever had a girlfriend? You know? In high school? A steady one?"

"Didn't have time for it. My daddy got sick, I had to work,

and… I just didn't have the time."

Tucker crunched on a chip, nodded. "Yeah, me neither. I had sports and was workin' the ranch all the time. Guess when we get to Vietnam, we can pass notes to each other like they was from a girlfriend back home."

Fogg laughed. "From one foxhole to another."

"That's it. Damn, I wonder if we'll be together? What if they separate us?"

Fogg hadn't thought of that possibility. More immediate was the question about a girlfriend. Couldn't tell him the real reason. "I guess we'll worry about that when we get there. You see the lights of Wichita?"

Tucker looked out the windshield. "Yessir. Spread out all over the place. How far is it to Laramie?"

"Oh, maybe six hundred miles. Another nine hours, I guess."

"Bet your daddy will be happy to see you."

"Maybe," Fogg said. *Maybe not.*

Tucker drove the long, flat stretch of road through Kansas and eastern Colorado, a seeming eternity across prairie and not much of anything else. When they got to the outskirts of Denver, they stopped again for gas, both used the restroom, and they grabbed some chips, a candy bar apiece, and a pop. Fogg took the wheel, and was soon headed north on I-25. In another two hours they would be in Laramie.

As dusk was fading, Fogg knew what he'd find, though he'd hoped for something different. His daddy lived in a tin house atop cinder blocks. Not ten miles from Laramie, the trailer park appeared as though it'd been lost to time, somehow sagging closer to the earth. The prairie and the forever wind had taken its toll on the place since the last time he'd been there nine months before, though nature hadn't broken the six or seven pickets in the fence he'd put around the tiny yard before he'd left. Maybe critters, he thought, as he motioned for Tucker to stay in the car.

Maybe kids.

He climbed the wooden steps and thought he ought to knock on the door. If his daddy was up to something he shouldn't be up to, that'd give him time to prepare himself. He knocked, waited a moment, then knocked again. When he heard nothing from inside, he tried the door. It opened.

The odor was like nothing he'd smelled before. Walked in, saw the stacks of dirty dishes in the sink and on the counter, held his hand over his nose and mouth. Stepped into the tiny living room and his father sat slumped in his easy chair, plastic tubes over his ears and below his nose, his mouth contorted into a grotesque toothy grin. Fogg guessed he'd died two or three days before. He studied the scene for a moment—a nearly empty bottle of Jack Daniels on the little side table, a glass on the floor, the carpet stained, cigarette butts overflowing the ashtray, that smile, and that odor. God, that odor. He thought about walking down the hallway to what was once his bedroom, but what would be the point of that?. There was a picture of his mother there, the only one he'd ever had.

His mother had been a somber and silent presence in his life. When Fogg was six years old, she disappeared. His daddy didn't tell him why until he was fifteen. "Prairie fever," his daddy had said. "She just walked away one day and never came back." Not long after that, Fogg's daddy misread the slant of an irrigation furrow, tried to ease the tractor through it, and found himself under the goddamned Deere, his spine fractured in three places, his hip broken in two.He applied for disability, and the ranch went to hell after that, then to the bank, then to a hedge fund manager from Boston. They then moved to the Happy Acres Park outside of Laramie—a single-wide, two-bedroom tin house on cinder blocks amongst others dotted here and there on what used to be unspoiled prairie. Fogg finished high school with only one intent—to get the hell out of there, away from his daddy, the tin house, and everything his life had become.

Fogg once again looked at his daddy, then glanced down the hall. Figured the picture of his mother would only serve to remind him of things he was trying to forget. He turned, walked out, and shut the door behind him.

"That didn't take long," Tucker said from behind the wheel.

"Let's go back down to that gas station we passed coming in here."

Tucker started the Chieftain, backed it up, and then headed back the way they'd come. "Your daddy okay?"

"No, he isn't. Or maybe he is. He's dead in there, Tucker."

"What?" Tucker shot a glance at Fogg, his voice a register higher than normal.

"Only forty-seven years old. Must have died a couple days ago."

"Jesus… What happened?"

"He just died. Probably drank himself to death. Pull into the station over here."

Tucker guided the Chieftain past the pumps and parked at the side of the building.

"Have to call the sheriff," Tucker said, opening the door. As he stepped out of the car, he bent down and looked at Tucker. "They got pop and candy bars in there if you want some. I think we oughta find a motel before we head to Greybull. Get some sleep? Shower?"

"Okay," Tucker said. "Sure."

Fogg walked into the building, saw the pay phone, and dug into his jeans for some change. "Yes," he said when he heard a voice on the other end. "Want to report a… There's a man who died in his house." He recited the address, and just as he was about to hang up, the voice on the other end asked for his name. "Just a passerby, is all," he said as Tucker walked into the storefront and opened the cooler door.

"You want a pop?" Tucker asked.

"Nah. Maybe a beer."

"We ain't twenty-one."

"That's okay. I know a place."

"Okay." Tucker grinned, nodded, and put his pop back in the

cooler.

"Goddamn, a '55 Chieftain," a voice came from the one-bay garage as they walked back outside. Fogg and Tucker stopped by the car, looked toward the garage.

"You got the 287 V8 in that beauty?" Wearing greasy overalls with the straps over bare skin, his black hair spiked and oily, a thin stream of smoke rising from the cigarette dangling from the corner of his mouth, the man rubbed his hands with a red rag and walked toward them.

"Yes, that's what she's got," Fogg said.

The man ran his hand lightly over the front fender. "Where'd you get her?"

"Leesville, Louisiana."

"You're shittin' me? Fort Polk?"

"Yessir," Fogg said as Tucker grinned.

"I was there. Not for long, but I *was* there for Basic. U.S. Army and me didn't see eye to eye. Stupid goddamned nonsense if you ask me. Leesville you say?"

"Yes."

"How'd you find this beautiful lady in that little nigger town? Nothin' but slutty whores runnin' around stealin' a man's money and—"

"We gotta go," Fogg said. He walked to the driver side and opened the door. Tucker climbed into the passenger side. "You ever hear of Sergeant Jefferson Qualls?" Fogg asked, standing by the door.

The man slanted his head slightly to the right. "Can't say I have."

"He made it through Basic, went to Vietnam, and died in battle. He owned this car, and I bought it from his mother."

"Okay." The man slowly removed the cigarette from his mouth. "So?"

"I think he was a better man than any of us," Fogg said. "He was a negro. From Leesville. And, he's come to Wyoming with us."

    Fogg got behind the wheel and started the Chieftain. Couldn't help but smile when Tucker displayed his middle finger to the man as they pulled away, the man straining to see if that third passenger was in the back seat.

    And, in a way, Jefferson Qualls *was* back there. His mama had given Fogg a small white box when he'd come to drive the Chieftain away. "It's just some of his things," she'd said. "When you get to Wyoming, could you find a nice place to put them? Somewhere peaceful. You know?"

    Fogg had taken the box, a white one with a blue ribbon tied around it. "Yes, I will, Mrs. Qualls. A peaceful place."

///

    They reclined against the headboard of the king-size bed in the Cowboy Motel just at the edge of Laramie's town center, both holding a beer can, Fogg with a Lucky Strike smoldering in an ashtray next to him.

    Fogg had stopped at the liquor store where he'd worked part time as a stock boy. The owner, Mrs. Taylor, a heavy-breasted woman who'd embraced Fogg as a son—she knew his dismal history—welcomed him with tears and a hug. Told him to keep the beer in the sack until he got back to the motel. Didn't cry when Fogg told her about his daddy, but simply nodded, said the Good Lord had a reason for taking him so young. Fogg didn't disagree.

    "Tell me somethin' about your childhood, Lester." Tucker sipped his beer and turned toward Fogg.

    "What do you want to know?"

    "You know. Just what it was like growing up."

    Fogg dragged on his cigarette, put it back in the ashtray. "Not much to tell. My mother left us when I was six. I went to school. Learned to cook after my mama left. Well, not cook, exactly, but how to fry bologna, hamburger, bacon, and eggs. Helped my daddy with chores. Got some part-time jobs when I got older. My daddy had his accident and we moved to the trailer."

"Nothin' that made you happy?"

"Nah… Yeah, there was one thing. My daddy took me to the circus every time it came to Cheyenne. Guess he thought since he couldn't give me much of anything else, a trip to the circus was the key to being a good parent. Hah! Always felt sorry for the animals. I did love the clowns. Used to wonder, though…"

"What?" Tucker said when Fogg paused.

"Nothing. Just stupid… stuff."

"C'mon, Lester. Tell me."

"Okay," Fogg said, reaching to the floor for another beer, pulled the tab and sipped. "When I was a kid I wondered if those clowns ever cried. I don't know why, but that was something I thought about. What about you? What was your childhood like?"

"My entire childhood was a great big circus," Tucker said. "Four brothers and three sisters. I was the youngest, and let me tell you, Lester, that was a damned circus from sunup to sundown."

"Wow. I can imagine. You get teased by your brothers?"

"No. They kind of ignored me. My sisters, though, treated me like I was a toy or a little puppy. They spoiled me, I guess."

The silence they shared for a moment witnessed strangers moving into rooms on either side of them—muffled voices and car doors banging.

"Tell you what," Tucker said. "These beers have made me sleepy." He scooted off the bed, and picked up the empties on the floor. "I gotta piss, then I think I'll turn in."

"Yeah, me too." Fogg grabbed the ashtray, slid off the bed. He put the ashtray on the side table, along with the beer he'd just opened. He bent down and picked up the three empty cans on his side of the floor. Piled them on top of the ones Tucker had just stuffed in the trash can, and then pulled off his t-shirt and jeans. He waited for Tucker to finish up in the bathroom, then went in there himself.

They lay for a time back to back in the big bed. Fogg listened to the strangers on the other sides of both walls settling in for the night. Heard toilets flush. Still the muffled voices. Felt Tucker move, sensed his closeness, stiffened slightly when Tucker reached over him placing his palm on Fogg's chest. Fogg rolled over. Not a word was spoken with each kiss, with each hand exploring the other's body. They stifled their simultaneous moans when the time came.

Their morning was filled with embarrassed glances and shy smiles as they prepared to leave for Greybull, Tucker's home, nearly three hundred and fifty miles away.

///

Fogg had never seen so many blue-eyed, fair-haired people together at one place at one time, all of them resembling each other—smiling the same, laughing the same, all finishing each other's sentences, all celebrating a familial quirkiness Fogg had never before experienced. All of Tucker's family greeted them when they arrived, except Jake, the next to the oldest brother, who was himself in Vietnam serving with the Marine Corps.

The Beene Ranch was seven miles outside of Greybull, a small town that sat at confluence of the Bighorn and Greybull rivers, nestled between the Bighorn Mountains and the city of Cody. The Beenes had worked the land for six generations, raising cattle, growing hay and alfalfa, keeping horses, and, at different times over the years, even offering dude accommodations for urban wannabe cowboys and cowgirls. The home place, the big house where Tucker grew up had six bedrooms and three bathrooms. Tucker's mama told him to take his old bedroom, and they'd get the rollaway in there for Fogg.

Fogg figured they could stay with the Beenes about four days before they headed west to Oakland. Figured, too, that he and Tucker had begun another kind of adventure with an uncertain destination.

Breakfasts were a blur of blue eyes and fair-haired people talking a storm, laughing, and shoveling eggs, bacon, sausage, toast, fried potatoes, melon pieces, and biscuits and gravy onto large plates. They shared stories about this and that, but mostly about Jake who was only three months into his thirteen-month tour in Vietnam, who'd written twice a week since he'd gotten there. Tucker, too, was singled out for stories in which he was the star. Seemed to Fogg that through all the laughter and smiles, the chatter, the jokes, and the humorous embarrassing moments they related about Tucker's past, there was a sadness, maybe a fear below the surface they all dared not reveal with words.

The rollaway was carried into Tucker's bedroom, dressed in linens and a comforter. Each morning before Fogg and Tucker came out of the room, they mussed up the rollaway so it'd look like someone had slept there. Kept the towel they used to clean themselves hidden in Fogg's duffel bag.

As the aromas of another breakfast wafted from the kitchen, Fogg and Tucker dressed in the bedroom. "If we're leavin' tomorrow," Tucker said, pulling on his jeans, "we got to do something with that box Mrs. Qualls gave you."

"Yeah, we do." Fogg tied his tennis shoes. "You think we could ride out a ways? You know, on horseback and leave it somewhere special?"

"Sure we could. There's a bluff not too far from the river. Used to go up there a lot myself."

"Sounds good. I want to leave early tomorrow, so let's get all our stuff ready to go."

"Eve said she'd do our laundry."

"Eve's nice." Fogg reached for the still-damp towel on the bed. "Don't believe I'll let her let her have this, though. You and she seem to have a… You two seem to be close. Closer than your other brothers and sisters." Stuffed the towel in his duffel bag, then zipped it closed.

"We are. C'mon. I'm sure they're waitin' for us."

"Okay." Fogg studied the room for a moment. Pulled the sheet down on the rollaway, then nodded. "We're set."

///

Dear Mrs. Qualls

I wanted to let you know Tucker and I made it to Wyoming. We're staying with Tucker's family, and this is the last night we'll be here before going to Oakland. He's in the living room with his family now, and I excused myself so I could write this to you. This morning we saddled two horses and rode about three miles to a place Tucker said was the perfect spot to leave the box of things you gave me that were Jefferson's. We got to a bluff, a small hill that's in the Bighorn River Valley, a beautiful place that overlooks the river, with the Bighorn Mountains to the west. Tucker said the Lakota Sioux and Crow and some other plains Native people lived around here and probably used the bluff as a lookout point. And this is a place that's seen lots of cowboys and cattle too. We rode up the bluff, got off the horses, and just looked at the scenery for a minute. Tucker brought a shovel with him, so we picked a perfect spot and started digging a small hole. I opened the box for the first time and found what I think must be some silver buttons from that marching band uniform you said Jefferson got when he was in high school. Found the Purple Heart and Silver Star ribbons, too. I'm glad you kept the medals. They're special. I'll bet you crocheted the little hankie in the bottom that showed a mountain and some trees and Jefferson's name on it. I hope you won't mind, but I took the picture of you and Jefferson in his Army uniform standing by the Chieftain. I'm going to keep that with me. Maybe it'll give me luck when I get to Vietnam. Besides that, it's a memory of you. I want to thank you again for letting me buy the Chieftain. It's been good to me and Tucker, and I don't doubt it'll get us where we're going. Oh, almost forgot. We buried the box and piled some rocks on top of it. It's right at the edge of the hill. Right where you can see the entire valley, and the mountains in the distance. Tucker said a kind of prayer, which was nice too. He told me his ancestors were Mormon, but his mom and dad gave that up and instead used to take his brothers and sisters to a different church every Sunday. They went to the Catholic, Episcopal, Community, and Baptist churches, and would even drive thirty miles to the Methodists. He said he liked the Baptists best because they raised hell. Hah! Anyway, his prayer was nice, and I think you would have liked it.

Love, Lester Fogg

///

Tucker had asked his mother not to make a big breakfast, but just a batch of those sweet rolls with the white icing on top. He'd told his family he and Lester were heading out by sunup, and by sunup the Beene family and Lester had finished their coffee and rolls and were outside in front of the house saying their goodbyes.

Eve, Tucker's oldest sister, took Fogg off to the side, slightly away from all the others, put her hands on his shoulders and smiled. "Thank you for bringing Tucker all this way."

"You're welcome. Us both being from Wyoming and all, it just seemed—"

"Lester," she interrupted. "You're Tucker's best friend. He told me that. He thinks you're pretty special. I hope you think the same about him."

"Yes. Yes, I do."

"Good." She grabbed his hand. "Let's walk over here a ways." And, as they walked, Eve asked Fogg to take care of Tucker. "Watch out for him if you can," she said. "His brother, Jake, is over there and, well… Jake is a Marine. He's always been a Marine, even when he was a little boy. You know what I mean?"

"I guess."

"Tucker was never that way."

"Okay."

"Jake can take care of himself over there. But Tucker…" She stopped walking and turned to Fogg, once again putting her hands on his shoulders. "Just try to watch out for him," she said, looking directly into Fogg's eyes.

"I will do my best."

She nodded. "You two be safe on the road. And bring Tucker home when this is all over."

"I promise I'll do my best."

"That's all I can ask."

"C'mon Lester," Tucker called out.

"Looks like we pick up I-80 at Fort Bridger," Tucker said. He refolded the map and stuck it into the glovebox.

Fogg turned the Chieftain's lights off as the morning rose in brilliant hues of red and oranges. Pulled his Luckies from his shirt pocket. He tapped the pack on the steering wheel, and pinched one between his lips. "It's a long haul to Oakland," he said as he pushed the lighter in to heat it up.

"Yeah, but we got time to enjoy it."

When the lighter popped up, Fogg reached for it and touched the orange end to the tip of his Lucky. "We got Utah, then the whole state of Nevada to cross. Not sure if there's much in Nevada to enjoy."

"We're on the road, Lester. In the Chieftain. Just you and me. That's somethin' I'm enjoyin' the hell out of."

"Eve talked to me before we left."

"I saw you two over there," Tucker said.

"She told me to take care of you."

"She would do that."

Fogg sucked on his Lucky, exhaled, and glanced at Tucker. "Your family know about you?"

"That I'm queer? No one except Eve. I told her a couple years ago."

Fogg again glanced at Tucker, whose face was turned, looking out the side window. Fogg didn't like that word Tucker had used so easily—*queer*.

"Need to ask you something," Fogg said. He'd wondered about this ever since it happened. "How did you know I'd let you touch me in the motel? In Laramie?"

"I knew from the first time we looked at each other in Basic," Tucker said.

"How is that?"

"It's in your eyes, Lester. And you're a gentle man. I've been queer forever and… I just knew the first time I saw you. Besides that, in Basic and Tiger Land, we were a pair. Hell, Drill Sergeant Amos even started callin' us girlfriends. 'Get your girlfriend, Beene,' he'd say, 'and kill me somethin''. You remember that. We were always together. You and me. You wanted it as much as I did—the togetherness. "

"That doesn't mean I'm… that way."

"What we been doin' together since Laramie seems pretty queer to me."

Fogg looked at Tucker. He'd spoken while still looking out the side window.

"Yeah, well… It's complicated, Tucker."

After they'd passed the busiest part of Salt Lake City, Fogg pulled off the highway for a fill up. It was past noon, and Tucker hadn't uttered a word since morning. When Fogg came back from using the restroom, Tucker was sitting behind the wheel.

"We ought to stop somewhere for lunch," Fogg said as he got in the passenger side.

"My mom packed us sandwiches." Tucker nodded toward the back seat.

"Okay. You want me to get us a cold pop?"

"Sure."

Fogg got back out. Walked into the station and grabbed two Cokes from the cooler, asked for a pack of Luckies from the old guy who was tending the register, paid the bill, and walked back outside.

Fogg gave Tucker his pop, stuck his own between his legs and opened up the map. "Let's go as far as Elko and find a motel."

"Okay. How far is that?"

"Looks like about two-hundred miles more. Oughta get there about five o'clock." Fogg refolded the map and stuck it back in the glovebox.

"We could go farther than that."

"That'll be about eight hours of driving. That's enough for one day, and we're in no hurry."

"I guess," Tucker said. He unfolded the waxed paper around his sandwich, took a bite, laid it to his side, and started the Chieftain. "Let's get movin' then."

They checked into the Phoenix Motel in Elko, Nevada, after stopping at a saloon that offered half-pound hamburgers and mouth-watering cuts of beef. Slot machines dinged and flashed and burped coins into metal trays, and a trio—two cowboys and a cowgirl—sang country songs amplified over the din of diners and gamblers.

The motel was a three-story affair made of cinderblocks, walkways on each floor looking out on a swimming pool where a lone woman swam a slow backstroke, her head festooned with a pink cap covered in multi-colored flower plastic petals.

Tucker had made a point to ask for a room with two beds when the desk clerk inquired. Fogg knew what that was about. Didn't know how he was going to tell Tucker what was on his mind, but knew he had to do it. Tucker deserved an explanation.

They couldn't gamble, they couldn't legally drink alcohol, so they sat a while down by the pool and soon watched the woman doing the backstroke get out of the pool. She took off her colorful cap, shook her head, and then picked at her butt where her suit had gathered up. They sipped on Cokes, Fogg smoked his Luckies, and Tucker slumped down in the deck chair. The Nevada heat loomed dry and oppressive past sundown.

"Is that AC all the way up?" Fogg said. He'd taken the bed farthest from the front door, kicked off his shoes, and watched *Gomer Pyle, USMC* in black-and-white.

"It's on max," Tucker said. He pulled off his jeans and shirt and draped them over the back of the lone chair in the room, then grabbed the bedspread and yanked it down to the foot of the bed. "I'm tired," he said as he slipped under the sheet.

"Yeah, me too." Fogg stood, took off his clothes, turned off the TV, then did what Tucker had done with the bedspread. He turned off the lamp on the side table and crawled into bed.

Tucker had lain on his side, his back to Fogg. Fogg looked at him, his shape defined by the soft blue neon glow from the rising Phoenix sign outside. Replayed the conversation they'd had in the Chieftain about intimacies they'd shared ever since Laramie. Knew he'd not explained himself to Tucker's satisfaction, or eve his own.

"No, Lester," Tucker said when Fogg got out of his bed and slipped into his.

"I've got to tell you something."

"It's okay. I understand," Tucker said, still with his back to Fogg

Fogg put his hand on Tucker's shoulder. "Please let me do this."

Tucker rolled over, faced Fogg. "What?"

"When I told you I'm not queer?"

"Yeah."

"I… I don't know what I am."

"C'mon, Lester, everybody knows—"

"No, no. I don't. All I know is… I need to touch someone, Tucker. The only person except you who ever really touched me in a loving way was Mrs. Taylor. The lady who owns that liquor store in Laramie? The one where I bought the beer? I don't even remember my mother doing it. My father sure as hell didn't do it. I've got this… I guess… I guess I've never really felt loved in my entire life until Mrs. Taylor and then you. It doesn't matter if I'm queer or not. Two people who have feelings for each other, who touch each other, who make love together… I didn't mean to hurt you when I said what I said. I know how you must have felt when I said it. I'm so sorry, Tucker. I…" He reached over with both arms when Tucker began to cry. Scooted himself closer, wrapped his arms around Tucker, and pulled him closer.

They walked to a hole-in-the wall café a block from the motel where breakfast was advertised on a handwritten sign in the window to be just like mother makes it. And it was.

All morning, ever since they'd gotten out of bed, Fogg sensed something had changed between them—a subtle shyness, or maybe it was just that they both were a little embarrassed about what had happened the night before, just like in Laramie.

Fogg chose to drive first, noting they were about five hundred miles from Oakland. "Should take about eight more hours," he said, handing the map to Tucker.

"Looks like we'll go through Reno," Tucker said.

"Yeah. We can stop there if you want, or just keep going. We've got a day to spare before we have to report at Oakland." Fogg started the Chieftain and pulled out of the motel's parking lot.

"We'll see when we get there."

Fogg took the ramp to I-80 West, glanced at Tucker who folded the map and stuck it back in the glovebox. "Sounds like a plan to me." He merged onto the highway, giving a moment's thought to why he hadn't cried last night. Couldn't remember when he'd last cried.

They kept going once they got to Reno. By nightfall, they'd arrived in Oakland where they drove by the Oakland Army Base. Fogg spotted a USO storefront nearby and told Tucker to pull over. "Let's just go in and see if they know of a decent motel. Unless you want to report at the base?"

"Nah," Tucker said, pulling over to the curb. "I guess I'm in no hurry for that."

"Hello," a white-haired woman greeted the as she stood from behind a little desk near the entrance. "Welcome. Come on in. There's coffee and lemonade over there and some cookies, and I think there's still some of Doreen's fudge on the table. I'm Clara." She held her hand out and Fogg shook it, introduced himself and then Tucker.

"You young men due to report?" Clara said.

"Yes. Tomorrow probably, though we've got one more day before we have to," Fogg said as Tucker walked over to the table where the goodies were.

"Good. I can give you some vouchers for a discount at the motel around the corner."

"That would be great."

Fogg started to follow Tucker, then he turned back to Clara and asked the question that had been on his mind since they'd left Louisiana. "Is there anywhere nearby I could store my car while I'm in Vietnam?"

"There's a couple lots. Not sure how safe they are, and you'd have to pay monthly, I think."

"It's got to be a safe place. I can't just leave it anywhere."

"Most leave their cars at home," Clara said.

"I don't have a—" Fogg realized what he was about to say. Knew it was true but didn't want to say it. "That's not possible. And… The car is special."

"Well, you tell me why it's so special," Clara said. She stepped back behind the desk, sat down, and motioned for Fogg to sit on the chair in front of it.

Fogg sat and told her the story. When he was done, Clara smiled. "That car is special. Tell you what. I live just across the harbor in Alameda. Not twenty minutes away. I'll keep your car for you. I've got the space, and I'll take care of it."

"I can't expect you to do that."

"I want to do it, and that's what we'll do." She stood and grabbed her purse from under the desk. "Doreen," she raised her voice, "I'll be back in about an hour."

Fogg and Tucker unpacked the Chieftain, putting their duffel bags inside the USO office. They then followed Clara to a nicely kept stucco home across the harbor. She told Fogg to park the Chieftain off to the side in the driveway so she could still get her own car in and out of the garage. Fogg did that, gave her the keys, and also pulled the title from the glove box and handed it to her. Told her he expected to come back from the war, but he couldn't guarantee it.

Before joining Clara in her car for the ride back, Fogg and Tucker spent a few moments just looking at the Chieftain as if to preserve in their minds an image of it, and perhaps, too, of the memories it evoked.

They spent the night in a motel around the corner from the USO, where their room was discounted because Clara had given them a voucher. They slept together that night in the same bed, both knowing it would be their last intimacy for probably the next thirteen months.

"What do you think Vietnam will be like?" Tucker said. Both of them lay on their sides, both seeing the other's face as a shadow against the seep of dim lighting from the parking lot outside.

"Hot and humid, Tucker."

"I mean the war."

"I suppose it will be bad. Never heard of a war that wasn't." Fogg propped his elbow on the pillow, raised his head and leaned it against his fist. "Probably worse than Tiger Land."

"Yeah, I expect. Never thought it wouldn't be bad, but… What if one of us dies out there?"

"That's a possibility."

"Can't imagine you dying, Lester. What would I do?"

"You'd go get the Chieftain and drive it back to Greybull."

"No. What I mean is…"

When Tucker didn't finish his thought, Fogg leaned over and kissed his forehead. "I know what you mean. And I'm not going to get killed in Vietnam. Neither are you. We're going to be okay. We'll get out of there and then get the Chieftain together, head down to see Mrs. Qualls, and then we'll take our time going up to Wyoming."

"What about after that? You and me?"

"We'll deal with that when the time comes."

"If it does," Tucker said, almost a whisper.

"It will, Tucker. Just wait and see if it doesn't."

///

Leaving Tiger Land, they'd received orders assigning them to the 4th Infantry. Idle talk at Tiger Land had suggested the 4th Infantry was the place to be, and the 1st Cavalry was the place not to be. The 1st Cav had sustained a lot of fatalities and seemed to be the most active unit in Vietnam. Now, as they processed into the Oakland Army Base, they were told their assignments could be changed according to need.

Fogg and Tucker were directed to what appeared to be an air-

plane hangar, but inside hundreds of cots were lined up across the floor. They were told to choose a cot, stow their belongings under it, and to report to an outside formation at 1300 hours. They did that and were soon divvied up into small groups and assigned duties ranging from washing dishes and mopping floors to policing the grounds and helping with the laundry—a myriad of tasks to keep them busy while they awaited their fate. Their fate? Each morning formation included a calling of names to identify who was to move to the deployment holding section.

After two days, both Fogg's and Tucker's names were called, and after another day they were on a plane to Honolulu, then the Philippines, then to Pleiku in Vietnam—in all, nearly twenty hours of flight. They were bussed to a processing center where they stayed the night. The next morning, they were called to a formation where an NCO announced the 1st Cav had experienced some losses over the past few days, and the following personnel were being reassigned from the 4th Infantry to the 1st Cav. When Tucker's name was called, Fogg flinched and looked at Tucker who stared straight ahead. When Fogg's name wasn't called, Tucker glanced at Fogg and shook his head. The four young men who'd been reassigned to the 1st Cav were given time to address postcards with their mailing address to their families. Tucker grabbed an extra one and gave it to Fogg, telling him to write when he could. They barely had time to say their good-byes before Tucker climbed into the helicopter that would take him to the war.

That afternoon, Fogg climbed into a helicopter, too. He didn't address a postcard to anyone.

///

"Hey! Fuckin' new guy!"

Fogg heard the call from his right. Before he'd climbed into the helicopter that took him to the base camp landing zone where he joined the first platoon, he was assigned an M16, combat boots and jungle fatigues, a helmet and camouflage helmet cover, and flak jacket. Now, having reached the LZ, he'd been assigned the tools of war—ammo pouches, backpack, canteens, grenades, entrenching tool, a claymore mine, and twenty magazines of cartridges for his M16. He'd reported to the company's lieutenant and was trying to find a place to sort out his equipment, when he looked to his right and saw the black soldier who'd called out to him.

"Come over here," the soldier said. He sat with his back against a rock, his helmet at his side, and his M16 across his lap.

Fogg felt as conspicuous as he looked. His fatigues were brand new, deeply green, while those worn by other soldiers who'd been there a while were nearly gray, torn, soiled by mud, sweat, dust, and blood. Fogg's face, too, was clean, lately shaved, while the others were smudged, unshaven, their eyes weary.

"Sit down here," the soldier said. "You've got to be fuckin' kidding me." He looked at Fogg's nametag when Fogg stepped over to him. "Fogg? F-O-G-G? Jesus fuckin' Christ!"

Fogg didn't know what to say. He read the soldier's nametag. "And you're Emerson."

"Will you just please sit the fuck down! And, no, I'm not Emerson. I'm Digger. You'll get a new name, too. Or maybe not. You already got a good one." He patted the ground to his side, and laughed. "You got a good goddamned name already. Hah!"

Fogg laid his equipment on the ground, then sat. "Nicknames, I guess."

"No, not nicknames. You got a special skill, or you're a stupid fuck, or you're… Shit, if you're foggy, that'll be your name. I'm Digger 'cause I dig into any fuckin' situation we got. No swingin' dick gets into a situation like I do. You ain't foggy are you?"

"No."

Emerson pulled a pack of Pall Malls from the strap around his helmet, tapped it against his other hand, and held it out to Fogg. Fogg took one and reached into his pocket for his lighter, surprising Emerson when he held his flaming Zippo out to him before he could get his own out.

"Where you from?" Emerson said.

"Wyoming."

"Ooo-eeee. Cowgirls with bowed legs. I'm from Detroit." He reached his hand out to Fogg. "Welcome to the first platoon."

Fogg shook his hand. "Nice to meet you."

"Well… Don't get too attached. I could be dead in an hour. Your cherry ass could be too."

"Digger." Sergeant First Class Kline stopped in front of them holding a clipboard. "Fogg is your cherry. Got it?"

"That an order?" Emerson said.

"That's an order. I paired him up with you before he got here. Fogg, you'll be a pimple on Digger's ass for a while. He's your squad leader. You go where he goes. You do what he does. And, if you're lucky, he'll show you how he's managed to stay alive in this fuckin' sty for the last six months."

"Yes, First Sergeant," Fogg said, thinking Kline was older than any soldier he'd yet seen. His white stubble, bloodshot eyes, and the hardness of his features spoke of a deep weariness.

"Good. You take care of him, Digger. You hear me?"

"Loud and clear," Digger said, raising his hand in a lazy salute.

"He's pretty old," Fogg said when Kline walked away.

"Nah." Emerson spit, then crushed out his cigarette in the dirt. "He fought in Korea. He's on his third tour here. I think he wants to die in Vietnam after he gets the chance to eat the heart and lungs out of some fuckin' gook. He's a mean machine. He loves this shit."

Fogg envisioned Kline bending over a body, pulling the organs out with his teeth.

"You join the army or you drafted?" Digger said when the first sergeant walked away.

"I joined."

"Why?"

"Fight for my country, I guess."

"Hah," Digger laughed. "You gonna kill communists, huh? Save the fuckin' world for democracy and all that shit?"

"Yeah. I—"

"Listen," Digger said as he grabbed his helmet and put it on. "One and only one thing you gotta concentrate on now that you're here—you kill the motherfuckers before they kill you. Forget that bullshit about fighting for your country. You kill those little shits that want to kill you. You kill to stay alive and to keep your buddy and your squad alive. That's all there is to it. And," Emerson grabbed his M16 and stood, "here's what you're gonna do since I'm your fuckin' babysitter. You walk where I walk. You drop to your belly when I drop to my belly. You stop when I stop. You run where and when I run. You shit and piss when I shit and piss. You don't talk unless I talk. Man, you don't even scratch your nuts unless I do it. You understand that, Fogg? You do what I do!"

"Sure. Yeah." Fogg stood and brushed the clingy-thick dust off his ass.

"And you don't even do that unless I do."

"What?"

"What! You! Just! Did!" Emerson's words were emphatic. "You want to go home in twelve months, you remember what I just told you!"

"Okay. Sorry."

"Your sorry cherry ass will be dead if you don't. And another thing. Lose your underwear. Crotch rot grows in your underwear."

"Okay."

"Now. Where we are is the rear, the base camp. Choppers are gonna come and take us to the war where we're gonna search for gooks and destroy the little motherfuckers if we can find them. You remember everything I told you or you're gonna die. Understand?"

"Yes, I understand."

"Sheeeit," Emerson huffed out as he helped Fogg attach all the implements of war onto his body.

The enemy was a phantom, there, then not there, slipping into the triple canopy jungle as if they became the jungle. The moist heat embraced Fogg like a boa, squeezing out every last drop of sweat as if it could be sated only by that last drop, by bringing men to their knees, boiling their brains, turning their faces the color and consistency of a fish's belly. The stench of the place was primordial—the odor of rotted things, swamp gas, rice paddies fertilized with oxen and human waste, of men bathed in days or weeks of their own excretions. Nightfall was an omniscient blackness that read a man's fear and infused his senses with the certainty of doom.

Fogg followed Emerson's cautions. Then, one morning when their platoon was approaching a smattering of thatch huts from where they believed sporadic gunfire had come, Emerson stood from a protective crouch, took a step forward, jerked his head back with the sound of another shot fired, and then collapsed as if he had succumbed to a surge of enormous gravity below him. Fogg fell, too, as Emerson had cautioned. Fogg inched over to Emerson and saw that his face was planted against the ground. Waited. Waited a moment more, then asked Emerson if he was okay. No answer. Reached over and slapped Emerson's helmet. Asked again if he was okay. Still, no answer. Placed his hand under Emerson's chin and pulled it toward him to get his face out of the dirt. Saw the hole below Emerson's right eye, his eyes open, his mouth gaping. Saw his platoon advancing, called for a medic, took one more look at Emerson, then stood to a crouch and ran on, toward the hooches, toward the motherfucker who'd killed his friend.

Irritated by months of searching for and losing gooks in the jungle, with only occasional opportunities to confront more than a few of them at a time, Fogg's frustration intensified his hatred of the enemy. Losing a sense of what humane restraint meant little by little, each new death of someone Fogg knew, someone he'd traipsed this particular hell with, someone whom he would kill for and who would kill for him, accelerated the process of redefining the Sixth Commandment. Thou shalt not kill except if you're killing gook motherfuckers.

Fogg watched passively as Collins—a blue-eyed, blond-haired, all-American boy from west Texas—sliced off the ears of his kills, then took the ears as trophies, stuffing them into the butt pack that hung from his web belt. Watched as two of his squad took pleasure in sighting their M16s by killing skinny dogs who'd wandered outside the perimeter of a village. Asked Corporal Dent—a red-headed kid from Iowa—why he'd strapped a puppy to the front and business end of a Claymore mine, and then detonated it. Dent said he'd gotten bored, that it was just something to do. Boys were becoming men without consciences, warriors in a place and time skewed by a reality that beckoned the heart's darkness.

The boredom was worse than the one-foot-after-another humping, the firefights, torching huts, blowing up wells and bunkers, and killing chickens and oxen just for the hell of it or, as they justified it, to deny the enemy sustenance. Boredom gave them all time to think, to reflect on where they found themselves, where they'd rather be. Idle time wasn't restful at all. The daytime snipers and the nighttime rocket and mortar attacks precluded that. Fogg would try to read. He'd become the recipient of a passed down, dog-eared edition of The Catcher in the Rye, but concentration eluded them all. Most would reread letters from home or look at pictures of their girlfriends or family. Fogg had neither. Just the book. Wished a thousand times he and Tucker had taken pictures as they'd driven west.

When in base camp, sometimes in the hole he'd dug for the night in the jungle, Fogg made a point to write to Tucker, to tell him about the war he was seeing, to reflect on their trip in the Chieftain, to ask him what his war was like. After four months of not receiving a single letter from Tucker, he stopped writing. He assumed the worst, but didn't want to actually know the worst. He'd learn the worst in another month—his letters marked undeliverable.

At first, Fogg wondered how he would make it through twelve months in this wretched place without losing his mind. After the fourth month, though, it was as if his body assumed control of his brain. Movement was by rote, thoughts were of any place that wasn't Nam, of anything other than the persistent one-foot-after-another, up-one-hill-down-another trudge.

Still, though, the fear of booby traps, mines, punji stick pits, bouncing betties with their two charges, one to lift the horror from the ground three to four feet, the second to blast shrapnel in every direction preyed on Fogg's and every other soldier's mind in spite of ratcheting down thought over movement. Once you'd seen the soldier not far in front of you lifted into the air, his legs or arms torn from his body, the limbs flying higher than the torso, you never forgot it. The process of picking shrapnel from your body, of wiping off the splattered remnants—skin, bone, brains, and God knew what else—of the dead, high-flying soldier was horrific. Yet, they'd make a joke of it. "Dixon was a smart guy. Should have ate me some of his brains while I had the chance." "You see how high his foot went? Goddamn, Dixon could jump!"

   When the monsoons came, Fogg's world became water. Black nights became frigid with the cling of fatigues to skin. A foot or more of rainwater would collect in the hole he'd dig to sleep in, and sleep became fits and starts against the freeze, against the knowledge that he couldn't hear the creep of the enemy for the patter, at times the gush of water from the sky and the jungle canopy. If the sun appeared in the morning, the mosquitos became relentless, feeding on faces, arms, hands. The bites would fester, ooze pus. Slogs through thigh-high standing water left them all with leeches on their legs, buttocks, backs, and crotches, frantically trying to rid themselves of the grotesque blood suckers once they paused. They shed their pants and shirts, each helping the other to remove the fattened worms by touching them with lit cigarettes, or a dose of bug spray, or covering them with salt.

   The diarrhea, the lice, the jungle rot on their legs and arms, the festering boils on their feet, the shrapnel wounds, the heat, the rain, the humidity, and a thousand other discomforts Fogg shared with his fellow soldiers, but ascribed them to his circumstance. Thought he couldn't expect better when his purpose was to kill or be killed—the essential purpose of war.

   Still, through it all, Fogg would watch the sun rise upon the spread of rice paddies, the shadows rising and falling against the green hills and mountains, the traipse of old men in conical hats leading oxen across the golden glowing fields below, lis-

ten to the birds sing, feel the uncommon morning breeze against his neck. Still, through it all, Fogg would marvel at the beauty of the place.

Fogg, now tenth months into his tour, saw the uniformed NVA soldier fifty yards ahead running down a thick-foliaged trail from Fogg's squad, assigned the point position in a search and destroy mission. Logan, a beefy soldier they called "Mississippi," raised his M16 and shot a burst into the fleeing NVA soldier.

"He dead," Mississippi whispered to Fogg, who kneeled next to him.

Fogg nodded. This kind of mission required them to be as quiet as they could be. They knew the enemy was nearby, but they didn't want to alert them to their presence. Mississippi had blown that caution to hell. But body count mattered to the brass, and, by God, Mississippi had chalked one up for the cause.

The squad inched forward, and Fogg stopped to look at the dead NVA soldier who had managed to sit upright with his back against a bamboo tree.

He wasn't dead.

Fogg stood over him, studied his face. Couldn't be more than eighteen. Starring at Fogg, red bubbles popped from his lips as he said, "Ma, ma, ma."

"Mother?" Fogg asked as he knelt down.

"Ma, ma, ma, ma."

Fogg noticed what appeared to be exit wounds on his chest and legs—the holes through the fabric, the blood.

"Ma, ma."

Fogg stared at the young man's eyes. Tears seeped from them, making little channels through the dust and dirt on his face.

"Kill or be killed," Fogg said. "That's Nam. Sorry, little buddy."

Over the last ten months, Fogg had seen death and dying as an increasingly normal occurrence, something inescapably commonplace. Had never had the opportunity, as he did now, to actually concentrate on the last moments of a gook's life. Wondered if this was the motherfucker who'd killed Emerson or maybe he was the one who had killed Tucker, if that's what had happened to Tucker which he still didn't know. Hell, he could have been a casualty of friendly fire or died from a snake bite. It didn't matter, he thought, as the bubbles from the gook's mouth ceased, as the eyes now stared with the vacancy of death.

Fogg raised his foot and planted his boot on the soldier's body, shoving it away from the tree.

The suddenness of the multiple explosions on either side of Fogg sent him to his belly, hugging the earth. He looked up and saw Mississippi running back toward him.

"Ambush!" Mississippi yelled.

Fogg got to his hands and knees and scampered toward the nearest thick groundcover. As he again went to his belly, he heard the unmistakable sound of AK47 fire coming from the trail. Beginning to position himself to return fire, an immense weight fell on him, knocking his head into the ground.

When Fogg regained consciousness, he again became aware of the weight on his back. He turned his head slightly toward a slip of daylight to his left and saw two bodies clad in American fatigues on the ground, sandaled feet moving around them. And there, hanging from a chain right next to his head was the unmistakable shape of a dog tag. Heard sing-song Vietnamese chatter, and a fierce battle—AK47s, mortars exploding, M16s—in the distance.

It dawned on him the weight on his back was Mississippi. Dead weight.

Now, the sing-song chatter increased. Fogg saw a hand pointing a pistol at the head of one of the American bodies. The pistol popped. Then the sandals moved to the next body. Another pop to the head. The sandaled feet were now inches from Fogg's line of sight. Another pop. He felt the impact to Mississippi's head as a dull thud.

///

"I swear to God, when lard-ass Mississippi started movin' out there I nearly shit my shorts. Goddman! Mississippi was comin' back to life!"

Peterson, a fair-haired Iowa crotchscratcher who'd been one of the first to reach the area where Fogg's squad and two others had been ambushed, stood amongst five other soldiers and recounted the scene he'd witnessed. "I mean the guy was dead. Really dead. Lookin' like a fuckin' beached whale layin' on its belly. Then he starts to move. Just a little bit at first, then, Goddamn if he don't roll over. Hah! We all backed up wonderin' what the fuck is goin' on. Then we saw you, Fogg. Goddamn, that was one fuckin' trip."

Fogg had spent the last three days at base camp rehydrating himself and sleeping, besides being interrogated by the platoon lieutenant and the company commander about what exactly had happened to him. He'd recounted what he could remember, including the two days he did not dare move except to breathe, watching the sandaled feet and listening to the sing-song voices around him. He tried to smile at Peterson's narrative, but couldn't. "Mississippi saved my life."

Boyles, a mean-spirited, small man who wore sergeant's stripes, grinned at Fogg, and said, "I'm just wondering what you two were doing when the shit hit the fan. He have his pecker up your ass, Fogg?"

They all laughed except Fogg. "Like I said, he saved my life."

"Well, there it is." Boyles raised his arms and voiced the conclusion they'd all come to at one time or another. *There it is.* Three words that encapsulated the war in all of its guises and reflected the impossibility of coming to terms with it in any rational way. Seasoned soldiers would view the aftermath of a napalm drop on the countryside where a village had once been and see the bare, lifeless spread of nothingness before them, nod their heads, and at least one of them would always say, "Well, there it is." They'd study the body parts strewn from here to there after a mortar had been tripped. "Well, there it is." They'd burn leeches off their body with cigarettes, watch the wiggling black slugs die at their feet. "Well, there it is."

Fogg then got off the makeshift bench and walked toward the perimeter of the camp where the view opened up on the beauty of the land—the jungle, the hills, the mountains, the snaky curl of rivers. He stood at the edge of the perimeter where spools of razor wire had been strung. Looked at the expansive vista and wondered how hell could look so pretty from afar. He'd be home—wherever he chose to make a home—in less than a month. Took one last look at the countryside, silently thanked Mississippi again, still knowing that Mississippi and he, too, hadn't done anything extraordinary. The lard-ass had just died on the run, and he, Fogg, had simply been in the right place at the right time. *There it is…*

Now

Fogg understands idle time is spent in dangerous places. He'd retired from the cardboard box factory where he found the kind of work he knew would keep him occupied, but not arouse his demons—senseless work done with his mind turned off. He'd finished his last two years as a supervisor, and they gave him a nice certificate and a small plastic doodad that looked like a cardboard box with the words *In Recognition of Your Valued Service* printed on the side. Now, he devotes his weekend days to Lester the Clown, and his Saturday evenings to a small group of friends he's kept in contact with after first meeting them at VFW pot luck dinners or other gatherings at the post not far from his home. He volunteered shortly after his retirement to do whatever the honchos at the post needed to have done that he was capable of doing.

He found the Vietnam vets notable not just because of their age, but because of the look in their eyes—the hard stares of soldiers and Marines who'd seen the devil's wink up close and personal. Fogg knew commiseration with their experiences was not something they valued but needed to share their stories with others who'd been there, done that, and had brought the same gruesome baggage back home, back to *The World*, as they'd called anywhere that wasn't Nam when they'd been there. He knew all this because he'd been there himself. Knew how he'd managed to keep his own demons at bay once he'd come home from it all. The spirits had helped with that. Lester the Clown had, too. He wanted to help others do the same.

Over time, the Wednesday group had been whittled down to four people who could sit in a tavern for an hour or two without consistently stumbling out of it. Booze was a transitory comfort, but as these four understood, it was only palliative. They needed more than that. And, of course, there'd been other whittlings—one member just disappeared, another blew his brains out, two had been institutionalized by family members who couldn't deal with it anymore because they belatedly realized after almost fifty years their loved one was crazy as a loon, mad as a March hare, or some other happy-crappy conclusion that belied how negligent they and the VA had been in dealing with their loved one's demons for all these years.

///

Still driving the Chieftain, which now brings admiring stares from folks who appreciate the old and well-kept behemoths, Fogg returns home from his appearance at a child's birthday party. He settles the Chieftain in the garage, then walks inside his house. Removes his makeup, showers, and dresses in comfortable clothes. Decides to walk to the tavern and pulls on a jacket. The dark clouds he'd seen creeping from the Rocky Mountains to the west and the coolness of the evening breeze had bespoken things to come.

The tavern is one of those dark places that oozes an odor of stale moistness—beer, piss, clogged toilets, mildew, too many tears shed when another quarter is slipped into the Wurlitzer near closing time, the strains of "A Whiter Shade of Pale" evoking memories of another place and time. Gray duct tape covers the rips and holes in the aged red leather-cushioned booths along one wall. The oak floor creaks in places, slightly sags in others. The jukebox still spins 45s, the singles stuck in a bygone era. The bar itself is mahogany and, as Fogg has often thought, too ornate for the space it occupies, too grand for the neighborhood clientele who open the front door, step in, and pause a moment to let their sight catch up with their circumstance. And when it does, most turn right or left to find an empty booth or table, or they walk to a stool at the bar, sit, and prop their elbows where they'd been the day or just the morning before.

Fogg sits at the corner booth farthest from the front door, nearly hidden from the rest of the tavern. A vent has been placed in the ceiling above the booth that grabs smoke from folks who do—the only space in the tavern where that is allowed. Two of Fogg's Saturday night group smoke, including Vincent, the bar's owner, who steps out of the storeroom, sees Fogg, and follows behind him.

"Goombah," Vincent says, his voice rasping as he slides in across from Fogg and extends his hand. "Semper fi!"

"How's it going, Vince?" Fogg grabs Vincent's hand and squeezes it.

"Can't complain." Vincent tugs a pack of cigarettes from his shirt pocket, lights up, raises his head and exhales.

Fogg glances at the scar on Vincent's cheek where a mortar fragment had entered it, immediately cauterizing the wound from the white-hot heat it had generated. Knows the exit wound scar on the other side is larger, uglier. Vincent often enjoys retelling what the medic told him at the time. "'Fuckin' miracle,' Doc said. Said I must'a had my mouth open when it happened. Passed right through, taking just the tip of a molar with it. Goddamn miracle!" Vincent runs his hand through his lightly gelled gray-black hair. Remnants of severe teenage acne pit his face, giving him a dangerous appearance, or so Fogg thought when he'd first met him at the VFW months ago.

"The others coming?" Fogg asks.

"Far as I know. You do the clown thing today?"

"Yeah. Bunch of kids."

They both look toward the front door when a slip of outside light intrudes. It's Lily, but without Sam.

Lily is a tall, thin woman who was a surgical nurse in Pleiku where a combat evacuation hospital had been established during the war. She sits next to Vincent and snatches his pack of cigarettes and lighter. She's done her gray hair up in a single braid that hangs in front of her shoulder.

"Good evening, gentlemen," she says, lighting a smoke. She sucks her cheeks inward with her inhale, and she, too, raises her head to exhale.

"Where's Sam?" Vincent asks.

"Well…" She pauses a moment, eases back in the booth, and smiles. "Pretty much what the others said before they stopped coming."

"That sharing wasn't helping?" Fogg asks.

"Yeah," Lily says. "That and his third wife just filed for divorce. Think he's drinking again."

"Stupid fucker," Vincent says, exhaling again.

"For not coming?" Lily says. "Or for drinking and ruining another marriage?" She rests her hand on the table, the cigarette held upward.

"For not coming and drinking." Vincent says. "I'd be a great one to judge somebody else for fucking up a marriage. Why'd you never marry, Lester?"

"Never wanted to chance it," Fogg says. "Like you, I brought the war home with me. Couldn't see any worth in always having that ugly third party in a relationship."

Fogg has never mentioned he *did* try once to live as others did. She'd been willing to touch him, to hold him like Tucker had. Brought her to his old house where she eventually measured the windows for new curtains. His silences and moods cut short that April to July fling. He wonders for the ten thousandth time what might have been if Tucker had made it home, and agreed to move to Denver as he had decided to do once he'd driven the Chieftain back to Leesville only to find Mrs. Qualls gone. He'd then turned around, knowing he could go wherever he wanted. He retraced his and Tucker's journey to Greybull where he told Eve, Tucker's oldest sister, he was sorry he hadn't kept his promise to her, that he and Tucker had been separated on day one. Eve told him it wasn't his fault. Explained that Tucker's older brother, Jake, had returned from the war broken in body and spirit, and that it was all the family could do to take care of him—the ostomy bag, the prosthetic below his knee, his blindness and deafness on the right side.

"Amen to that, Lester," Vincent says. He pats the top of Lily's hand. "How's your old man?"

"He's fine," Lily says. "Remind me to chew a mint before I leave."

She met her husband in Pleiku where their shared experience—slicing off limbs, treating deep jungle rot ulcers, removing eyes made worthless from projectiles or firestorms, plucking shrapnel from bones and organs, and a thousand other gruesome procedures they conducted side by side—had given them a clinical view of hell.

"When's he going to retire?" Fogg asks.

"I think he'll give it another year. He'll be seventy-two next month."

Vincent turns toward the bar. "Charlie," he hollers. "Three drafts."

"I was remembering," Fogg says, "how dark it would get." *And how frightened of the dark I was.*

"Jesus," Vincent says. "That fucking jungle. The blackest black I'd ever seen. It was as if there was… I don't know. As if the universe had turned into nothingness. As if you'd been struck blind." He taps ash into the glass tray.

"Here you go." Charlie, another vet who Vincent served with in the 9th Marines, sets the beers on the table one by one. He'd brought them from the bar, two of them cradled against himself with his left arm that ends at the elbow.

"Thanks, Charlie." Lily slides a beer to Vincent and Fogg.

"My pleasure," Charlie says, raising his remaining hand as he walks back to the bar, his purely white hair set off by his black skin.

"I used to lay there in my hole," Vincent says. "You couldn't see a thing. Half the hole full of water. Nothingness around me. When it wasn't raining, I'd listen. Hell, we'd all listen to the jungle and hear impossible things. Fuckin' rocks would whisper things that didn't make sense."

"The rocks, the ground, the grass," Fogg says. "Listening for any rustling that might be gooks coming up on us. Then the whispers. You couldn't see where they were coming from, but you knew there'd been a rock or a tree there when it was daylight. Siren songs from the rocks and trees telling you all kinds of shit. Sometimes I thought I could hear leeches crawling toward me, and—"

"Jesus Christ!" Vincent says. "Don't get me started on the leeches. Tiny goddamn motherfuckers. We thought they were even fallin' from the trees!" He leans over the table, stares at Fogg as if Fogg has become the source of his ire. "They were waitin', just fuckin' waitin' on the elephant grass or a puddle to take a ride on somebody as we humped to nowhere in that fuckin' worthless jungle where we were savin' the world from fallin' dominoes."

He leans back, reaches his hand to the table, and taps three times. "Oohrah! Up one hill. Oohrah! Down another. Oohrah! Dig in. Do it all over again. Over and over. All of us swingin' dicks humpin' up and down hills, even mountains. Fuckin' goddamned jungle. Layin' in mud that reeked of death. Layin' in ox shit, people shit, in mud with a thousand years of rotted leaves all churned up in it. Goddamn fuckin' bugs eatin' on you constantly. Dust like soup that you ate, drank, breathed... Cuttin' ourselves on the grass, then squeezin' the pus out of the cuts when they festered. We'd take a hill from the gooks, and then the brass would tell us to hump over to the next one. Didn't matter that we'd secured some real estate for Uncle Sam. The man didn't want real estate. It was the body count that mattered. Fuckin' body count."

Fogg waits for Vincent to continue. He knows he will. Glances at Lily who shares a knowing smile.

"We'd report three confirmed gook dead," Vincent says, "and by the time it got to the brass, hell, it'd be ten, fifteen dead enemy shits. According to the brass, we'd won a fierce battle. Three or four of our guys get killed? Well, the brass called that an incidental encounter with acceptable losses. Fuck acceptable losses! Then, by God, we'd be ordered to hump back up the hill we took the week before and take it again."

He sucks on his cigarette, shakes his head. "But them leeches, man. Pull up your pant legs, or take off your shirt every time you stop to dig in, and there they were, those tiny little shits had puffed all the hell up, suckin' your blood. Huge fuckin' things hangin' on your skin. A goddamn blood feastorama! I mean… Goddamn, Lester! God! Damn! It!"

"Removed three or four from as many urethras," Lily says matter-of-factly.

"I know," Vincent sighs. "You told us before. Disgusting."

"Occupational hazard," Fogg says. "Nobody wore underwear. The jungle rot was… pervasive. Everybody had emersion foot."

They are silent a moment. Each sip their beers.

"All the goddamned death," Vincent says. "We'd place our dead or what we could find of them on one side of the LZ wrapped in their ponchos. Slicks would eventually come—fuckin' loved the *whop, whop, whop* of their rotors—and we'd load 'em into the birds as gently as we could. Tossed the gook dead on the other side, one atop another. If we had the equipment, we'd dig a big hole and toss them in."

"Choppers took us in, but they always got us out." Fogg says.

"Goddamn right, Lester. Whenever I'd hear that sound—*whop, whop, whop*—it was like Santa Claus was comin'. Food, water, ammo, new guys. Hell, on Thanksgiving they even brought in hot food and cold beer. Goddamn!"

Again there is silence.

"Some of the boys called for their mothers before they died," Lily says, smashing out her cigarette. "The stench—body odor, shit, piss, mud, pus from their ulcers, blood, and God knows what else—would hover over them. A horrible odor. I wanted to hold them, touch their cheek, and maybe kiss their forehead. All I could do... All I could manage to do was hold their hand."

"Watched an NVA regular die," Fogg says. "He'd been shot in the chest and legs. Young kid. Maybe eighteen. Maybe younger. He must have been covering a retreat, as he was the only one left on the trail. He kept saying ma, ma, ma. I assumed he was calling for his mother. Didn't find out until later ma *is* their word for mother." Fogg doesn't tell the whole story. There are demons there.

Vincent sighs again and shakes out another cigarette from the pack. "I guess it's good to talk about this shit." He lights his smoke, raises his head. Exhales. "I don't know. I guess it helps. Shit! It's been half a century, my friends. But still... It's still there."

"Like a hole you try to avoid," Fogg says.

"No," Lily says, "you shouldn't avoid it. You need to lay it out. Study it. Talk about it. Make it... Just make it less important."

"I can't make it less important," Vincent says. "I've tried for fifty years. Can't do it. All I can do is shove it to the side, put it in a dark corner and hope it stays there a while. But it doesn't. It never has. Ask my two exes about that. Ask my kids, for fuck sake."

"But Vincent," Lily says, "look at you. Look at this place. It's a veritable mausoleum to your thirteen months in hell. The pictures on the walls, the flags, the banners, the music, all of it remains inescapable to you. You haven't put it in a dark corner. It's here. All around us."

"Hah!" Vincent rasps. "Do you know that the yup-yups who live in those ticky-tacky shiny metal and glass boxes they built down by the river have started coming in here? Hell, they weren't even born when Nam was goin' on. They love all this." He sweeps his arm from left to right. "They look at the pictures. Play the 45s. Drink their drinks. Hell, Charlie has made a fuckin' fortune in tips lately. They think it's the old curiosity shop. Young women look at some of those pictures and say, 'Ooooo, he's cute.' And what they're lookin' at is O'Hare, or Dingbat, or Rodriquez, or that blond kid we'd named Lame Duck because he couldn't do anything right. All of 'em smilin' for the camera, all of 'em or what was left of 'em shipped home in a box. What's here is where my life got stuck, Lily. It's the memories. Good or bad, they're important. The things I put in that dark corner are the screams, the odors, the dismembered arms and legs, the fuckin' terror that… That dark corner is where I put the times I was so fuckin' scared I could hardly breathe. The times I pissed myself because I couldn't… because none of us could move a fuckin' inch while we lay on our bellies hoping the gooks wouldn't hear us. That dark corner is where—"

"I get it," Lily says, touching Vincent's back and gently rubbing it. I *do* get it. We all deal with it in our own way."

Fogg remembers. *Mississippi saved my life.*

Charlie comes from behind the bar, feeds the jukebox some quarters into it. The machine clicks, and there's Creedence, imploring Suzie Q to remain true.

"How come Charlie never sits down with us?" Fogg asks.

Vincent glances at the bar where Charlie is stepping back behind it. "Charlie grew up in Alabama. Jim Crow. All that shit. He doesn't talk about Nam except when some shit-for-brains wants to toast him for his service. He tells them to save it for someone who cares. Tells them he was the same nigger in Nam that he was in Mobile County. If I'm in the area, he'll raise his voice and say, 'We was all niggers in Nam. Ain't that right, Vincent?' And I'll say, 'Truth told, Charlie! Truth told!'"

"Jesus," Fogg says.

"He's not wrong, Lester." Vincent says.

"I know." *She told me Jim Crow wasn't welcome anymore.*

"War takes on many faces," Lily says.

"One time, some dipshit wanted to toast Charlie's service, and Charlie told him if he wanted to raise a glass to anything it should be the Corps. Guy asks, 'What core?' I braced myself 'cause I knew Charlie was gonna leap over the bar and kill the guy. But all Charlie did was shake his head and tell the guy to forget it."

Don Cherry's rendition of "Then You Can Tell Me Goodbye"

CLOWNS NEVER CRY

comes to life, softly amplified across the room.

"C'mon, Lester," Lily says, scooting out of the booth. "Dance with me."

"I can't dance," Fogg says.

"Sure you can. Just follow my lead."

Fogg slips out of the booth. They walk a few steps away, hold each other and, as Vincent turns to watch, Lily and Fogg slow dance in a tight circle. Lily raises her hand and gently presses her finger against Fogg's tattoo.

Fogg smiles as Lily rests her head on his shoulder. Remembers his afternoon at Mrs. Braithwaite's lovely home where the patio overlooked the Denver Country Club's ninth tee. Thirty or so friends of Emily's—Braithwaite's daughter, who, Fogg thought, was a rather plain-faced girl—were gathered to celebrate her eighth birthday. Balloons, colorful tents, a downsized working carousel, three Shetland ponies, a four-piece live band that provided Disney-inspired tunes, and other delightful accoutrements were spread out behind the house. Children ran here and there as the mommies or nannies watched from the patio. Fogg entranced them, except for two boys who were in timeout for bursting balloons behind the grazing ponies, the horse's teenage handlers scrambling after them.

As the children sat on the lawn before him, Fogg pulled those magic quarters from front row ears, produced strings of brightly-colored handkerchiefs from under his sleeves, created a rainfall of tiny silver and gold stars, shaped balloons into poodles, and told a story about a tortoise and a hare. When it came time for pony rides, all the children but one scampered away. Fogg looked at the brown-haired boy who was staring up at him and asked him if he didn't want to ride a horse.

"Why do you have a tear there?" The boy stood, then pointed at Fogg's tattoo.

Fogg knelt down. "Why do you think it's there? You can touch it if you want."

The boy gently pressed his finger against the tattoo. "I think," he said as he lowered his arm, paused, looked into Fogg's eyes,

"I think maybe it's there because even clowns cry sometimes."

Fogg nodded. "Yes," he said, smiling. "They do," he lied.

As he holds Lily, as Cherry's words flow, as nothing matters at all except this moment, Fogg knows that clowns never cry. If they did, they'd never stop.

Simple Gifts

'Tis the gift to be simple, 'tis the gift to be free
'Tis the gift to come down where we ought to be,
And when we find ourselves in the place just right,
'Twill be in the valley of love and delight.

"Simple Gifts" – A Shaker song – Elder Joseph Brackett (1848)

Three giant and ancient elms stand as sentries, solemn, strong, serious, in front of our house, towering over the grass and the spruce hedges, shading the grass and the spruce hedges until slightly before sundown, until slightly before the sun is hidden by the purple juts of the Front Range of the Rocky Mountains barely twenty miles from the front door of our old house. I have watched the elms through five years of changing seasons. Spring, summer, fall, winter, each of the seasons evoking from me some concern for the trees. Too cold. Too hot. Too dry. Too wet. The trees and I seem somehow intertwined with one another, dependent upon one another, feeding upon one another. I treasure the quiet strength of the trees, their beauty, their relationship with the seasons and, consequently, their secret unseen intimacy with the Great Maestro. In return for what they give to me, I trim their errant branches. I spray the tiny beetles that invariably arrive in mid-summer to suck the chlorophyll from their leaves. And I wonder through hours of musing, sitting on the front porch of our wonderful old house and listening to the hypnotic, somehow comforting sspit, ssspit, sssssssssssssssss-pit of the brass sprinklers, yes, I wonder if my giant and ancient elms ever wonder about me.

David has suffered years of my tree soliloquies. He will listen to my peculiar musings and will usually agree that, yes, the trees possess some intelligence and that, yes, it is possible that human beings are no more important than the thinnest blade of grass in the eyes of the Great Maestro who conducts the Cosmos rhythmically, following the Great Score exactly as written. David understands the importance of the unknowable to me, just as I have acknowledged that David's life would be empty, useless without music.

"If I accept your relationship with the elms," David said when I first told him of my feelings for the trees, "then it is not unreasonable for you to accept my relationship with Bartok and even, and I know this is stretching it, Schoenberg."

"Schoenberg is absurd," I responded, smiling, knowing the comment would get a rise out of him.

"No," he said quite seriously, "in that case, wondering if trees are wondering about you is absurd."

"All right," I said, deciding to, as they say, smooth the moment. "I will grant you your attachment to Bartok, who is ridiculous, and to Schoenberg, who is absurd, without further comment if you will grant me that there might be more to the elms than meets the eye."

David considered this for a moment. He waited for me to smile, and then he said, "Granted." He then stepped into his music room and pulled a CD from the rack, and amplified the Schoenbergian din past the windows of our neighbors' bedrooms.

Of course, thereafter David could not listen to Bartok or

Schoenberg without the image of me and my elms at the periphery of his consciousness. I do not know this to be a fact. We have never discussed it. I would like to believe it, though. I would like to believe that what we mean to one another is embodied in ten thousand convoluted associations, which appear unbidden at the unlikeliest moments—the firings of engrams that belie explanation or cause. Such, I would like to believe, is the *stuff* of love. I do know that after I told him about my feelings for the trees, I have not been able to be think of them without the faint, atonal noise of Schoenberg or Bartok filtering through my consciousness much like the momentary, minuscule but irritating whine of those damnable dog days mosquitoes quickly dispatched with the flick of the hand or a shake of the head.

Now, this spring, my sixth with the elms, soon my seventh with David, my relationship with the giant and ancient ones and the sounds of Schoenberg and Bartok have finally become inarguably commonplace, and grudgingly compatible under the roof of our lovely old house.

I sit on the front porch and watch the mid-spring breeze stir the new leaves so brightly green upon the branches of the trees. As Sibelius surges from within David's music room, I sit on the white wrought iron chair and look past the elms to the park that abuts our property thirty yards beyond. At the other side of the elms, at the edge of our property, the joggers jog on the foot-worn path that circumnavigates the park. Already—though the last fleeting presence of the Big Freeze still whispers its parting farewell: "I leave you now, but I *will* return. I will *always* return!"—the boys, the joggers have stripped their shirts from their backs and, their chests bare, pump their thighs below the sweet, muscular jut of their buttocks covered only by the barest flaps of nylon. Now, for the third time, the dark-haired boy in the blue shorts crosses my vision. The dark-haired boy looks for the third time at the porch, at me. I smile. The dark-haired boy returns my smile and runs on.

David and I have occasionally discussed the possibility of erecting a fence at the edge of our property this side of the jogger's path. Usually one or the other of us will bring the subject up after returning from a weekend at the cabin and finding that someone, some *family*, some ignoble bevy of humanity has left the remains of their picnic—beer bottles, chicken bones, ant-encrusted chunks of potato salad—at the base of one or two of the elms. When, about once a week, an inspection of the fringe of our lawn this side of the path reveals the remains of several canines' hefty meals, the fence question will usually arise again. After nearly six years in our old house, though, the fence question remains a point of discussion—not built.

"Chain link would be so…punitive," I have told David several times. "And wood would obstruct the view of the park."

"Yes, and that of the boys," has been David's consistent response through five years of the fence question.

And, indeed, it is David who receives more pleasure from the visual, the untouchable. The high-powered telescope that sits before the park side window in his music room is testament to his visual appetite.

I, on the other hand, would rather touch.

The dark-haired boy in the blue shorts joins a volleyball game in progress near the middle of the southern edge of the park. A jogger, an older woman with orange hair and huge, bouncing breasts, traverses the edge of our property and smiles up at the house, at the porch, at me. I smile back as I watch her substantial mounds of butt tremor excitedly as she chugs on, slowly, almost slower than a fast walk. Yes, I realize, I know this woman as I see the arthritic Irish Setter hobbling into view behind her. She is the woman with the Irish Setter, our neighbor from three doors down. Her husband is a lawyer who has made a great deal of money defending the wealthiest and guiltiest businessmen of four states. He owns two liquor stores, and has an interest in the racetrack in Commerce City where the sleek, muzzled Greyhounds chase a mechanical rabbit named Rusty. The lawyer is fat and bald, and he drives a blue Mercedes. Yes, the lawyer and his orange-haired wife are the ones who have fenced in that portion of their yard abutting the park.

"Good fences make good neighbors," the orange-haired wife

told me after their fence had been completed.

I had smiled then at my mind's image of Old Mister Frost peeking over the Great Maestro's shoulder, and waiting for me to say the words that desperately needed saying. And I had said then, "Something there is that doesn't love a wall," echoing the old poet's conclusions about fences.

The orange-haired wife had said, "Excuse me?" with her forehead furrowed, a curious expression on her face that suggested she did not know if I had just said something in Swahili or Russian or street jive.

"Robert Frost. M*ending Wall*," I said, in explanation.

"Yes, yes," the orange-haired wife had said, smiling and saying it again, "yes, of course."

The lawyer had wanted David and me to sign a petition to have the city erect a fence between the path and the private property along its perimeter.

"No, I don't think so," I told the lawyer, who had held the petition in front of my face.

"But, what about the dog shit and the debris?" he had fumed.

"Simple gifts," I had replied, smiling, following David into our old house and closing the door in the lawyer's face.

As I watch the Irish Setter hobble beyond my sight, Heidi, my and David's thirteen-year-old Old English Sheepdog rises to her feet in the middle of the yard where she has lain for over an hour soaking in the warmth of the new season. She shakes herself and as if on cue, Pepi, a fourteen-year-old Toy Poodle and Jessica, the baby, a three-year-old Siberian Husky rise to their feet, shake themselves, and turn their heads to Heidi—big sister. Yes, it is time.

"C'mon, kids," I say, standing from the wrought iron chair. I open the screen door and let our children into the house. I then follow them to the back door, where I let them out into the back yard where their food and water is, where they are secure from the encroachment of joggers on their territory, or stray dogs who release their scent at the base of the elms. I allow the children the freedom of the front yard about three times a week. It has proven oppressive duty for them; remarking their territory, nervously alerting to any human or animal sound or smell. They seem happy to return to the back yard. We love the animals, the children. Like the elms, like David's music, the dogs, our children are, in David's words, "...sacredly inspired arpeggios..." which enhance the humanity, the beauty, the sanity that David and I have struggled for so long to preserve in our lives.

I return to the front porch and sit in the wrought iron chair. It will be twilight soon. The dark-haired boy in the blue shorts has left the volleyball game. Where do they go? Where do the beautiful boys go at twilight?

David opens the screen door and comes out onto the porch. He sits in the matching chair. "Wonderful evening," he says.

"Yes," I say, hearing Debussy from his music room. "Spring is definitely here."

"Ah, and a young man's fancy turns to thoughts of..."

"Dark-haired boys in blue nylon shorts."

"You saw him, too?" he says.

"Of course. Did you have him under your microscope?"

"Yes. I happened to glance up from the Sibelius score and there he was, playing volleyball. You do realize that he was not strapped down?"

"I guessed as much," I say, smiling. "And you, my dear, will probably have wet dreams for a week."

"Yes, whenever I put on the Sibelius."

"I just get cold whenever I hear Sibelius."

We sit silently for a moment. After six years together, we have become comfortable with one another's silences.

"You know," I say, "I was wondering where all the beautiful boys go at twilight after they...expose themselves in the park. Where did the dark-haired boy in the blue shorts go?"

David smiles with the certainty that I am doing it again. David knows that it is not actually a game or a capricious fancy with me, my compulsion to create situations in which I place strangers whom I have never met or seen before; my attempt to grasp truths to which I am not privy; to know the unknowable. "I suppose," David says, always willing to indulge, "I suppose he simply went home."

"Yes, yes," I say, formulating the imagery that unless shown otherwise will be my perception of the unseen life of the dark-haired boy in the blue shorts. "I see him living on the third…no, the *fourth* floor of an unfashionable but clean building on Capitol Hill. He has a one bedroom apartment with green shag carpeting, and the walls are painted off-white."

David smiles. "A semi gloss that washes easily."

"Yes, a semi gloss. And they paint the walls each time a tenant moves out regardless of whether they need it or not. A point of pride, incidentally, for the resident manager. And they paint the walls without removing the ceiling hooks for plants, or without taking the covers off the electrical outlets where upon attempting to plug his stereo in for the first time, the dark-haired boy discovered the prongs of the plug would not make a connection because of the thickness of the paint. And I see the dark-haired boy saying…" I pause, gesturing with my hand for David to supply the word.

"Fuck!" David says.

"Ah, and the dark-haired boy said, 'Fuck!' and, upon discovery of this wee problem, he pulled a screwdriver from an unpacked box and removed the outlet cover so that the stereo could be plugged in because as we all know, that is always the first thing unpacked, set up and…plugged in."

"Life is simply not worth living without a functioning stereo," David says.

"Exactly." I nod. "And the dark-haired boy placed the removed outlet covers in a bottom drawer in the kitchen from where, before he moves out, they will be retrieved and put back on the walls because we are talking about a four hundred and fifty dollar security deposit, here. And I see…I see a bed without a frame sitting on the floor in the dark-haired boy's bedroom."

"Oooooo, we're in the bedroom," David says.

"Yes, the bedroom. There are dumbbells on the floor where, as the dark-haired boy enters the bedroom, he slams his big toe into the iron weight and says…"

"Fuck!"

"Ah, our dark-haired boy has one hell of a vocabulary. And, the dark-haired boy says, 'Fuck!' as he pulls his sweaty, sweetly-thin blue nylon shorts from his body and…"

"And?" David says.

"And, yes… I'm seeing it now. There, attached full-length to the closet door, a mirror reflects the dark-haired boy's naked body to his observant, perhaps adoring eyes. The dark-haired boy slowly pivots, keeping his eyes on the mirror as he examines his body as both artist and connoisseur. Smiling, pleased with his image, the dark-haired boy goes to the bathroom and…"

"Pisses," David says.

"…a long and steady stream from the head of his substantial—quite thick but not too long—penis into the porcelain-encased pool. A soft rush of aromatic air passes, fffsssssssst, from the sweet, tight hole between his voluptuous asscheeks, something for which only the Dairy Queen hot dog he ate earlier could be responsible."

"Our beauty farts?" David smiles.

"Indeed," I say, nodding my head. "He flushes. He then steps into the shower. And, yes, I am there, soaping the boy's body and feeling his soap-slick skin much as Michelangelo Buonarroti must have caressed the finished *David*."

"Frank," David says, standing, "you have left me out of it once again. Couldn't we, just once, *both* be soaping up the boy, or at least I could be watching."

"Of course you could," I say.

"Good. Now I can go inside and abuse myself."

"You're putting Schoenberg on, then?"

"Oh, you're incorrigible," he says, opening the screen door and stepping inside.

I remain on the porch and watch twilight descend, remembering another dark-haired boy who, it occurs to me, was also fond of wearing blue nylon running shorts. He was a swimmer, something that he and I had in common besides our sexuality. His name was Pat, and he was fond of wearing those nylon shorts over his Speedo racing trunks. Sometimes as I would watch Pat swim—a precise and effective, yet easy, relaxed freestyle—I would conjure a further, deeper relationship with him.

This was all pre-David, and, no, Pat and I never did really have a relationship.

Pat developed HIV early, in those darkly frightening early days when the bogeyman's curse was simply that: a curse from which no one recovered.

I often wonder what would have happened had Pat and I developed something…intimate. My wonder is not so much about the kind of relationship we would have had because it would have been wonderful, but, rather, would I have survived it? Would I have lived through it?

I watch the setting of the sun behind the Rocky Mountains. Twilight softly effuses.

In all the years that have passed since I last saw Pat, and the others who passed before their time, my memory of them reemerges as the sun dips below the mountains. At twilight, Pat and the others always appear smiling in those lovely pictures my mind still holds, secreted in that special place in my brain against the day when memories may become more precious than life itself.

The music coming from David's music room is Prokofiev, the finale to the First Symphony. David has explained to me that this movement is required by the composer to be performed *molto vivace*, very spirited, and has hurried the demise of many a flautist. He, a flautist since childhood, loves the exuberance of this work that during the last five minutes of which is, and there is no other way to describe it, breakneck. That I would have wished for a less robust piece at this time of day, is something left unsaid. It will end soon enough.

Twilight. I stand and open the control box to the brass sprinklers. I turn them on. I sit back down, and listen and watch. *Spit, sspit, ssspit, ssssssssspit.* The red and purple hues of the coming night. The darkening outline of the Rocky Mountains against the red and orange hues of the sky. *Ssssssssssspit.* The blackening of my giant and ancient elms that not twenty minutes ago had been so brightly green with their new growth. The car lights of the cruisers already popping on as they, the cruisers, circle the park looking for… What? Life? Love? Simply a distraction to help them make it through the night?

I will be forty-one this sixth year of the elms. David will be twenty-nine. Gene, Rex, Ronnie, Michael, Pat will never be old. Ever.

I am sure that when I go back into the house David will ask, "Talking to the trees, again?" And I will probably say, "Yes," and smile back, carefully controlling the urge to tell him that life is so precious. David has heard this recitative before. But I will want to paint the oral picture again of the lawyer's wife with the big muzuggas, of the old Irish Setter hobbling behind, and the brilliant hues of twilight and, yes, I will want to tell him that I love him.

I sigh as I stand from the wrought iron chair. I believe… Yes, I believe I should touch my giant and ancient elms, and ask them to grow strong and healthy this seventh spring. The trees are over a hundred years old and flourished well before my intervention. My obsession with them becomes no more than quaint if viewed from afar. I do not apologize, though, for the immediacy of my passion for them, their lives. Yes, perhaps I will ask them, as conduits to the Great Maestro, to put in a good word for sweet young men who left life too soon; for sweet young men who, perhaps, never had the chance to reckon the simple gift of a tree.

Fixing Fence

Sighing, Gus Klynkee studied the sagging fence line through the pickup's cracked windshield. The fence had sighed a bit itself against the nature of winter in the high lains of north central Colorado—snow, felled aspens and pines rested on the barbed wire and had snapped it in places. The passage of critters over, under, and through the fence had taken its toll as well. Gus put most of the blame on the damned elk. He huffed a gray plume against the windshield from the nub of the Camel glowing between his lips. Pushed his SHELL ballcap up a bit, brushed his palm against his three-day growth of stubble, and massaged the ache in his neck. Hell, he'd seen them do it. Unlike deer and antelope, elk wouldn't even try to jump the fence. What's a goddamned fence to a nine hundred pound bull elk, anyway? Critter would walk right through it like it wasn't even there.

He'd known even before sipping his first cup of coffee that morning, he'd see more or less of what he always saw this time of year. Fences, like people, were vulnerable to the passage of time, the elements. He wished for less vulnerability. Always the wishing. Didn't pray on it. He reserved prayers for good harvests, fat calves. Intact fence remained just on the wish list.

He'd grabbed his ballcap and denim coat from hooks to the left of the kitchen door. "C'mon, Joe, get the lead out."

///

"Fence ain't gonna fix itself."

Gus pulled the pickup alongside the sagged fence, cut the ignition, and let the truck glide to a stop. He waited for a response from his grandson, Joe. When none came, he turned, saw Joe's chin resting on his chest—deep breaths, even a little snore. Kid would sleep through a train wreck. He studied the boy for a moment. Joe's black hair, eyes the color of almonds behind the now closed lids, the slightly brown skin, all of it coming from the boy's mother, a Greek beauty who'd captured his son's heart. Though she'd been the daughter of a sheep rancher from Craig—Gus had followed his own daddy's distaste for sheep and those who herded the ravenous critters—Gus assented to the marriage knowing his son would do it even if he objected.

Gus now, as he'd done a thousand times, looked for some little hint of his son in the boy's face. Maybe his nose, Gus thought. He shook his head. *Maybe his heart.* Gus stepped out of the truck, paused a moment and turned his eyes—hard and gray as iced-over river water—toward the sunrise, his squint lining his face like crinkled paper, deep set lines earned from sixty years of worry about the lives and deaths of cows since he was ten. He took off his hat, ran his fingers through his still full head of purely white hair, put it back on, coughed, then spat. Saw blood on the ground. Pulled his red hankie from his back pocket and wiped his mouth. He already knew the prognosis.

"No sir, fences just don't up and fix themselves."

After he had said the words again, Gus slammed the door. The sound jerked Joe halfway out of the few winks he was catching since climbing in and slumping down into the passenger side of the battered pickup. The jolt of the door slamming sounded like a rifle shot, fired close, too close. Joe slid up, opened his eyes and remembered the orthodontist.

The orthodontist, like all of them—doctors, lawyers, CEOs,

Wall Street traders who had yet to lose their shorts in the downturn—fancied themselves hunters of wild game, at least for four or five days out of the year when they headed for the G-K Ranch. Most of them were return customers who valued the homey accoutrements offered by Gus and Anna Klynkee. Gus and Anna kept three cabins clean, warm, and rid of varmints; all for the purpose of supplementing hay and cow income with East-Coast-dreams-never-die money from fat cats intent on inventing or reinforcing their perception of their own manhood by killing wild critters. Their targets were elk, deer, and some antelope, all of which lived a good part of their lives in the high scrub meadows of the G-K. Gus and Anna Klynkee were happy for the opportunity to take the fat cats' checks, skin their kills, ship deer and elk racks back East. Back East where bold stories, lies mostly, of death and danger would flow over the jingle of ice caressed by single malt Scotch, as one fat cat or another explained the story behind the disembodied head with glass eyes and a ten-point rack affixed to the wall above the mantle.

The orthodontist had stubbed his toe exiting the cabin. Joe'd been standing right outside the damned door at the time. The orthodontist reflexively squeezed the trigger of his Ruger in response to the pain in his toe, killing a weathered wooden windmill, a goose twirling wings with the wind that Joe's grandma had stuck in the yard in front of the cabin just for the homey quality of the thing. Joe had slightly, not enough he thought for anyone to see, wet his pants that day when the old goose caught the .30-30 slug right between its eyes. Joe had missed getting the slug in his head or chest by an inch or two as he stepped onto the cabin's porch, sent by his grandpa to see if the weekend wonders were ready to hit the trail, kill some critters.

The bevy of doctors, dentists, CEOs would laugh like hell about it all over a campfire later that night.

Now, there was again that close-in enormous pop he'd never forgotten as a lesson learned, encompassing the essence of city folk—an unpredictable lot not to be trusted.

Joe was now fully awake. He'd slept most of the way lulled by the bounce and sway of the pickup over ruts and gullies, dirt mounds, and sagebrush; the prairie and pastures offered up as personalities, not unlike the kitchen floor in the home place, left untended now through generations of the footslog of the Klynkee family. No want or need to fix it, to even it out. It was fine just the way it was and would remain.

///

Joe had finished his chores just before sunup. He'd sipped some hot coffee, ate some eggs and bacon, then followed his grandpa to the barn. They'd thrown the fence stretcher, shovel, pliers, wire cutter, pry bar, posthole digger, and spade in the bed of the pickup. His grandpa then drove the pickup past the corrals, let the old heap idle, and loaded the bed with fence posts and rolls of barbed and baling wire, all taken from the hidden acre just south of the corrals. Gus had named that hidden acre The Rest Home, a place set back out of sight where the detritus of ranch life had collected through four generations of the Klynkee clan. Never knew when you might need something from it someday. A bolt, a transmission from a 1937 DeSoto, a steering wheel from a 1950 John Deere, rusted roll of prickly wire, railroad ties, fence posts cut from fallen or felled trees soaking up motor oil mixed with creosote in fifty-five gallon drums.

Joe could do without hearing *waste not, want not* again from his grandparents, but, then, there was a practicality to it all. Don't have to buy what you've already got. Don't have to buy what you can't afford.

Joe figured he had seventy, eighty more years ahead of him… not something most thirteen-year-old boys thought about. But he'd come to consider the specter of mortality early. The daddy he'd never known was dead. Goddamned tractor had toppled over, crushing the life out of him. His mama gone, just gone, because ranch life wasn't worth it anymore. Never had been, actually, but she did love that hard case cowboy, Joe's daddy, and would follow him anywhere except to death, which was the sorry outcome of that situation.

///

Joe pulled up on the latch, opened the door. Mirrored his grandpa's squint against the rush of sunrise from the east. His grandpa had already started digging up the underground rot of a failed post.

"You helpin' or takin' a leisurely South Sea cruise to the land of sun-baked women, naked at the tits?"

Joe stepped out of the pickup, smiled, ran his fingers through his sleep-mussed hair. He glanced over his shoulder at the Flattops eleven miles away, still dusted with snow, still holding an allure wrapped in truths and fables about the Colorado Yampa Ute tribe, who favored the area before the white man favored it more.

Joe turned to his grandpa. "Grandpa, them South Seas can wait till I'm old and feeble like you. How come we're doin' this section, anyways? And, where's Mitch and Billy?" He pulled the back of his hands across his eyes.

His grandpa stopped digging, rested his hand on the top of the spade. "Well, mister-thirteen-year-old-hot-shit-know-it-all, I guess the difference between hay and scrub meadow just ain't somethin' taught down at Yampa Elementary. Guess some old and feeble dipshit hard case needs to explain it all so you can understand what the hell you're doin' when your grandpa takes off for them South Seas and sun-ripened women. And the hired hands is over on the old Reineke spread, fixin' fence up north."

"All I asked was…"

"I know what you asked. For the record, if you're keepin' score, we fix fence on this section 'cause we're floodin' this hay meadow come next week." He pointed down, exaggeratedly raising and lowering his index finger in front of Joe's face. "Then, we're turnin' the herd out into the high meadow, into them aspen groves and pine forest, 'til this here section is growed, cut and put up. Point is we don't want Mister Hill's cows comin' into this meadow as it grows. Besides, a man's straight and true fence line says somethin' about that man, says somethin' about family, too. Me, my daddy, his daddy before him, all of us…"

"I know," Joe said, stepping close, smiling, grabbing his grandpa's gloved hand. "I know what we're doin'. I know why we're doin' it."

Both studied the other. Both understanding truths caressed by the caring clutch of family. His grandpa smiled.

Joe looked east, squinted. "Mister Hill and his boy comin' this year?"

Gus glanced east, toward Finger Rock. "Said he would. That's the arrangement, anyways."

"I see 'em," Joe said, pointing.

Gus looked again. Saw his neighbor. "Yeah. That's them." He turned back to the work at hand. "Gimme one a them posts behind you."

"Yessir," Joe said, watching Mister Hill and his boy, Mark, inch closer, become larger, as their red Ford pickup slowly chugged to the fence line.

Gus and Mister Hill had an understanding about repairing the fence. Neither remembered when that understanding had first occurred, but it remained irrevocable. They had shaken on it at one time. Such was the habit of men who had come to value the truth of themselves, honed by lives lived on the land, seeing hay harvest teeter between good and bad, the caprice of seasons, the loss of children before their time, the unending single-minded plod of cows upon the good earth.

"Don't want to use that baling wire if we don't have to," Gus said, concentrating on the post. "Snip about two feet of that roll of prickly wire, Joe. Use them wire cutters. You got your gloves on?"

Gus hooked one end of the fence stretcher on the severed end of the barbed wire already fastened to the new fence post he'd secured into the ground. Mister Hill grabbed the other end of the torn wire and hooked it into the business end of the stretcher. Ratcheted it tight. They waited for Joe to hand over the splice piece. Gus and Mister Hill twisted the ends of the splice wire into the existing, used pliers to secure the tie, gradually eased the fence stretcher's hold, and watched the posts on either end for give. Seeing none, they moved on, repeating their task as needed.

"You boys get busy on the stays, them floaters," Gus said. "Got pieces of aspen in the truck. Use them staples."

The boys, same age, each grabbed an armful of three-foot lengths of aspen and a bag full of rounded staples. They bent down, one on either side of the fence, placed the aspen posts vertical against the taut wire. They used their pliers and a hammer to secure the posts to each of the four strands, both knowing their purpose was to make sure no damned calf was able to slip through the gaps in the wire if the stays held true. Such was their primary responsibility as boys. Later on, they'd move up the chain to actually replacing posts, stretching wire. They understood their contribution to the effort mattered. As they worked, they gabbed about the prospect of returning to school after spring vacation. Shared plans for the summer ahead.

What they didn't talk about was the time they spent together alone, sometimes within a copse of aspens near the high meadow just above the Klynkee family cemetery, or sometimes in one of their bedrooms when they were allowed to invite the other for a sleepover. Those times were journeys of discovery, their interest in the other's body an inevitability of pubescence, a trek into their own being, their psyches. Joe was more intent on the discovery than Mark, and he knew what that meant—he would go to hell for it.

They'd both learned the meaning of and the stigma attached to the word *queer*, an epithet often heard at Yampa Elementary to categorize the most despised human beings on earth. Joe prayed nightly he would be changed, that his queerness would be swept from his soul by the God Pastor Gunn preached about every Sunday at the First Baptist Church on Main Street. Though the Klynkees were and always had been Lutherans, Gus had refused to drive the twenty-five miles to the nearest Lutheran church in Steamboat after his son had died. Joe's grandmother, though, hadn't given up on God altogether as Gus had, and each Sunday she'd take Joe to the First Baptists. She felt it was her duty to raise her grandson as best she could, something that included a weekly walk with the Lord. Joe would sit with her in the pew, listening to Pastor Gunn's promise of damnation for those who weren't saved in Jesus's name, and that those giving comfort to the devil would perish in hell. Joe knew his thoughts and deeds on those sleepovers and up in the high meadow were exactly what Pastor Gunn was talking about.

///

"You stop that fidgetin', Gus." Anna Klynkee seasoned a pot roast. Had fired up the oven. "And that cough a yours needs tending. Need to see a doctor."

Gus sat at the kitchen table, sipped coffee, drummed his fingers. "Damned doctors ain't gonna know more than I do. Think I'll ride the fence. Where's Joe?"

"In his room, I suppose. And you do need to see a doctor."

"Ah, hell..." Gus stood up, walked through the hallway, and opened Joe's door. "Wanna ride fence?"

Joe turned from his homework, scooted his chair from his pint-sized desk. "Sure. We takin' the truck or the horses?"

"Horses." Gus walked back to the kitchen. "You saddle up Flapjack. I'll get Clementine," he said, knowing Joe was at his heels.

"Supper in a couple hours or so," Anna said, not looking up from her task, knowing her men, the center of her life, would probably not return until nightfall. She was used to such things. She'd keep the food warm, sip coffee until they returned.

Fall had come to the G-K, turning aspen groves into bouquets. The sun lingered just above the Flattops, bathing the hay meadow stubble in a golden sheen. The five thousand acres of the G-K was readying to hunker for the winter.

"Let's head up the hill," Gus said, reining the bay mare south. Joe followed, scratching Flapjack's withers as the chestnut gelding blew, farted, and shook its head. Joe read the signs of a horse happy to be moving.

After they'd crossed the hay meadow, Gus sidled up to a gate, bent down and unlatched it, shoved it open. Beyond the gate was a tire-rutted trail leading up to the high meadows where aspen and pine hovered over puffs of sagebrush, wild grass now gone brown. Joe reined Flapjack tight, knew the five-year-old gelding was probably working on a notion to bolt and get out front of the old mare.

"How many city folks comin' to hunt?" Joe'd had the question in his mind for a while. Wondered if the orthodontist would return.

"A number of 'em," Gus said. "That damned dentist ain't comin' back, though. I seen the spot on your jeans that day, Joe. Prob'ly woulda done the same myself. Told him he wasn't welcome no more."

Joe was silent. Had placed the incident at the back of his mind as an embarrassment he'd thought was his alone.

"Times past," Gus said, pausing to cough, spit, "the family would gather about Memorial Day. Nephews, nieces, cousins, hell, about forty of our kin would come from points east and west to help with fixing fence. Your grandma would prepare the food three days prior. A family time. Everybody knowing the worth of taut fence. But, hell, last couple years the family has begun to snipe like crows, all wonderin' whose got the inside track on inheritin' the G-K, all figurin' I'm on my last legs. Worth millions now, Joe. But them millions don't even skim the surface of the worth of it all. Seems family is just broke apart by avarice."

Gus reined Clementine, coughed again.

Joe saw him spit blood and wipe his mouth with the back of his hand. Gus clicked his tongue against his cheek, got Clementine moving.

"Thing is, Joe," Gus continued, "just like them hunters, the family has lost sight of the G-K as anything other than a pleasure trip, somethin' havin' meaning only in the worth of their own egos and their pocketbooks. You understand that, Joe?"

"Sure, grandpa." Joe reined Flapjack alongside Clementine. They had reached the top of the hill that overlooked the southernmost hay pasture spread out below their pause. Gus pulled a flask from his coat pocket, unscrewed the top, and then sipped.

They studied the pasture below. Neither spoke. Flapjack blew again, anxious to get moving. Clementine, older, perhaps wiser, simply lowered her head, pulled up brown grass and munched.

Gus put the flask back in his pocket, again clicked his tongue against his cheek, and nudged Clementine with his heels. "Fence line down here, between this scrub and the hay meadow, is lookin' a little sad."

Joe didn't have to urge Flapjack to move. He eased back in the saddle, leaned his weight against the cantle as Flapjack followed the old mare down the hill.

They rode the fence line west between the base of the wild scrub and the hay meadow that defined the southern perimeter of the G-K.

"She'll need work come spring," Gus said, coughed again, this time grabbing the red hankie from his back pocket and wiping his mouth.

"Grandpa, you all right?"

"Sure am." Gus put the hankie back in his pocket. "Soothin' to just see the line of fence. Sure, needs fixin', but still…"

Gus coughed hard, bent over and grabbed the saddle horn, turned his head and spit, felt the drool slide from his mouth. He started to grab his hankie again, felt the pain of something heavy and hard in his chest alongside the left of his body. He leaned over, kept hold of the saddle horn with his right hand. "Joe," his voice ragged, "take my reins."

"Grandpa," Joe said, reining Flapjack up close to the mare. He grabbed the reins from his grandpa, slipped them over the mare's head, and looked back. "Grandpa, what's the matter? We need to stop?"

"No, no stoppin'. Just get us home." Gus's voice seemed to come from an ancient, dark place Joe knew he'd probably find in nightmares the rest of his life.

///

The family came, paid their respects, sat anxiously through the services for the later reading of the will. Most were uncomfortable with Anna Klynkee, the matriarch of the family, sitting in the first pew with her arm around the black-haired boy, so unlike themselves.

They gathered at the home place, heard Gus Klynkee's words read by the rumpled old lawyer who'd come from Oak Creek to reveal the last wishes Gus had given his signature to a month before.

"All my earthly belongings," the lawyer said, "the ranch and everything upon it, divided equally, I bequest to my precious wife, Anna, and my grandbaby, my friend, my son's son, Joseph Gustav Klynkee." The old attorney paused, peered over the tops of his reading glasses, saw disappointment, even anger in the eyes of most of those gathered. He continued, "To the rest of my family, I bequest a wish that they someday find a sense of themselves that gives no quarter to mendacity and greed."

To the stone-cold silence in the living room of the home place, Anna Klynkee stood, turned to her relations. "Next spring, I want to fix the fence around the plot in the aspen grove, up above the hay meadow, where we'll bury Gus's ashes. His forebears are there already. I figure a good fence, taut and true, would be a fitting thing to do in Gus's memory. I hope you all will come and help."

///

Another spring, Joe and the hired help, Mitch and Billy, busied themselves with cows dropping calves, helping with the births when needed, valuing the look and spunk of the newly born as they found their feet for the first time. Anna hovered in the background, aware of the responsibility left to her from her husband, appreciating the work of her hired help and her grandson, Joe. She viewed the births of calves as a thing of wonder, just for its simplicity in the whole scheme of things encompassed by the G-K.

Day came when it was time to fix the fence surrounding the family cemetery. Anna prepared food, stocked up on beer and wine. Figured the whiskey drinkers would bring their own.

Joe, now fourteen, fired up the old pickup and drove to The Rest Home. Threw the implements and supplies necessary for the task at hand into the back of the truck. He glanced at the small marble headstone on the passenger seat, shifted on the four-wheel drive and inched up the incline to the aspen grove. There he saw his grandma alone, sitting on a felled stump with her hands clutching the silver box, his grandpa's ashes within. He got out of the truck.

"Maybe just you and me, Joe." Anna placed the box on the ground, stood up and waited for Joe to come to her.

Joe wrapped his arms around his grandma. "Grandpa would'a prob'ly wanted it that way. We can get it done, grandma." He glanced up the hill where he and Mark had often spread their clothes on the ground, where their exciting discovery of each other's naked bodies was something Joe now felt not ashamed of, but inappropriate given the proximity to where his grandpa would be buried.

They both turned at the sound of motors revving to climb the incline, and they saw three pickups, a couple ATVs behind, all chugging up the hillside.

Joe saw the red pickup leading the others. Mister Hill and Mark were the first in line. The others Joe recognized as neighboring ranchers and other folks from Yampa, Oak Creek, Kremmling, Heeney, and Topanas, who'd known Gus Klynkee for much longer than Joe'd lived on this earth. His grandma broke their embrace, stepped toward the vehicles fanning out and stopping in the open space just the other side of the grove. She greeted them all as they stepped out of their trucks or climbed off their ATVs.

When she came to Mister Hill, she stopped short and took in

the sight of him and his son standing next to each other. She felt her eyes give up the hold she'd had on her emotions since Gus had passed. She sobbed freely for the first time since the death.

Mister Hill stepped to her, wrapped his arms around her shoulders. "Me and Gus had an agreement, Anna. We're here to honor that."

Joe moved up to where his grandma and Mister Hill were standing. He smiled at Mark. "Thanks for coming."

Mark reached his hand out, grabbed Joe's and, as they shook, Joe, like his grandma, caved in to the emotion. He began to sob. Mark stepped closer, kept his hand clasped in Joe's, wrapped his other arm around Joe's shoulders and said nothing as he pulled Joe close.

///

Joe turned the old pickup and backed up a bit nearer to the fence line. He'd pulled the back strap taut on his grandpa's SHELL hat, felt it caress his head as a blessing of sorts. He opened the door, stepped out of the truck and looked west, toward the Flattops, still topped with snow, still whispering the secrets of the Ute. He then turned east, saw the sunrise and the ruined fence line between the hay meadow and Mister Hill's spread. Damned elk, he thought. He then smiled with the specter of it all, wondered if his grandpa was smiling down on the springtide of seasons, on the promise of another beginning for the G-K. Fat calves and good harvest.

Joe pulled the spade from the back of the truck and started digging around the base of a failed post. He heard the engine whine first, looked east, saw the red pickup crossing the Hill's meadow.

"Told Mitch and Billy to head over to the south pasture," Joe told Mister Hill and Mark as they stepped out of the pickup. "That fence was the last thing grandpa worried about, somethin' he saw as needin' a fix. Grandma's gonna hire another hand to help out when I go back to school."

Mister Hill looked at Joe, the SHELL ballcap, the denim jacket hanging loose with the sleeves rolled up to the wrist. "Well then," he said, paused a moment, "I guess we ought to get movin' on this fence."

"Grandpa said you'd shook on it once, on your agreement that he'd meet up here with you and do the mendin'. Think we oughta do that again. Me and you. Mark, too."

Mister Hill stepped to the fence line, reached his hand over. "Good thought, Joe." They shook hands. Joe then grabbed Mark's hand.

"Okay," Joe said. "Mark, you come over on this side, cut the splice wire. Me and your daddy'll take care of the posts and fence stretcher. We'll do the floaters last."

Mister Hill smiled, nodded. "You heard what the man said, Mark."

///

Sipping coffee at the kitchen table with his grandma, Joe scratched his head, drummed his fingers on the tabletop.

"What's on your mind, Joe?"

Joe hesitated a moment, stopped his drumming, looked at his grandma's eyes. "Them hunters that come up here in the fall. I been thinkin' we tell them we ain't open for huntin' no more. I think if we get some fishermen rentin' them cabins, maybe some hikers, you know, folks that just want to get the feel of the land is what we ought to do. Don't really need them hunters no more."

Anna Klynkee looked across the table, studied Joe's eyes, those deeply brown eyes that appeared as pools of something kind, a gentleness she'd seldom seen since that day Gus Klynkee had offered her a future, a lifetime by his side on the G-K.

"Okay, we can do that. We'll lose some money at first. But we'll make do."

Joe smiled. "Thanks, grandma."

"Joe, I've got something to tell you. Might be a little hard to hear it. But it's gotta be said. It's about your mother and your grandpa, too."

Joe folded his hands on the table, quit the drumming, stared at his grandma. "Okay."

"Well, I got this letter yesterday." She pulled an envelope from the pocket of her apron and placed it on the table. "It's from your mother. She heard about your grandpa dyin', and of course she offers condolences…to us both. But somethin' we, your grandpa and I, never told you, but I think you're old enough now to hear it, was that we worked for years to find your mother ever since she left you here after your daddy died. Somethin' else you prob'ly don't know is your grandpa wanted to give you up at first."

Joe lowered his head, stared at his hands.

His grandma reached across the table, put her fingers under his chin, raised his head, then covered his hands with her own. "This is important, Joe. Ever since Gus died, I've struggled with this. Should I tell you or not. I think Gus would have wanted me to tell you. He was out of his mind with the loss of your daddy, Joe. Can't blame him. He was angry at God, at your daddy for dyin', at your mama. He was even angry with me for a time. He saw you as a reminder that your daddy had picked a woman he hadn't approved of, Joe. But after his anger passed, after he was able to grieve the death of your daddy, he saw you as a precious gift your daddy had given to him. And you were a gift, Joe. You wasn't even a year old when your mama left. Goodness, she was only just barely eighteen at the time. So, we figured we'd find a way to make you our son, in a legal sense. And we started lookin' for your mama. She'd have to give you up 'fore we could adopt you. And we found her. She signed the papers just before your second birthday. Now this letter from your mother is meant more for you than me. She says she never stopped loving you, Joe. But she went and got a new life, a new husband. She has two children now. Lives in Denver. Has a good life there. But back then, well… She did what she thought was best…for both her and you. So," she raised her hands from Joe's, grabbed the letter, held it out, "I 'spose you ought to read it. Keep it for your lifetime as something of your past, of where you come from."

Joe unfolded his hands, gently grasped the letter, stared a moment at his grandma's eyes. He nodded, got up from the table, walked down the hallway to his room and closed the door. He sat on his bed and looked at the handwriting on the envelope—the blue ink, the little flowery turn to some of the letters. He teared up, tore the envelope in half, and then in half again. Tossed it in the trashcan next to his little desk.

"Joe," his grandma stood outside his door, "you all right."

Joe pulled the sleeves of his shirt across his eyes. "Yeah, I'm fine, grandma."

She opened his door and sat down next to him on the bed. She put her arm around his shoulders, looked for the envelope, saw the torn edges in the wastebasket. She knew she'd later retrieve the letter, Scotch tape it back together, and put it up in the box she kept on the top shelf of her bedroom closet.

"Grandma," Joe placed his arm around her waist, "I think I wanna be called Gus from now on. That is my middle name given by my daddy. That okay?"

Anna Klynkee turned, looked at those eyes staring back at her, those eyes she'd never really get enough of, never tire of letting herself get lost in. "That's fittin', Joe," she said, her voice breaking a bit. "Gus fits you fine. Your grandpa would be proud."

"Somethin' else I oughta tell you."

"Okay."

"You told me about grandpa not wanting me at first?"

"Yes."

"I guess that's a secret you had that wasn't easy to tell, but… I guess you had to tell me 'cause it's the truth."

"Yes, it was, Joe."

"Well, I think I gotta tell you about me."

"What about you, Joe?"

"I like boys."

"That's nice, Joe."

"No," Joe said. "I like boys 'cause I'm queer."

Anna Klynkee reflexively tightened her grip on Joe's shoulders.

They sat on the bed for a while, neither speaking, both listening to the creaks and moans of the home place.

The Story of Myrtle Roady

Myrtle Roady took a toy
Drank some rum
And ate a boy
Myrtle Roady stole a curl
Drank some rum
Then ate the girl

It begins…

By December 31, 1882, Hiram Clop, a fair-haired boy of seven, had already broken one leg from the hand-fashioned wooden horse his daddy had given him for Christmas. Carried the cherished, albeit lamed, steed he'd named Fury to the canvas tent-covered odiferous hole fifty yards from the pine-framed and canvas-walled and roofed structure he knew as his home. His mamma and daddy had told him to hurry up his business as the New Year's Eve celebration would soon commence in the large communal tent down the road and, "You still gotta change your clothes, Hi," his mamma had said.

He pulled the flap open and smelled the odor that always

aroused his druthers to step off into the blackly-hued scrub either side of the path to the outhouse where he could squat, do what he needed to do, and then run back to the warmth of the iron wood stove that centered their unfinished house. He'd been admonished to be civilized, though, by his mamma who'd caught him more than once, "…actin' like a savage," and "…decent white men use the privy."

And he did. Stepped under the flap, kept hold of Fury in his right hand and pulled his pants and drawers down with his left. He quickly finished his white man's duty to decency, wiped with a handful of feather grass, pulled his pants up and stepped back out of the awful place.

He saw the yellow glow from inside his house, heard the voices of those already gathered in the Crawford town center. Smiled with the remembrance of last New Year's Eve, when the townspeople had sat down to a fine supper after the blessing from Pastor Gumm had ended. He took one step into the run he knew would get him to it all a little faster, when he felt something clamp against his mouth as Fury was ripped from his hand. His whole body rose as he was tightly embraced by an arm around his middle. He tried to scream, but couldn't. Kicked his legs and flailed his arms. Knew he was being carried away from the proximity of his home and even farther away from the happy sounds of those anxious to bring in the new year with good food, a warm fire, a little cider, and declarations that the Good Lord would bring them a better year ahead. He felt no pain when the hand upon his mouth quickly snapped his head backward to an unnatural and mortally conclusive life-ending droop. Hiram Clop was dead, and Fury found a new home amongst other childish things—ragged baby dolls and ribbons, curled locks of hair, six-shooters of wood, and wooden blocks painted gaily in reds and greens.

///

Myrtle Roady left life on January 1, 1889, in a town of a hundred and fifty souls called Crawford in southwestern Colorado, a place where scrub oak, cacti, sagebrush ,and saltbush were plentiful upon the land, and where the mountains and canyons beyond provided stingy embracement of Pinyon Pine, juniper, yucca and Mountain Mahogany. Where cottonwoods suck sustenance from washes here and there, and sunrises come late against the rise of the West Elk Range of the Colorado Rockies to the east.

Story is that Captain George A. Crawford passed through the area at the end of December in 1882, mentioned to a Baptist preacher/resident, Henry Gumm, that this would be a fine place for a town and the preacher and his flock heartily agreed as they watched Captain Crawford disappear into the sunset. They then and there named the place where they'd settled Crawford and set up a post office for good measure. Didn't occur to the folks who now had a name for the place upon which their ragtag assemblage had squatted, that Captain Crawford—who didn't even find it necessary to dismount as he smiled down at Pastor Gumm and gave voice to those encouraging words—that patronization was a convenient way to just get on with more pressing business that, in Captain Crawford's case, eventually included the founding of more hefty burgs like Grand Junction and Delta.

Myrtle Roady was amongst the group who watched Captain Crawford ride away that day. And, finding the silly hurly-burly of the gathered Baptists distasteful, she spit an epithet barely heard by the rowdy group, walked north past the outskirts of the wee settlement, climbed one hill, walked down the other side, then trudged up another topped by her one-room roughly-hewn pine abode, which she entered, mightily farting as she closed the door. Charley, a raccoon of mild temperament who had half-buried himself under the three deer hides spread upon Myrtle's sleeping corner on the floor, raised himself from his loll, studied Myrtle's entrance, cocked his head with her malodorous release and stood up on two feet—wide-eyed and bushy tailed, as they say.

Myrtle nodded, said, "Go back to bed, Charley," and Charley did, once again digging into the bedclothes as a badger to a hole. "Goddamned Bible-thumping sonsabitches," she said, not knowing it would be thirty or more years before her pejorative would gain prominence. Didn't care about such things as her priorities tended to focus on the here and now. And here and now she figured it was time to once again hone the edges of her cutlery, including the two axes she favored.

She tossed two thigh-long and doubly thick pine logs into the river rock fireplace where orange embers still sizzled. She grabbed her cutting tools, placed them upon her all-purpose table, sat down on the broad-based two-foot tall log chair, and began filing the edges with a hand-crafted rasp, working rhythmically as she sang, "Oh, dem golden slippers! Oh, dem golden slippers!" She stopped her scraping, held up the axe, licked her finger and slid it against the business end of the implement. Shook her head, grinned large, and got back to work, taking up the ditty where she'd left it. "So it's good-bye, chillun. You will have to go. Oh, dem golden slippers! Oh, dem golden slippers!"

She'd long since forgotten all the lyrics and, besides "Dixie," it was the only other song she knew, and she'd not really intentionally changed the words but had found they'd somehow changed themselves over the years. "So it's good-bye, chillun," she now hollered, spitting out the words to the four walls. Charley didn't stir from his slumber after having long since concluded Myrtle's quirkiness was a benign thing for him, and perhaps other small critters as well. But those other larger critters Myrtle fancied more dead than alive? Well, that was another thing altogether, one as exotic and exciting as the tasty tidbits Myrtle would toss his way as she sliced and chopped. In his quiet, calculating, nocturnal scrounging way, he understood night feeding as well as any likeminded critter. Myrtle surely did know how to bring home the bacon…so to speak.

///

Pastor Henry Gumm had not really seen the worth of settling upon the spot that would become Crawford, but after leading his flock of thirty-five from Ash Flat, Arkansas—an apt name for a dreary place even the most robust of Baptists could no longer countenance—across the even more dismal flatlands of the Indian Territory into what he had identified as the Promised Land of Colorado, he knew his and his congregation's fervor for travel had hit rock bottom. Colorado may have offered more ideal places to settle, but the road had been long and the collective enthusiasm for continuing their exodus had turned sour as sun-baked milk. So, tents were raised, plentiful water was found, deer were shot, and timber was felled and cut for the coming winter. They'd found their Promised Land. Eden it was not, but it'd have to do.

Myrtle Roady, certainly not partial to religious folks, especially Baptists, had tagged along on the journey when Pastor Gumm had reached the Panhandle of the Indian Territory where she joined the group, more as a matter of expedience rather than any notion life might be rosier in Colorado. Seems Myrtle had overstayed whatever welcome she'd found at the Cimarron cut off for the old Santa Fe Trail, where more than a few travelers from points east rested for a day or two before resuming their westward trek.

Myrtle had been born to her fourteen-year-old mother in 1860. Her father may or may not have been her uncle, but such things were common in Tennessee at the time, and her mother didn't live past the birth to affirm or deny it. Myrtle grew up among the Roady clan, an ever-blossoming family that lived off the land and the critters upon it. She favored the natural urges of the male side of the family rather than the female, abjuring motherhood as a waste of time. Was drawn to girls more than boys, and dallied here and there with the prettiest ones—the girls responding with surprise, but not repugnance as Myrtle was, after all, a gentle lover. By the time she was in her twenties, this peculiarity brought accusatory scrutiny from itinerant Methodist preachers who certainly understood the lessons of Leviticus 18. Myrtle was robustly condemned in the name of Jesus. Just as robustly, she set out on her own in a westward direction.

Preferring pants, knee-length boots of soft hide, a silk top hat ragged with wear, and a wool coat two sizes too large, Myrtle had tarried at that offshoot of the Santa Fe Trail for two weeks, where she gained some little respect from the prairie pioneers for her cutting and carving upon newly-slain game. Elk and deer mostly, and one domestic hog that had apparently gone mad from ingesting nettles, kept Myrtle busy and valued by the fairly steady flow of folks upon the trail.

She was glad to do what she could, and certainly had the equipment with which to do it. Folks took notice, though, that Myrtle didn't like children. Seemed she'd determined children were "…no good for nuthin' and oughtin' ta be on the road screamin' and smellin' like vermin." 'Course Myrtle hadn't smelled herself for some time, given that she'd long since become immune to her own odor. Folks began to wonder, though, about Myrtle Roady, who'd take to her cutting and carving with the same song upon her lips. "Oh, dem golden slippers," the chopping part of her butchery always punctuated with a heightened tone. Seemed her axe always managed to separate the head from the critter's body with those words: "So it's good-bye, chillun! You will have to go!"

The day after Pastor Gumm and company arrived at the fork in the trail, Priscilla Purdy, a red-haired six-year-old wandered away from her mamma who was washing clothes on a board in a bucket at the sandy bank of the Cimarron River. Priscilla, who carried her straw-stuffed baby, Victoria, in her arms, did not return when called, and the search party didn't find her. Some of the fretting mamas began to glare at the chillun' hating Myrtle Roady, so when Pastor Gumm and the Baptists headed out early the next morning, Myrtle saw the good sense of moving on with the Baptists regardless of her distaste for them. And the Baptists had welcomed her after she'd lied to Pastor Gumm that she'd been washed in the Waters of the Lord back in Tennessee. That was just fine and dandy for the pastor and his minions to accept Myrtle as they crossed into Colorado and headed northwesterly to the place where Captain George A. Crawford would eventually plant the seed of a town in the minds of the Faithful.

///

By December 31, 1888, and after eight years of doggedness

in the pursuit of making Crawford a town to be proud of, the residents—now including two Mormons, seven Methodists, forty-five Baptists, and twelve others not self-identified by their faith—determined to make the last year of the decade even better than the one they would tie up tonight at the annual New Year's Eve celebration. That the Baptists still organized the event didn't bother the others, who looked upon the good sense of strength in numbers, and weren't disinclined to share some of their food stores as well.

What *was* bothersome, though, and had affected all souls in the town in one way or another, was that New Year's Eve had also become the time when a child would be lost. Not just lost, but forever gone without a clue as the why or wherefore of it. Five children in all, and a peculiar thing no one had yet to put a meaning to, was that with the disappearance of each child, something belonging to that child had also disappeared. After the first one vanished on New Year's Eve, 1882, Pastor Gumm wrote in the front of his Bible: *12/31/82 Hiram Clop – 7 yrs – wooden horse.* The list had grown by the New Year's Eve day in 1888 to five entries including Hiram Clop: *12/31/83 Mary Day – 6 1/2 yrs – blue ribbon around a ringlet of her baby hair; 12/31/84 Rachel Moore – 8 yrs – doll with painted eyes; 12/31/85 Henry Poole – 7 yrs – wooden axe; 12/31/87 Richard Sawyer – 9 yrs – rawhide Indian headband.*

Myrtle Roady had never participated in the nonsense that annually erupted a mile from her hilltop, and had, over the years, instead fancied her own celebration of sorts consisting of uncorking one of the three bottles of rum with which she'd begun her journey west. She'd managed to secure a half-full fourth bottle from the owner of the hog she'd butchered at the Cimarron cut off, which was now the only remaining bottle. Her temperance was disciplined to the point that the last six years had seen her imbibe only once a year, and today was that day. She'd finish the bottle after she'd made her kill, rendered it to edible strips and chunks and then warmed up her home to a lavishly comfortable temperature—another once-a-year indulgence.

Her mouth watered, and drool seeped down her chin in anticipation of the scrumptious morsels after they'd been slightly roasted over the fire, then the rum to wash it down. Oh, she'd throw Charley some of the smaller bits after he returned from his own hunt. Charley could, of course, smell the particular sweet aroma of the roasting practically the moment the first waft of smoke curled out of Myrtle's chimney, and he'd come a lumbering up or down whatever hill he'd happen to have been traversing at the time, stand tall, scratch against the door and wait until Myrtle opened it. Certainly, Charley had no sense the special smell marked a special day, but did remember what that aroma had promised from years past.

Just as the sun began to slip from what had been a mild day with a cool breeze from the north since noon and a meager cloud cover since two, Myrtle pulled on her coat, slipped her Bowie knife into its sheath on her belt, and tied the rawhide strips hanging from the rosewood covered tang of her serrated, clawing knife to the loop of her pants. She grabbed her axe, considered the sufficiency of logs she'd carried inside for the later feast, smiled at the rum upon the table, clicked her tongue, said, "C'mon, you rascal," as sweet as she'd ever said a word in her life. "C'mon Charley, let's get to it. Oh, dem golden slippers," she began to sing as Charley slipped from the beneath the deer hides, waddled across the floor and preceded Myrtle out the opened door. "Oh, dem golden slippers. So it's good-bye, chillun!" She raised her head, shouted the words, heard them echo off the canyon walls beyond.

About the same time Myrtle Roady was beginning her hunt, Pastor Gumm was welcoming the spinster sisters, Charlene and Darlene Skivers, into the wall and roof-framed but not yet sided First Baptist Church of Crawford. The sisters had, for the past three New Year's Eves, taken charge of the immediate preparations for the later dinner and blessing and would do the same this year while Pastor Gumm, as had been his habit for as long as anyone could remember, sought some solitary time away from the townspeople.

He'd go off into the scrub and hills nearby where he would seek a personal confabulation with the Good Lord Himself, a self-cleansing of sorts, before returning to the church to share the victuals and give the blessing for the new year. As he headed for the outskirts of town, he saw Peter Drum and Harold Oaks had begun their vigil to assure no child was lost this day and, as had been agreed at this past Sunday service, to question any unusual activity by or behavior of anyone in or near the town. The question of what constituted unusual activity or behavior was voiced by Isabelle Constance, a schoolteacher from Missouri, who had always sought clarification of vague pronouncements. Pastor Gumm's response, "I think we'll know it when we see it," evoked nods from most and a silent sigh from Miss Constance.

Myrtle moved silently as the shadows of dusk crept toward the town's center. She knew from experience the aroma of the town's feast would draw out her prey. The repetition of her song, "Oh, dem golden slippers. Oh, dem golden slippers. So it's goodbye, chillun!" now sung only in her mind, over and over again. She hunched down, smelled her prey, and saw it directly in front of her.

On his solitary traipse, Pastor Gumm squatted in the scrub, mouthed his annual prayer beseeching Good News for the coming year, and saw movement to his left. He tensed, believing it was the Stivers' boy, Sammy.

Myrtle unsheathed the Bowie knife, knew she was upwind, crept closer, leapt upon it, wrenched its neck, swiftly buried the blade in its back, knew she'd struck the heart when it simply deflated upon the ground, a soulful whimper in its descent.

"Who goes there?" Peter Drum called out, his voice, sturdy and full of authority.

Pastor Gumm stood up, turned away from what he had earlier eyed—the Stiver's boy. Waved at Drum. "It's only me, Pete."

Harold Oaks approached Pastor Gumm from the other side, patted him on the back. "Thought you was the demon, Pastor."

"Good work, you two," Pastor Gumm smiled, watched Drum approach him. "'Spose we ought to get back to the church, huh?"

"Could eat a mule," Oaks laughed, as the three headed back toward the welcoming glow of the First Baptist Church of Crawford.

///

Myrtle Roady sliced and chopped, fashioned the meat into strips, cut the strips to her liking, stoked the fire, and sang her song, "Oh, dem golden slippers." She tugged a length of barbed wire through the fleshy strips, then stretched the wire high over the fire, securing each end through a gap in the river rock. She heard Charley's scratch, opened the door, watched him sniff and lick the pooled blood on the plank floor. "Gonna have the meat done in a bit, Charley," she said. "Oh, dem golden slippers…"

///

"Where's Sammy!" Mary Stivers screamed to the already feasting assemblage. "I can't find my boy!"

Sammy Stivers, a boy of seven, red-haired and with a temperament inclined toward to premeditated mischief, was nowhere to be found. His mamma, Mary, had delayed her short trek to the church awaiting Jimmy's return from the nearby pond where he'd been sent to wash up and make himself tidy for the celebration. His daddy, Samuel Sr., had already settled himself before one of the three tables in the church generously spotted with food offerings from nearly all Crawford's citizens. Samuel Sr. stood, toppling his pine stool to the floor, hollered, "It's her! It's that goddamned witch Myrtle Roady! We all know it! She's taken my boy!"

Pastor Gumm stood, spread his arms in a calming gesture, started to say something and was immediately silenced by the shouts of the God-fearing fathers amongst the gathering who, to a man, agreed heartily with Samuel Sr. "She's got him!" Harold

Oaks screamed. "By God, we can save him if we get up there right now!" Peter Drum huffed as he grabbed a knife from the table before him and started running for the tent flap door.

Myrtle sucked on the meat, sipped from the bottle, and watched Charley lick his paws after consuming each bit she'd thrown to him. "Good-bye, chillun! Huh, Charley?" she said, then cocked her head with the sound of voices in the distance. "Goddamned Bible-thumping sonsabitches!" she spat, sending Charley's attention also to the sounds he'd long since come to avoid. Myrtle stood, opened her door, saw too many shadows to count moving up the rise of her hill, heard distinctly the words: "I want my boy back, Myrtle Roady!"

Charley scampered under the deer hides as Myrtle braced her arms against the door frame. "Goddamned…" was the only and the last word Myrtle spoke before the angry men rushed her, stepped into her shack, saw the blood, smelled the meat, and knew for a certainty that Sammy Stivers' little life would be Myrtle Roady's crap in the morning. It was too much for Samuel Sr. He grabbed one of Myrtle's axes, smacked her across the head with the flat end and declared, "Let's string her up. She killed my boy! Oh, God-A'mighty, she killed my boy!"

///

In the earliest hours of January 1, 1889, Myrtle Roady's toes floated three-feet above the ground, her head drooped to her shoulder, her neck wrapped in the rope Harold Oaks had quickly untied from his mule, Clem, where it had hobbled the beast against the animal's annoying penchant for wanderlust. The limb of the oak over which the rope was thrown had audibly sighed when burdened with the weight of Myrtle's body. All eyes of all souls in Crawford, Colorado stared at the apt end to the killer of the innocents among them. Women sobbed and men cursed the demonic visage of Myrtle Roady. Pastor Gumm, while providing a faint attempt to cool tempers, had finally stepped aside and

THE STORY OF MYRTLE ROADY

lowered his head in prayer as Myrtle was sent to her just reward.

///

Sammy Stivers, having determined that hiding out within the newly constructed log post office one hundred yards down the road from the First Baptist Church might have caused some concern, hadn't counted on the Myrtle Roady twist to the event. Beginning to shiver against the near-freeze now that it was past midnight, he picked up the rawhide whip his daddy had fashioned for him and simply went home. He didn't know what all the hubbub was about and didn't care. He was cold and tired, and he crawled into his bedclothes where he was found by Mary Stivers shortly past three a.m. when she returned home from the hanging, her body spent, he eyes raw, her heart broken. The reunion was heaven-sent.

With Sammy Stivers accounted for, Pastor Gumm, Samuel Sr., Peter Drum, and Harold Oaks climbed the two hills to Myrtle's ramshackle house, studied the scene in the light of the new day of the new year, and saw the remains of what was clearly a small catamount, not a human child. They returned to the old oak where Myrtle still swung, cut her down, wrapped her in canvas, and duly buried her in the cemetery behind the church. The following Sunday services were attended by more than a few with atonement on their minds who found solace in Pastor Gumm's observation that the Good Lord surely does work in mysterious ways.

Charley had managed to scamper out of what he had come to know as his home up the hillside shortly before sunset the day after the mighty upset to his life as he'd known it for the past two years. He watched from afar as several two-legged critters set ablaze the little house on the hill.

A week into the new year of 1889, Pastor Henry Gumm stuffed

his few belongings and a goodly amount of dried meat and hardtack into three burlap bags, said good-bye to no one, and headed toward what he'd heard was the bloom of a bustling place to the west called Grand Junction. He reconfirmed the good sense in never marrying as he considered the particular course his life had taken over the years. After five hours into his journey, his sat down off the side of the rutted road, untied the top of one of his bags, reached in and pulled out what he believed was his favorite of them all—a wooden horse missing a leg.

The Return...

Myrtle Roady raised her axe
Then sliced the man
almost in half
Myrtle Roady screamed with glee
then she turned
and smiled at me...

Odorous and unkempt, unshaved and greasy-haired, his back and buttocks hued black like ripe eggplant, Wiley Pinnt leaned his head out the window hoping the breeze would momentarily shake off what he knew was coming. The approach of an oxycodone- bourbon-inspired collapse was just minutes away. He'd swallowed the pills two hours before, sipped bourbon since then, and now that he'd crossed into Colorado, he still had enough sense to know it was time to pull over.

For the most part, he'd managed to keep the old Dodge on his side of the highway, jerking it back when it slewed over the yellow or white lines. After leaving Albuquerque late in the afternoon, he'd gassed up in Durango where he bought a pack of Marlboros, gingerly climbed back into the pickup, lit up, took another sip, and pulled onto US 550 North. Dusk embraced the road about the time he passed through Silverton, an old mining town that still thrived by charming tourists and winter sports enthusiasts. Pinnt smiled at a fat man in Bermuda shorts with a camera hanging from his neck, and holding the hand of a woman attired the same but wearing a broad-brimmed sun hat. They were admiring a brightly colored four-foot wooden Indian standing at the entrance to a curio shop. "Hah," Pinnt said. "Go on in and buy somethin'. Hell, you can get a genuine Apache tomahawk in there for fifty dollars. Don't look at the label though 'til you get home. 'Harold,'" Pinnt raised his voice to near soprano, 'did you know this here tomahawk was made in Bangladesh?'" He laughed at that, then groaned with the accompanying reminder that mean sonofabitch in Albuquerque had given him two fractured ribs, and the fall had gifted him three fractured vertebrae.

Frenzy was the sonofabitch, a bull he'd sat for three seconds in Albuquerque. The bull was known to raise his head higher than most, then squirm his body almost into a figure eight, lower his head, then thrust himself into an arcing leap some swore was ten feet off the ground. Frenzy's neck had made contact with Pinnt's chest during the first second, while the remaining two seconds of the ride was devoted to Pinnt's plan for the fall. He hadn't intended to land on the small of his back, but what the hell…

After his x-rays and the diagnosis, Pinnt grabbed the blister pack of eight pills offered by the doctor. "That'll last you four days," the doctor said. "Now, before you put your clothes back on, take a look at your backside in the mirror."

Pinnt winced as he slid off the examining table. Looked over his shoulder at his reflection from the mirror on the door, and studied the blue-black butterfly imprint covering his ass to nearly his shoulders. "Seen worse, Doc," he said.

"S'pose you have. You mind those pills now. Only two a day."

Pinnt pulled on his jeans, his shirt, and then stuck his feet in his boots. Knew better than to lean down and tug on his Justins, and instead just wiggled his feet into them. Figured he wouldn't lean over for a while unless he had to. Walked out of the exam room, crossed the hall to the dressing room where he gathered his belongings, and told his buddies he'd see them next year as he passed them in the hallway. Once outside, he gingerly positioned himself behind the wheel, pried two pills from the pack, and swallowed them with a nice gulp from the bottle he always kept on the seat to his right.

The Dodge Ram had been sixteen years old when his daddy gave it to him on his sixteenth birthday. Shortly after both turned eighteen his Professional Bull Riders' membership card arrived, and he joined the rodeo circuit as the fulfillment of a dream he'd nurtured since his daddy first put him atop a young steer when he was four years old.

Now, after two years on the circuit, after coming away from yet another rodeo with no share of the purse, but with a nice collection of bruises and fractures, after crossing back into Colorado, Pinnt steered the Ram onto the apron where a dirt road led to a Ponderosa pine bordered road up a hill. Fifty yards in, Pinnt let the Ram coast to a stop. He turned off the headlights and the engine, slunk down a bit in the seat, and closed his eyes.

///

From the depth of a dark place he could not identify, Pinnt startled at the enormity of sound to his left, and a voice speaking muffled nonsense. He opened his eyes, felt the sting of daylight upon them, and raised his head.

"Help me! Please!"

The voice became clear, the articulation precise. Someone was pounding on his side window. Pinnt turned his head. A white-haired stranger with too red lips and blue eyes peered at him with a worried frown covering his face. Spittle seeped from the corners of his mouth. Again, he struck his knuckles against the glass.

"I need help," the man said. "She's coming!"

Pinnt felt the pain of his recent injuries as a full-body pulsing ache. Fished the page of oxycodone from his shirt pocket, poked a pill out of the cellophane packaging, grabbed the bottle to his right, popped the pill in his mouth, and washed it down.

"What the fuck!" Pinnt said, recapping the bottle. Looked at the man outside his window and shook his head.

"She's coming!" the man again said. "Myrtle's coming! Look what she did." He held up his left hand, bloodied and missing all the fingers.

Pinnt opened the window a couple inches. "Don't know what the fuck is wrong with you, and I'm—"

"Oh God," the man said, glancing behind him. "Jesus…" With that, he turned from Pinnt's side window, headed toward the thickset of pine trees and disappeared into the darkness beyond.

"Crazy motherfucker," Pinnt hissed as he craned his neck to watch where the man went. Felt the pain of that contortion, slowly turned his head back, and starred out the windshield a moment. He grabbed the page of pills he'd placed on the seat, and popped another one into his mouth. The bourbon burnt like hell going down. "Goddamn," he whispered, stuck the remaining pills in his pocket, and shook his head.

Pinnt opened his door, and turned his body to the side. Again looked at where the crazy man had disappeared into the trees. *Myrtle's coming!* What the fuck did that mean? Bracing his hands on the doorframe, he gently eased his feet to the ground.

"Motherfuckinggoddamn!" He spat the words as he arched his back, hoping against hope to get the fire-laden kinks out. The only thing it got out was a groan as his left side felt like a kitten from the inside had barred its claws against his chest. He closed his eyes, and raised his head. "Sonofafuckingbitch!"

"Nice mornin'."

It was a woman's voice. Pinnt opened his eyes, and there she was standing not three feet away, though her appearance belied femininity. She was a short woman, broad in the shoulders wearing pants, knee-length boots of soft hide, a silk top hat ragged with wear and crushed down, looking like the bellows of an accordion. Her wool coat appeared to be two sizes too large and it bulged to one side. She was a plain-faced woman, though her nose was wide, and her hair appeared to be long, but matted.

"Who—"

"You smell of bull," the woman said, leaning her head forward and sniffing the air between herself and Pinnt.

"Yeah," he said, feeling his body relax a bit as the oxy took hold. "I ride 'em. Who are you?"

"Myrtle Roady. You are?"

"Wiley Pinnt."

She stared at Pinnt, stuck her right hand beneath her coat, pulled out a short-handled axe from under her belt, and wiped the business end of it across the front of her coat.

"That blood?" Pinnt said.

"Might be. Why?"

Myrtle!

"Why?" Myrtle again said.

"Some fella was bangin' on my window. He mentioned your name."

"This fella?" Myrtle said, reaching into the bulged side of her coat and tossing the white-haired guy's head toward Pinnt. It rolled across the ground, picking up some pine needles before it stopped at Pinnt's feet.

Pinnt stared at the still open blue eyes, and the too red lips. He raised his head, looked at Myrtle as she took a couple steps toward him. He backed up against the truck.

"I'm lookin' for a ride to Crawford," Myrtle said. "I believe that's where you're goin'."

What the fuck! "Miss Roady," Pinnt said, hearing the shake in his voice, thinking her green eyes were more reptilian than human. She smelled of moist earth. He cleared his throat, and began again. "Miss Roady, I don't know—"

"You can call me Myrtle."

"Okay. Myrtle, I don't know what's goin' on here, but—"

"You are goin' to Crawford," Myrtle said and it wasn't a question.

"Well, yeah."

"Let's go then," Myrtle said, pulling back her coat and sticking the axe handle under her belt. She leaned over, grabbed the head by the hair, and, as she walked around the truck, tossed it into the pickup's bed. When she got to the passenger side, she opened the door and climbed in.

Pinnt shook his head, turned and looked into the bed. There it was, the eyes still staring at nothing in particular. He reached over the side and pulled part of the tarp he always kept there over it. Felt that kitten inside his chest clawing, clawing. He thought a moment about just knocking Myrtle in the head, pulling her out of the truck, and leaving her on the roadside. Moment didn't last long as he damned the sonofabitch in Albuquerque for precluding that kind of physical exertion.

"Oh, dem golden slippers. Oh, dem golden slippers. So it's good-bye, chillun! Oh, dem golden slippers..." Myrtle chanted more than sang the words, slapping her leg with the word *chillun*. She stared out the windshield at what was ahead, occasionally sticking her pinkie finger up her nose, and digging a bit.

Pinnt had climbed back behind the wheel, his entire body throbbing as he bent over to start the engine. He glanced at Myrtle, who stared straight ahead and looked like a fat Buddha with a hat on. He didn't know what the fuck was going on, or how he'd managed to get in the middle of it, but hell, if she wanted a ride to Crawford that was where he was going. The head under the tarp? He didn't even want to think about that. He gave the old Dodge gas, backed it up, turned it around, and got back onto 550 North.

"'Bout three hours to Crawford I expect," Myrtle said. She grabbed Pinnt's bottle and held it up. "Mind if I take a sip?"

"No. Sure," Pinnt said, and then thought better of it. *Her lips on my bottle!* "There's a cup behind the seat."

"Don't need a cup." Myrtle took a sip. "Rum is better," she

said reaching the bottle out to Pinnt. "Have some."

Pinnt took the bottle, set it between his legs, and dug in his shirt pocket for the pills. He kept his hands on the wheel and managed to work a pill out of the blister pack. Stuck the pill in his mouth, pulled the bottle from between his legs, and hesitated a moment. *Her mouth was on that.* Shit, he thought, he'd shared a bottle a thousand times with cowboys who thought oral hygiene was pulling a used up plug of tobacco from their cheek. He took a gulp, and damned the consequences. He held the bottle out to Myrtle. She took it and put the cap back on.

"What you got there?" Myrtle said, putting the bottle on the seat, and grabbing the blister pack from Pinnt's hand.

"Pain pills."

"Yeah, smelled it on you. Bull messed you up, huh?"

"He did."

"Oh, dem golden slippers—"

"What is that?" Pinnt interrupted her, annoyed with the stupid thing.

"It's a song. You ain't heard it?"

"Yeah. Of course, I have," he said, grabbing the blister pack and stuffing it into his shirt pocket. "But why do you— Shit. Never mind. That don't bother me as much as that head back there." He gestured with his thumb toward the back.

"That's Pastor Gumm. Not the original, but close enough."

"Why'd you... do what you did?"

"That head back there is Daniel Gumm, great-grandson of Henry who was one of the founders of Crawford. Baptist preacher, he was, and a killer of small children. Daniel's a preacher too, and I followed him and his little woman to Silverton."

"Followed from where?"

"His great-granddaddy went to Grand Junction from Crawford in 1889, married, had children, and the children had children and that's where the Gumm family still resides. Goddamn Baptists all. Found him down there and followed him to Silverton."

"Okay. How you know all that?"

"I just do."

Pinnt glanced at Myrtle who was pulling something out from under her coat. It was the axe. She plopped it down on the seat between them.

"Had to stop the bad seed at last," Myrtle said. "Was waitin' for 'em when they come back to the motel after their dinner. Sliced the little woman across the throat when she walked in the room. Henry's eyes got real big, and he just stood there. Told him who I was, and why I was there, and I'd give him a head start to see if he could get away. He reached for the telephone, and that's when I chopped off his fingers. Told him if he tried to get help I'd finish him off right then and there."

"Jesus."

Myrtle patted the axe. "This here is a genuine W.C. Kelly Perfect Axe with the original hickory handle, though I shortened it a while ago. Cuts like a razor except you never want to go for the head. Might get stuck in the skull bone. Oh," she said, reaching into the left side of her coat and pulling something out. "This here"—she held the item toward Pinnt—"is a genuine Apache tomahawk. Ha! That's what the label says. Goddamned dumb Gumm and his little woman got themselves a souvenir from a place called Banglesh."

"Bangladesh."

"What I said."

"Christ. You say you gave Henry a head start?"

"Yessir. He run outta that room, down the stairs, and out the front door. Tracked him all night, and finally caught him a while ago back where we were."

"I know," Pinnt said. The oxycodone was kicking in, and he realized he wasn't as bothered by all this as he probably should be. "So, why you want to go to Crawford?"

"That's where it happened," Myrtle said, a slight dreamy quality to her voice. "And there are others. The seeds have got to stop."

"Seeds?"

"Makin' more babies from bad seed. And, I've been given vengeance."

"Okay. Whatever." Pinnt saw the Uncompahgre Peak ahead and to the right. They were getting close to Ouray.

"Ouray up ahead," Myrtle said.

"Read my mind."

"Ha! I can do a lot more than that."

Pinnt supposed she could. She'd already smelled the bull leavings on him, and had some insight into what the bull had done to him. What else could she do?

"Where you from?" Pinnt said, glancing at her profile.

"Born in Tennessee."

"How come you know so much about Crawford?"

"Lived there."

"I been there a year. It ain't that big a place, and I never heard of any Roady."

"Died there, too," Myrtle said, her voice a whisper.

Passing through Ouray—U.S. 550 North ran right through the middle of town—Myrtle grabbed the bottle and took a couple sips. "Pretty place," she said holding the bottle out to Pinnt.

"Nah, better not, it'll just make me sleepy."

Myrtle put the cap on the bottle, laid it aside, and stared out the side window. "Had a raccoon once. Named him Charley. He was the best friend I ever had."

Pinnt thought about that. She had killed Gumm's wife with a slash across the throat, sliced off Gumm's fingers, then chopped off his head after tracking him through the forest all night, and her best friend was a raccoon. He shook his head and couldn't help from smiling.

"You think that's funny?" Myrtle said.

Pinnt felt her stare, heard the menace in her voice. "No, not at all. Raccoons are smart as can be. Never had one as a friend, but I can see where—"

"I know about your friend."

"What?"

"Tyler Oaks, great-great-grandson of Harold Oaks."

Pinnt snapped his head toward her, and met those green serpentine eyes with his. "No. No, ma'am. You—" He quickly looked back when a horn blared. He'd slewed over into oncoming traffic. Jerking the Dodge back onto his side of the road, he slammed the palm of his hand on the steering wheel.

"Oh, dem golden slippers."

"What the fuck. You leave Tyler out of this here craziness."

"Can't do that."

"I'll stop right here and kick your ass—"

Myrtle snatched the axe, swiftly scooted closer to Pinnt, and held the blade to his neck. "Nossir, you'll just keep on drivin'."

Pinnt tried to lean away from the axe, and Myrtle applied more pressure.

"Okay. Okay," he said. "Settle down."

"You're not on my list, Wylie Pinnt, but I can put you there." She kept the pressure on the axe.

"I said *okay*. Just ease up."

Myrtle slowly eased the axe down, and scooted away from Pinnt. "You mind your driving."

"Shit," Pinnt said, seeing the flashing lights behind him. After passing the end of town, he pulled over onto the apron. "You just keep your mouth shut, Myrtle."

"You mind your own words," she said, slipping the axe under her coat.

Pinnt rolled down his window and waited for the local yokel in blue to approach.

"Good morning," the officer said, leaning down and taking a good look inside the cab.

"Morning," Pinnt said.

"Driving a little erratic back there."

"Yeah. Sorry about that."

"Do I smell alcohol on your breath?"

"No sir. I—"

"Believe that's an open container on the seat."

Pinnt looked at the bottle. "Yessir, but I haven't been—"

"Turn off your engine, and step out of the vehicle."

"Christamighty," Pinnt said reaching for the keys. He turned off the engine.

"Just do what the man says," Myrtle said.

Pinnt looked at her. She was smiling. "You stay in the truck."

"Sir, step out of the vehicle."

Pinnt opened his door, and slowly turned himself to get out. Pain shot through his back and chest. "Sorry, I'm a little injured."

"Just come on out," the officer said, backing away a few steps, his hand on the butt of his pistol.

When Pinnt managed to get his feet on the ground, the officer ushered him farther onto the apron away from the highway, and back behind the side of the truck.

"I do smell alcohol," the officer said. "You have your license and registration?"

"My wallet is in the glovebox."

The officer stepped to the passenger window, made a fist, and motioned for Myrtle to roll down the window.

"Would you get his wallet from the glovebox?" the officer said once Myrtle had opened the window.

"Sure," Myrtle said, opening the glovebox. She grabbed the wallet, and opened the door.

"No need to get out, ma'am."

Myrtle ignored him, and stepped out onto the apron. She handed the wallet to the officer who then turned slightly away from her and flipped it open. He pulled out Pinnt's license, held it up, and looked from the license to Pinnt's face.

"Wiley Pin—"

All Pinnt saw was Myrtle's right arm in an upward thrust. The officer lurched forward a step, dropped the wallet and license, appeared as though he was trying to look behind him, and collapsed face down onto the apron. Pinnt saw the tear in the officer's clothing, right up the seat of his pants, and halfway up his shirt. Blood seeped through the material. Pinnt raised his head, and there was Myrtle, wiping the axe across the front of her coat. His voice failing him, Pinnt mouthed *What?*

"Get his arms," Myrtle said, slipping the axe under her belt, and bending down to grab the officer's feet. "We'll put it down that drop off." She nodded toward where the apron slopped down to a depression.

"It?" Pinnt said.

"Do it!"

Pinnt couldn't move. Looked back down at the body. *Right up his ass to his spine.*

"Goddamnit," Myrtle huffed as she pulled the body by herself to the edge of the drop off, kicked it twice, and watched it roll down to the sandy bottom. "Get in the truck."

Pinnt looked at her, and then toward the highway. No one had stopped. No one was passing by.

"I said get in the truck." Myrtle's voice menaced as she walked toward Pinnt with her hand inside her coat.

Pinnt raised his arms, motioned with his palms down. "Okay, okay." He walked around the Dodge's front, and got back in. He sat there a moment while Myrtle climbed in on the passenger side.

"Shut your door, and let's go," Myrtle said. "Less 'an two hours to Crawford." When Pinnt didn't respond, she stared at him. "Go!"

"Yeah. Okay." Pinnt closed his door, leaned over, and started the truck. Realized his pain wasn't so bad now. *Right up his ass to his spine…*

After a half hour of silence, Myrtle started in again: "Oh, dem golden slippers."

"Myrtle, please," Pinnt said.

"What?"

"Stop with that."

"Okay." Myrtle nodded, and grabbed the bottle. "Only a couple sips left," she said unscrewing the cap.

"It's all yours."

"Don't mind if I do," she said, draining the bottle. "Now,"—she put the cap back on, set it to the side, and folded her hands in her lap—"we still got to talk about Tyler Oaks."

"No, we don't."

"I know about you two."

"I don't give a shit. You know a lot about lots of things. Where the hell you come from anyway?"

"I told you—Tennessee."

"No. I mean lately."

"Don't matter. I'm here, ain't I."

"Oh," Pinnt said, shaking his head. "You sure as hell are. No doubt about that."

"You and Tyler Oaks been fuckin' for a while now."

Pinnt tensed. Stopped himself from saying that was none of her fucking business.

"How old are you?"

"Almost twenty-one. Why? How old are you?"

"Tyler Oaks ain't even nineteen yet."

"Would you stop with Tyler," Pinnt said, snapping his head to her, and glaring at her profile, his jaw muscles tensed.

"His mama know you're fuckin' him?"

THE STORY OF MYRTLE ROADY

"His mama knows we're workin' hard to keep up the ranch," Pinnt said, lowering his voice, picturing Tyler back home keeping his eye on things, probably worrying about cows soon to pop out calves.

"Does his mama know?"

"You forget about Tyler. Don't you mention his name again or I'll..."

"You'll what?"

"If I wasn't beat up I'd stop right here and pull you outta this truck and... And..."

"But you are beat up, and nothin' you can do will end my vengeance."

"What the fuck are you talkin' about? Vengeance? I mean... What the fuck!"

"Harold Oaks strung the rope up."

Pinnt quickly glanced at Myrtle, and shook his head. "What the hell are you talkin' about? Has nothin' to do with Tyler."

"Oh, yes siree Bob it does."

"Christ..."

"The last sound I heard was the creakin' of that old oak tree."

Pinnt immediately saw in his mind people tying yellow ribbons on oak trees, and heard the song that went with that image. "You're nuts," he said.

"Gumm killed all those little chillun. Not me. And Henry Oaks strung the rope, and Peter Drum, and Samuel Stivers helped him."

"Oh wait a fuckin' minute. You said the guy that killed children was that guy's"—Pinnt nodded toward the back of the truck—"great-granddaddy or somethin'."

"I did."

"Okay. So you're tellin' me that... Christamighty, you're sayin' that all this vengeance crap is because of somethin' that happened way back in, hell, I don't know, back in the eighteen hundreds?"

"I am."

"Goddamn." Pinnt shook his head and tried not to laugh. "You're nutty as a—"

"Last sound I heard was the creakin'—"

"Jesuschristamighty, Myrtle."

"Oh, dem golden slippers. So, it's goodbye chillun!" Myrtle screamed the last word, scooted over to Pinnt, and, inches from his face, said in a whisper, "And Henry Oaks strung the rope, and Drum and Stivers helped him."

US 550 became US 50, then, near Delta, Pinnt took Colorado 92, skirting the Gunnison Gore National Park eastward toward Crawford. He and Myrtle had settled into silence for the last forty minutes, and as they neared the town of Crawford, Pinnt dug the blister pack from his shirt pocket, and popped out a pill. He put it in his mouth, chomped down, tasted the bitterness of it, worked up some spit, and swallowed the pieces.

"Let me out here," Myrtle said.

Pinnt didn't argue. Though they were several miles from Crawford, the sooner she got out of the Dodge the better.

"Sure," Pinnt said, pulling to the side of the road. "Wanna grab what's left of Mister Gumm out of the bed?"

"I do." She opened the door, and stepped down to the ground. "Got some stops to make 'fore I come see you and Tyler."

"Yeah, right. Just get the fucking head outta my truck."

Myrtle's smile was something Pinnt hoped he could eventually forget. She slammed the door, walked to the back of the truck, and pulled Daniel Gumm's head from under the tarp. Pinnt watched her walk off into the roadside scrub through the rearview.

Pinnt continued on 92, turned onto Black Canyon Road, followed it for three miles, then turned onto Black Bear Road and, after two-hundred yards, made another turn onto his and Tyler's ranch. Well, it wasn't theirs exactly. The bank still held the note, and Tyler's parents were on the hook for that. They'd not been able to pay the cell bill for the last three months, and Pinnt wished mightily he'd been able to stop somewhere and tell Tyler what had happened. As he topped the small rise that gave a view of their house and barn, Tyler was standing there with his arms over his head waving a welcome.

Pinnt pulled the Dodge up to the house, and Tyler met him there.

"You look like shit," Tyler said as Pinnt opened his door.

"Feel like it too."

"You get stomped again?"

"Yeah." Pinnt sighed while easing himself to the ground.

Tyler stepped into Pinnt and wrapped his arms around his shoulders. "Welcome home," he said, touching his lips to Pinnt's.

"Whoa," Pinnt said. "Got some broke ribs."

Tyler backed off a step, and shook his head. "What bull did you get?"

"Frenzy," Pinnt said as he walked toward the house.

"Mean bastard if I remember," Tyler said, looking into the cab. He reached in and grabbed a little tomahawk from the seat. "This my souvenir from Albuquerque?"

Pinnt stopped and turned. "Ah, hell no," he said, again heading for the house.

"Says it's genuine Apache."

"Yeah, well… Don't believe everything you read." Pinnt stopped when he got to the porch, turned back, and studied the landscape for a moment. "Tyler, c'mon in the house. Don't want you out here by yourself."

"What? Why?"

"Long story. Just come in the house."

Tyler followed Pinnt in the house. "You need a bath," he said as he closed the door behind him. "I'll run the water."

"Okay. Listen," Pinnt said stopping in the hallway to their bedroom, "you really do have to stay in the house."

"Why?"

Pinnt walked into their bedroom, and gingerly began to take off his clothes. When Tyler leaned against the doorway, Pinnt stared at him for a moment, then closed his eyes and shook his head. "You sit with me while I take a bath. I'll tell you why."

"Good enough," Tyler said as he turned and walked the few steps to the bathroom.

The sound of warm water filling the tub was a comfort to Pinnt, and having managed through his pain to get his clothes off he reached for his shirt on the bed, pulled out the blister pack and stared at the remaining two pills. He pried one out and grabbed the water bottle Tyler always kept on the night table. Washing it down, he figured he'd take the last one tonight. Or maybe not. Myrtle was out there somewhere, and he needed to be alert. Hell, he thought, I shouldn't have taken this one.

"Goddamn, Wiley," Tyler said when Pinnt walked into the bathroom. "Look at your back."

"I know. Fractured my back, too."

"Goddamn," Tyler again said.

Pinnt braced his palm against the wall as he stepped over the side of the tub, slowly kneeled down, and then sat in the steaming water. "Feels good," he said. "Sit down on the toilet."

Tyler did sit, and handed Pinnt a washcloth he grabbed from the vanity. "So, I guess you didn't make eight seconds."

"Not even close." He soaked the washcloth, leaned back, rested his head on the edge of the tub, and placed the washcloth on his face. "Had a peculiar thing happen on the way back, though."

"Okay."

"Tell me about your ancestors here in Crawford."

"Don't know much about them. We were one of the first families to settle here. Grandma knows all about that stuff, though."

"Well, we gotta talk to Grandma then."

"Why?"

Pinnt took the washcloth off his face and sat up. He grabbed the soap, and rubbed it into the cloth. "You ever hear of somebody murderin' children way back in the early days," he said, scrubbing his face, then his shoulders.

"Sure. When I was bad my mama always told me I better be good or else Myrtle Roady would come in the night and eat me."

Pinnt stopped scrubbing and looked at Tyler. "She said that name? Myrtle Roady?"

"Yeah. It's all bullshit, though. That dead oak tree near the middle of town that nobody wants to cut down? Grandma says it's haunted ground, and anybody that tries to get rid of it will die."

"Jesus." Pinnt sighed. "Hand me that shampoo."

Tyler knelt down next to the tub and grabbed the shampoo from the far ledge. "I'll wash your hair. Just sit back and relax."

"I knew there was a reason I loved you."

"Just one?"

"Maybe a couple."

Pouring a handful of shampoo, Tyler set the bottle back on the ledge, and gently massaged it into Pinnt's scalp. "Need a shave too."

"Need to get you naked in bed, is what I need."

"We could do that." Tyler grinned, dunked the washcloth in the bathwater and squeezed it out over Pinnt's head, then did it again. "Here," he said, pulling a towel from the rack.

Pinnt wiped his eyes with the towel, and handed it back to Tyler.

"Thank you," Pinnt said. "I am serious about talkin' to your grandma. Sooner the better."

"Sure. I'll go call her." Tyler stood. "You need anything else?"

"Might lock the front door while you're in the livin' room. Get the back door, too."

"Why?"

"I'll tell you when I get outta here."

"Okay. And I should stay inside?"

"You should stay inside."

Tyler walked out of the bathroom, then came back and stood in the doorway. "You're serious, aren't you?"

"As a fuckin' heart attack."

"You should call the sheriff," Tyler said as he watched Pinnt pull on his jeans.

Pinnt had given him the short version of what had happened after he pulled over to sleep off the pills and the booze. Tyler had listened, sitting on the bed, his brown eyes wide with the story-telling.

Pinnt walked to the chest of drawers and grabbed a T-shirt. He raised it to pull over his head, and groaned. "No. Can't do it," he said. "Need help with this, Ty."

Tyler stood, held the shirt so Pinnt could slip his arms through the holes, and then gently pulled it over Pinnt's head. "You have to report it, Wiley."

Pinnt sat down on the bed. "Can you get my boots?"

"Sure," Tyler said, grabbing the boots, kneeling down, and sliding them onto Pinnt's feet.

"You think the sheriff is gonna believe what I just told you?"

"It's the truth." Tyler stood and helped Pinnt get to his feet. "You really look tired."

"I am, and I'll crash after we talk to your grandma. And," he said, wishing the old doc in Albuquerque had given him more pills, "the truth don't sit well when the story is unbelievable."

"I guess," Tyler said walking behind Pinnt as he walked out of the bedroom.

"You drive," Pinnt said, grabbing the keys from the side table by the door where he'd left them, and held them out to Tyler. "Oh, wait." He walked back into the bedroom, and felt the claws of that persistent kitten inside his chest as he reached up to the shelf above the clothes rack in the closet. He stuck the .38

THE STORY OF MYRTLE ROADY

caliber pistol behind his belt, and walked back out to the living room. Tyler was waiting for him outside on the porch.

"Goddamn, Tyler. I said not to go outside alone." Pinnt stepped onto the porch, and closed the door behind him.

"Myrtle ain't gonna get me. I been a good boy."

"She don't care if you been bad or good. And, it ain't no fairytale we're talkin' about. C'mon." Pinnt stepped off the porch and headed for the Dodge.

"Sorry," Tyler said. He walked to the truck, opened the door, and sat behind the wheel.

"Wish I was more clear-headed," Pinnt said, sitting on the passenger side, and closing the door.

"You might want to pull your shirt out over that gun," Tyler said as he started the Dodge and drove a drove a half circle to head back to the highway.

"Yeah." Pinnt tugged the bottom of his shirt out and draped it over the weapon. "Like I said, I ain't very clear-headed right now."

"Grandma ain't either. You know that. Right?"

"I do," Pinnt said as Tyler turned onto Black Bear Road. "But she's all we got, unless you want me to tell your mama about all this."

"Hah," Tyler laughed. "No, don't tell my mama. She thinks you're a strange one anyway. My daddy thinks you're queer."

"Hell, your daddy knows I'm queer, and I'm sure he's figured you out too."

"Maybe."

"Maybe my ass." Pinnt looked at Tyler, smiled, and, in that moment, knew he'd kill for that young man who was smiling back at him.

Tyler turned onto 92 North that would take them to town.

"Hey, Grandma," Tyler said, leaning down and hugging the tiny woman who stood just inside the doorway.

"Ty, you never come to see me," Grandma said, her soprano voice laced with a squeal. "And there's Wiley Pinnt," she said when Tyler let go of her. "Since you and Ty moved onto that ranch, I barely see my grandbaby anymore."

"Sorry about that," Pinnt said gently grabbing and squeezing Grandma's hands when she held them out to him. "We're pretty busy out there."

"I know. I know. You boys come on in here and sit down. I got some cookies set out for you, and coffee is brewin'."

Pinnt felt the oppressive heat inside the tiny living room, as he sat on the over-stuffed chair, covered with a pattern of faded flowers. Tyler sat on a matching chair, just inches from Pinnt. They both faced Grandma who sat on a padded rocking chair on the other side of the coffee table.

"Love to have you boys come see me," Grandma said, rocking slightly, and picking at the lace on her housedress. "You said you wanted to talk about family."

"We do, Grandma," Tyler said. "Wylie has some questions for you."

Pinnt cleared his throat. "Well, ah… I know the Oaks family was here in Crawford at the begging, way back in—"

"One of the first families," Grandma said. "My granddaddy Harold helped build the post office. That's why Crawford is here in the first place—a post office."

Smiling, Pinnt nodded. "Yes, Ma'am. But I'm wonderin' about stories that children back in those days were murdered and their bodies never found."

Grandma tensed, grabbed the chair's padded arms, and shook her head. "Lord," she said, her eyes closed, "what a time that was. Granddaddy told me about it." She opened her eyes and gestured with her hand. "Ty, go in there and get the coffee. Put it on the tray I got in there."

Ty stood, and walked into the kitchen.

"Put the cream and sugar on there, too."

When Tyler returned with the loaded tray, he set it down on

THE STORY OF MYRTLE ROADY

the coffee table.

"Fix up your coffee now," Grandma said. She leaned toward the table, and poured a little cream into a cup. Pinnt and Tyler leaned in too, sugar for Tyler, black for Pinnt.

Grandma sipped, and then held her cup atop the rocking chair's arm. "Five children between 1882 and 1887 went missing, one for each New Year's Eve. That's when she got 'em. Not one was ever seen again, nor was their bodies found. And something of each of the lost children ended up missing—a toy, a doodad of some sort, a hair ribbon. When my grandfather told me the story, he cried like a baby. His own son, your grandfather, Ty, was only two or three years old by then."

"You said *she*. Who did you mean?" Pinnt said, setting his cup on the table.

"Why, Myrtle Roady of course."

"How did they know it was her?"

"Well, who else could it have been? Myrtle Roady hated children, and told them so to their faces. Told them they stunk, and to get away from her. My grandfather said she was an odd woman who some claimed preferred her own sex to men. You know," she said, wiggling her left hand, "the crime of Sodom. She didn't mix with the normal people, and never attended Sunday service like everybody else. She lived alone up on the hill, killed her own meat, and granddaddy said she was a drunk. He also said most folks thought she ate those lost children."

"So nobody ever saw her do it?"

"No. Like I said, nobody saw nothing. Didn't have to see her do it. Everybody knew it was her."

"What happened to her?" Pinnt said.

"When the last child was missing on New Year's Eve in 1888, the men went up to her cabin and saw she had butchered something on her table. They just knew it was the missing child, and they dragged her out of there, and strung her up on the oak tree toward the middle of town—it's still there, Ty, you know the one. Granddaddy said it was his rope they used. But, I think he regretted that." Grandma lifter her cup, but didn't sip. She set it back down on the chair's arm, and gazed off toward the window.

"Why'd he regret that, Grandma?" Tyler said.

Grandma was silent for a moment, still looking at something only she could see. She lifted her cup, and this time she did sip. "Granddaddy told me that after they strung her up, a bunch of them went back to her cabin, and looked closer at what she'd butchered on her table. It wasn't a child, but some critter, prob'ly a mountain lion or bobcat. That, of course, didn't absolve her of her deeds, but I guess my granddaddy…"

"Why'd—" Pinnt said.

"My granddaddy had some misgivings about hangin' Myrtle. The boy they thought was missing was just playin' a trick on everybody. Granddaddy said it was the Stivers boy, Sammy. He wasn't missing at all. But all the others… Myrtle killed all those children. You can be sure of that."

"Did your grandfather ever mention Pastor Gumm?"

Grandma smiled. "Why, yes he did. Pastor Gumm led that group of people through the wilderness to right here where they founded the town of Crawford. He said Pastor Gumm just up and left, though, after they hanged Myrtle Roady. I guess he figured he'd done enough of God's work in Crawford—you know, after the killer was found—and just thought he'd move on to where he was needed more."

Pinnt glanced at Tyler who was finishing off his coffee. Realized he hadn't told him the whole story, particularly why she'd come back from wherever she'd been. *Back from the dead? Nah. Not possible.*

"The old oak, Grandma?" Tyler said.

"Yes."

"Is it really haunted?"

"No such thing as ghosts, Ty. You know that. That old tree is just… old. That's all there is to it."

"But you told me before that—"

"I know what I told you. And, yes, maybe through the years some things have happened around that tree. But it ain't ghosts.

It's... Well, I don't know exactly what it is except that some people have big imaginations." She started to pull at the lace on her housedress again.

"Grandma, you told me—"

Pinnt put his hand on Tyler's leg. "It's okay, Ty. I think we need to get back. Them heifers are due any minute."

"Oh, you got some calves comin'?" Grandma said with a smile.

Pinnt saw the obvious—Grandma was happy the subject had changed. "Yeah," he said, standing, "we got some coming. Might already be here."

Tyler stood, and placed his and Pinnt's cups on the tray. "Grandma, you done with your coffee?"

"Yes, I am." She held the cup out to Tyler, who reached over and placed it on the tray.

"I'll get this back in the kitchen," Tyler said as he picked up the tray, and inched past Pinnt.

"You take good care of Ty," Grandma said, lowering her voice as she stood. "Somethin' ain't right in the air."

Pinnt took a step toward Grandma. "I will," he said, placing his hand on her arm.

She looked at his eyes. "You know it too?"

"I do."

"We'll come see you again, Grandma," Tyler said coming from the kitchen. He kissed Grandma's cheek, and turned to smile at Pinnt. "You ready?"

"Yeah," Pinnt said stepping to the door. "Nice to see you, Ma'am."

"You boys take care of yourselves."

"We will," Tyler said.

Pinnt opened the door, and Tyler followed him out.

"She knows more than she told us," Pinnt said as Tyler turned the Dodge off Fir Street and onto D Street that would take them to Colorado 92, and back home.

"I know she changed her story about the oak tree."

"Yeah. Maybe she's got her reasons. There's the oak right now." Pinnt pointed to the small park that surrounded the infamous tree. "Somebody is over there."

Tyler looked toward the park. "What is that?"

"Pull over," Pinnt said, his hand on the door handle.

Tyler stopped the Dodge. Pinnt got out and Tyler followed. The oak was about a fifty yards in front of them.

"Get down," Pinnt said.

They both got to their knees; Pinnt winced with the effort, and watched as Myrtle swung her axe at a body hanging by its neck on the oak tree's limb. The man's legs, cut off at the thighs, laid on the ground below him. Myrtle was swinging at the man's left arm. Also hanging from the limb was a head. Just a head.

"Oh God," Tyler said. "Is that her?"

"That's her. You recognize the man?"

"It's Dick Stivers. I grew up with him."

"He an ancestor of that little boy who wasn't lost?"

"What?"

"What your grandma told us."

"Oh. Yeah. The Stivers have been here forever. Wonder whose head that is?"

The white hair gave it away. "That's Daniel Gumm—the guy from Silverton."

They watched as Myrtle lopped off the man's right arm. Nothing remained but the torso hanging from the oak. She then took a swipe at Gumm's head, chopping off the left side of his face. Wiping the axe blade on the front of her coat, she turned and stared, beaming a smile at Pinnt and Tyler.

"We gotta get outta here," Pinnt said as he stood. He returned Myrtle's stare for a moment until he heard Tyler's door slam. Pinnt walked back to the truck, grabbed the door handle, and looked again toward the old oak. Myrtle was gone. Dick Stivers wasn't.

"Shouldn't we call the sheriff?" Tyler said as he steered onto 92.

"No. Somebody'll find it soon enough."

"What about that guy in Silverton, and the cop?"

"I suspect they've been found already."

"Sure they have, but shouldn't you... You got to tell somebody, Wiley. You got to warn people about her."

"Now how do you think I'm gonna convince the authorities there's a crazy woman come from the past to avenge her own death by killin' folks with an axe? Hell, they'd prob'ly lock me up and throw away the key."

Tyler didn't answer for a moment. When the turnoff for Black Bear Canyon Road appeared ahead, he nodded, reached his hand over, and grabbed Pinnt's shoulder. "They'd prob'ly say that bull stomped you in the head."

Pinnt reached across and squeezed Tyler's thigh. "They would. You do realize she's goin' for the last male ancestors of those who strung her up?"

"I know," Tyler said, moving his hand from Pinnt's shoulder, and placing it atop Pinnt's hand resting on his thigh. "And, I know I'm one of 'em."

"She told me she had to stop you from makin' more babies from bad seed." Pinnt looked at Tyler and smiled.

Tyler glanced at Pinnt with his own smile. "You ain't pregnant, are you?"

"Not yet," Pinnt said, once again squeezing Tyler's leg, losing his smile, and staring out the side window. *She's out there somewhere.*

"We'll check them heifers together," Pinnt said as he got out of the Dodge.

Tyler got out, and walked around the back of the truck. "Only them three heifers is ready. They usually bunch up near the ditch." He continued walking toward the barn.

"Where you goin'?"

"Gotta get the birthing kit. Just in case—"

"Nah, leave it. I want to get them ladies into the barn."

"Okay," Tyler said. "I hope they ain't out there tryin' to push one out."

"See your point," Pinnt said, walking to Tyler. "We'll just get a hook rope."

"Sounds good. I'll head over to the ditch."

Pinnt grabbed Tyler's arm. "No, we'll stay together. *We'll* get the hook rope, they *we'll* head over to the ditch."

The heifers had yet to start their first birthing experiences, and Pinnt and Tyler managed to get them moving, and eventually into the barn. They separated them into unused horse stalls, spread hay, and gave each one a forty-gallon water stock tank. After closing up the barn, they walked back to house where Pinnt stepped up to porch, stopped and turned to Tyler.

"You stay right here, right in front of the door while I go in and check the place," Pinnt said.

"I guess we should have locked the door."

"Nah. Somethin' tells me she don't care about locks." Pinnt opened the front door, and looked back. "You holler if anything… Just holler if somethin' happens."

"I will."

Pinnt pulled his weapon from under his belt, held it out in front of him, and entered the house. He walked through the living room, looked into the kitchen, then walked down the hallway to the bedroom and bathroom. After checking the bedroom closet, he walked back through the house to the living room. "You can come in," he said before he got to the front door. When there was no response, he stepped to the doorway, and looked out. No Tyler. "Fuck it," he said, stepping out onto the porch, pointing the weapon in front of him.

"Whoa," Tyler said from the far end of the porch, holding his palms toward Pinnt. "I'm right here."

Pinnt lowered the weapon, and shook his head. "Damnit, Ty. I thought she got you."

"She didn't," Tyler said as he walked to Pinnt.

"C'mere," Pinnt said, spreading his arms. Tyler stepped into him, wrapping his arms around Pinnt's waist. Pinnt raised his arms around Tyler's shoulders. "This hurts like hell, but it's worth it. God, I love you."

"Love you too," Tyler said.

Pinnt broke the embrace, and motioned for Tyler to go in the house. "You go lock the back door and windows in there. Pull the curtains across the windows too. I'll get the bedroom and bathroom."

"It's gonna get hot in there," Tyler said walking through the living room.

"We'll get the sump cooler goin'."

"If it still works. Haven't used it for a year," Tyler said as he engaged the deadbolt on the back door.

"Yeah, it'll work," Pinnt said. He stuck the weapon back in his waist, and walked down the hallway toward the bedroom, jerking to a stop when the landline rang. "Jesus," he whispered. "You gonna get that?"

"Yeah," Tyler hollered.

Pinnt closed the two bedroom windows and clamped down the measly aluminum locks. *That ain't gonna stop her.* He then pulled the curtains across the windows. Hearing Tyler's side of the phone conversation, he walked back into the hallway.

"We're fine, Grandma. …Yes, I know. We saw it, and Wylie was just gonna call the sheriff. …Okay. …Yeah. …Okay. …You too, Grandma. I love you. …Bye."

"She saw it?" Pinnt watched Tyler stick the receiver back into its slot.

"No, she didn't see it. Heard a bunch of sirens, and her neighbor come over to tell her about it. Bunch of sheriff cars are there, and an ambulance."

"Why'd you tell her I was gonna call the sheriff?"

"Because her neighbor saw us stop and watch what was goin' on and she told the sheriff about that."

"Christ! So a sheriff is headed out here?"

"Prob'ly. It's that old bat Della MacElduff. Somebody farts near her yard and she's on the phone to the sheriff."

"Jesus." Pinnt walked into the living room, paced a few circles on the worn carpet, and then stepped over to the landline. "I'll call them. Gotta make it seem… innocent." He picked up the receiver. "What the fuck is the number," he said, turning toward Tyler.

"I think 911 would do it," Tyler said.

"Oh, yeah. Guess it would. That's the Delta County cops?"

"Only ones we got out here, Wylie. You want me to do it?"

"No, I'll—"

They both turned toward the front windows. A car was moving over the pebbled drive just outside.

Tyler hurried to the window, and looked out. "Shit. It's Norman Drum. Super cop in his own mind."

"No," Pinnt said almost in a whisper. "*The* Drum? His family been here forever too? Maybe an ancestor named Peter Drum?"

"Yeah, his family is one of the originals too."

They looked at each other as a car door slammed.

"You go back in the bedroom," Pinnt said.

"Why? I wanna stay and—"

There were three quick, forceful knocks on the door. "Deputy Drum," a deep-seated voice called from outside. "Need to talk to you."

"Okay," Pinnt said. "You get behind me, Ty." He pulled the weapon from his waist, cocked the hammer, and held it behind his back. "She might be out there." He inched toward the door, disengaged the lock, and opened it.

THE STORY OF MYRTLE ROADY

"Hello," said the six-footer wearing a dark green uniform, a gold badge, and a huge smile. "I'm Deputy Drum, and I—"

There was a barely audible thump, causing the deputy to take a step forward. Still smiling, he reached a hand to his shoulder, and craned his neck to look behind him.

Pinnt and Tyler watched as the deputy turned his gaze back to them, and, still smiling, his irises rolled upwards, his legs folded under him and he fell face down onto their living room floor. Myrtle Roady stood on the porch. She too smiled as she wiped the axe's blade against the front of her coat.

"Oh, dem golden slippers. Oh, dem golden slippers. And it's good-bye... You!" Myrtle pointed at Tyler, then stuck the axe under her coat, turned, and walked down the steps.

Pinnt shook his head, looked down at Deputy Drum's back where a three-inch diagonal cut to the mid-point of his spine now seeped blood.

"Shoot her," Tyler said.

"What?"

"Your gun! Shoot her!"

Pinnt looked at Tyler. *Yeah, yeah. I've got a gun.* He looked outside, aimed for Myrtle's head, and pulled the trigger, then again, and again, and again, and again.

"Stop! Stop! Stop it, Wiley!"

Pinnt heard Tyler's voice first as a far away, meaningless echo. When he realized it was Tyler, and understood the words, he lowered the weapon.

"She's gone, Wiley."

Looking beyond the porch, out across the fronting acreage, Pinnt saw that Tyler was right. Myrtle wasn't there. He looked at Tyler, then back outside.

"She just... I don't know," Tyler said. "It was like she vanished when you fired the first shot."

Pinnt looked down at Drum's body. "There's one left."

"One what?"

"You. You're the only one left on her list." Pinnt turned to Tyler.

Tyler looked from the body to Pinnt. "What're we gonna do?"

"We have to…" Pinnt walked to the couch in front of the window and sat down. He placed the weapon on the coffee table, then put his palms to his face and shook his head. "Let me think, Ty. Just let me think a minute."

"We gotta call the sheriff."

"No, no, no. Can't do that yet. Besides, they'll know he's missin' and where he went. They'll prob'ly send somebody out here soon enough."

"But we got to—"

"No," Pinnt said as he stood and, nodding his head, motioned for Tyler to help him. "Let's get Drum out of here." He carefully stepped over the body, and onto the porch. "Don't think we can lift him, but we can pull him. Come on. Help me."

"Wiley, I don't know…"

"I know this ain't right, but we gotta do it. I got a plan. C'mon, help me."

Tyler edged to the body, carefully stepped over it, and joined Pinnt outside.

"Get the other leg," Pinnt said, leaning down and grabbing hold of Drum's left leg.

Tyler did help, and they managed to pull the body off the porch. Both winced as the head thudded down each step.

"Just off to the side of the house," Pinnt said when they got Deputy Drum on the ground.

Once they got the body to the side of the house, Pinnt walked over to the Dodge, and pulled the tarp out of the bed. He came back and Tyler helped him cover the body.

Pinnt tried to arch his back in an effort to release some of the pain that now interminably throbbed. That only made it worse. "Goddamn," he said, bending over slightly, feeling his stomach working on an upsurge of whatever was still in there.

THE STORY OF MYRTLE ROADY

"You okay?"

"Yeah. Might have to barf."

Tyler stepped to him, and placed his palm on Pinnt's forehead. "You oughta be in bed."

Pinnt grabbed Tyler's wrist, raised his head, and kissed Tyler's hand. "Thank you. I'll be okay. But we have to go over to that dead pine near the ditch."

"Why?"

"Somethin' there I need to get."

"What?"

"Just trust me, Ty. It might be the only way we're gonna get through this."

"Okay," Tyler said as Pinnt stepped away from him.

"Grab some gloves from the barn," Pinnt said over his shoulder. He then stopped, and turned around. "No, you go in the house and grab the gun, and get that box of shells from the closet. I'll go get them gloves." Tyler started to walk back to the house, and Pinnt said, "No. Damnit! We gotta stay together. Let's get the gun, then the gloves. Need to grab a bath towel, too. And, I need to get that last pill."

///

Pinnt lay on the couch, and Tyler sat with Pinnt's legs atop his thighs.

They'd come back to the house after finishing preparations for what Pinnt thought might be the only way to keep Myrtle from finishing what she'd set out to do. After locking the door, Pinnt collapsed on the couch. Tyler grabbed two beers from the refrigerator, gently lifted Pinnt's legs, and sat down under them. He twisted the caps off the bottles, and handed one to Pinnt.

"Thank you," Pinnt said.

"Welcome. You think it'll work."

Pinnt took a sip, and then set the bottle on the coffee table. "I hope so. This is crazy-assed, messed up shit, Ty. Just hope that little bit of my pill don't wear off too soon."

"You think she's out there right now?"

"Prob'ly."

"You think she can get in here?"

"Prob'ly."

Tyler picked at the bottle's label. "Appears bullets can't hurt her."

"Maybe."

"You think—"

There was an enormous thud against the front door. Pinnt slipped his legs off Tyler's, and both stood, staring at the edge of an axe blade slicing through the door from top to bottom as if the pinewood was butter. There was another thud, and the door separated from the middle inward. Deputy Drum's head flew in the room, and rolled across the floor into the kitchen.

"Get behind me, Ty," Pinnt said, pulling the pistol from his waist, and stepping to the middle of the living room.

Ty moved behind Pinnt, and both watched as Myrtle stepped through the doorway, the axe held at her side.

"Oh, dem golden slippers," Myrtle chanted, swinging the axe back and forth alongside her leg.

Pinnt raised the pistol, aimed at Myrtle's head, and fired.

"Hah!" Myrtle said, raising her left hand and sticking her pinkie into the bullet hole in the middle of her forehead, working it around a bit. "Ain't gonna work, Wylie Pinnt." She pulled her pinkie out and sucked on it. "Mmmmm."

"Get outta here, Myrtle," Pinnt said firing again. A hole appeared on the back of Myrtle's hand.

Myrtle pulled her pinkie from her mouth, held her hand up, and peeked through the hole. "I see Tyler Oaks. He's the one I come to get. He's the last one I come to get." She lowered her hand, exposing a new hole just above her lip. She then perked her head, raised it, and began sniffing the air. "What I smell?"

THE STORY OF MYRTLE ROADY

she said, taking a step forward. "I know that smell. I know—"

Pinnt backed himself and Tyler up to the side chair sitting near the hallway, facing the couch. He reached down and pulled the bath towel off what was under it.

Myrtle startled, stared at what was on the chair.

"It's Charlie," Pinnt said.

"You killed him!" Myrtle said, looking from the raccoon in the chair to Pinnt.

"No I didn't. He's just sleepin'. He's been lookin' for you, and we found him. Pick him up, Ty."

Ty stepped to the chair and picked up the raccoon, cradling it like a baby. He handed Pinnt the end of a wire that encircled the animal's neck.

Myrtle took a step forward, her eyes glaring at the raccoon.

"No!" Pinnt said, moving in front of Tyler. "You hurt Ty, and I pull this wire and kill Charlie."

Myrtle backed up. "You can't kill Charlie," she said, her voice soft, a barely perceptible quiver.

"Yes I can."

"Charlie is my friend."

"Ty is mine."

They all turned their heads with the sound of four car doors slamming just outside the front door, then a yell: "Police! Come out with your hands in the air!"

Before Pinnt and Tyler were aware that Myrtle and the raccoon had vanished, two officers in green uniforms and brandishing weapons were screaming at them to "Get down! Faces to the floor!" They both immediately complied; both noticing as they lay down the W.C. Kelly Perfect Axe with the shortened original hickory handle was on the rug between them.

Manufactured by Amazon.ca
Bolton, ON